# the Celebutantes
## IN THE CLUB

## ALSO BY ANTONIO PAGLIARULO

*A Different Kind of Heat*

*The Celebutantes: On the Avenue*

Antonio Pagliarulo

the *Celebutantes*

IN THE CLUB

*Delacorte Press*

Published by Delacorte Press
an imprint of Random House Children's Books
a division of Random House, Inc.
New York

www.randomhouse.com/teens

Educators and librarians, for a variety of teaching tools, visit us at
www.randomhouse.com/teachers

Library of Congress Cataloging-in-Publication Data

Pagliarulo, Antonio.
The celebutantes : in the club / Antonio Pagliarulo.
p.   cm.
Summary: Wealthy triplets Madison, Park, and Lexington Hamilton are shocked
when one of their classmates at St. Cecilia's Prep is killed during the opening of
their father's newest nightclub, but even after they narrow down the suspects to the
members of a secret campus role-playing club, the murderer is not obvious.
ISBN 978-0-385-73473-8 (trade pbk.) — ISBN 978-0-385-90472-8 (Gibraltar lib. bdg.)
[1. Murder—Fiction. 2. Wealth—Fiction. 3. Triplets—Fiction. 4. Sisters—Fiction.
5. Role-playing—Fiction. 6. Catholic schools—Fiction. 7. Schools—Fiction. 8. New
York (N.Y.)—Fiction. 9. Mystery and detective stories.] I. Title.
PZ7.P148Cd 2008
[Fic]—dc22
2007007931

The text of this book is set in 12-point Filosofia Regular.

Book design by Angela Carlino

Printed in the United States of America

10 9 8 7 6 5 4 3 2 1

*For my aunt, Antoinette,*
*with love and thanks*

FOR IMMEDIATE RELEASE:
TO: The Editors, *Socialite* magazine
FROM: Madison Hamilton (and on behalf of
        my sisters, Park and Lexington)
RE: A few nasty lies


The recent flurry of publicity that has descended on me and my sisters has been anything but acceptable. We didn't enjoy being targets of a killer, nor did we find the sight of two dead bodies particularly appealing. Have you ever tried to outrun a gun-toting madman while wearing heels? It isn't generally our style to pay attention to nasty lies, but this time, the media's attempts to tarnish our reputations were cruel, unusual, and incredibly tasteless. And if there's *one* thing we won't tolerate, it's people who have no taste.

EXAMPLE NUMBER ONE comes from the pages of *The New York Daily*: "Apparently it's not enough that celebutantes Madison, Park, and Lexington Hamilton appear daily in gossip columns all over the world. They've just launched the Triple Threat clothing line, hogging even more press in their customarily shameless way. The lesson: when bloody scandal erupts, spin it into a lucrative business."

Let's get something straight: my sisters and I launched the Triple Threat clothing line because it happens to be an extraordinary fashion product. In just over one month's time, Lexington's styles have become a global brand. And we don't "hog" attention shamelessly—we manage it gracefully because the press can't get enough of us. The *real* lesson: when sisters stick together, the world becomes their playground.

EXAMPLE NUMBER TWO is from *Hollywood Spotlight,* the unintelligible nightly newsmagazine that hires failed B-movie stars and musicians as reporters: "The recent crimes attached to the Hamilton triplets inevitably raise questions about their credibility. Will the public ever be able to trust Manhattan's adored golden girls again?"

What a vulgar way of trying to get ratings up. Before attempting to insult our credibility, take a nice long look at your journalistic stupidity. If you're going to insult us, please do it with a smidgen of intelligence. As for the public . . . well, we *adore* our public. Not only are my sisters and I credible—we're *incredible* when it comes to loving our many fans.

EXAMPLE NUMBER THREE, from the pages of *Celebrity* magazine: "It seems the ever-amusing Hamilton triplets can add another job to their fancy resumes; having solved a gory double homicide, they are now the most fashionable crime-fighters on the planet. But have they traded in their Fendis for forensic microscopes?"

Ever-amusing? Try ever-enchanting. Or maybe ever-enlightening. We don't set out to amuse—we just hate to lose. Solving a double homicide is all in a day's work. When we realized the police couldn't handle the job, we decided to take the case. We were only looking out for our fellow New Yorkers. And, for the record, we think fashion and forensics go hand in hand, because we're always dressed to kill.

*See you...*
*In the Club*

# Where Madison and
# Lexington Meet

She reached for her sunglasses.

Madison Hamilton dug into her tan Triple Threat hobo bag and felt instantly relieved as she touched the smooth silk lining. After a harried morning that included a press conference and two final exams, she needed a little fabric pick-me-up. She also needed to hide the worry glowing in her eyes. The last thing she wanted was someone asking her why she looked so downright frightened.

She let her fingers skim through the bag for a few moments, the silk a cool kiss against her hot skin. It was like a shot of champagne straight to the veins. A feeling of serenity washed over her, but it was quickly eclipsed by the small note sitting on the table in front of her. She stared down at the perfect script and swallowed hard.

*Please report to the principal's office at once.*

Sighing, Madison snatched her sunglasses from the bag and slipped them on. Oliver Peoples couldn't be beat when it came to covering up. She lifted her face and glanced around the ornately furnished room. The student lounge at St. Cecilia's Prep was decorated lavishly in dark wood and Oriental rugs, in shiny plasma screens and marble countertops. Its four windows overlooked the medieval courtyard, but a thick trail of ivy wound over the glass panes, blocking out the bright June sun. The long shadows that fell across the floor didn't matter: sunglasses were a priority when it came time to make the walk down the fifth-floor corridor that led to the principal's office.

Thankfully, the student lounge was fairly empty so late in the afternoon. Madison shot a glance at Jessica Paderman, who was sitting at one of the mahogany desks beside the bookcase. Short, scrawny, and blessed with a mane of thick red hair, Jessica was the heiress to a huge pharmaceutical empire; she was a quiet, studious, timid girl who never got into any kind of trouble. Madison had spoken to her only a handful of times. There was no reason to suspect that Jessica knew about the note from the principal's office, so she let her gaze drift to the left side of the room, where Aaron Linney was snoozing fitfully on one of the plush love seats. The light snoring sound wafting through the air was typically Aaron. Also the heir to a sizeable fortune, Aaron had a habit of smoking too much

6

weed and drooling onto his wrinkled white uniform shirts. Madison doubted he'd heard anything about the note either, or much else, for that matter.

Getting summoned to the principal's office wasn't really a big deal at St. Cecilia's Prep. The school had the wealthiest student body in the world, which left little room for disciplinary action or useless things like detention or suspension. Punishments were handed down, but they were rarely ever meted out. A single phone call from a disturbed parent usually swept a problem under the rug. And because a large chunk of the students were celebutantes with very public social lives, the nuns who staffed the school couldn't really argue their holy points. Incidentally, these were the same nuns who received generous donations and academic endowments from parents eager to buy a little silence.

But Madison was still totally wrecked by the note. She had no idea why she was being called to the office of Reverend Mother Margaret John—the stern, disapproving principal. Madison was a stellar student. She was even an obedient student, smiling and nodding and dipping into a quick curtsy when the older teachers walked by her in the halls. More than once, she had volunteered her free time in the school's development office, giving her expert advice on fund-raising and special-event planning. Her black-and-red-checkered uniform was perfect: crisp shirt, navy blazer buttoned just above the waist, tie knotted firmly at the neck, skirt flowing past the knees. Like everyone else, Madison hated the uniform, but she never followed the examples of her female classmates, who had their skirts professionally altered nearly up to their butts. Thighs must be seen to properly show off a tan.

7

So why the note?

*I can't be in trouble,* she thought. *I haven't done anything wrong.*

She had been sitting in the student lounge for fifteen minutes, trying to delay the inevitable. Now it was time to get up and face whatever awaited her on the fifth floor. She pushed the sunglasses further up on the bridge of her nose and reached for her bag. But before she could rise out of the chair, she saw a tall, gangly male figure jump through the doorway like a giant grasshopper, stomping his feet and breaking into a funny dance. His practical joke shattered the silence in the room.

Jessica Paderman nearly shot out of her chair.

Aaron Linney opened one eye, recognized the culprit, and resumed his snooze.

It was Madison who laughed. "Damien Kittle," she said with a shake of her head. "When will you *ever* grow up?"

Instead of answering, Damien Kittle launched into a new dance, spinning around, kicking up his knees, banging his head as if he were at a heavy metal concert. He held his arms up and out and twitched his fingers, playing an imaginary guitar. "You won't be finding me actin' like an adult anytime soon, Miss Hamilton," he said.

Madison couldn't help but smile. Watching Damien Kittle in action was an event that rivaled front-row seats at a Cirque du Soleil performance. As she stared at him, taking in his wild antics, she felt some of her anxiety melt away.

Damien was a senior at St. Cecilia's Prep—and probably the only true blue blood. He had English royalty in his veins. His official title was Duke of Asherton, but he hated admitting it to people. In fact, he liked to project an image that was entirely at odds with the prim and proper role of the British throne. Perfect posture? A staid demeanor? Tea in the afternoon? Hell, no. Damien was a self-avowed adrenaline junkie, a class clown who enjoyed harassing teachers and scaring the quiet kids. He was also a world-class charmer.

Madison simply adored his bravado. She would never forget the time he had stripped down to his boxer shorts—or, as Damien called them, knickers—and gone prancing through the science lab as old Sister Martina tried to keep herself from fainting. Or last year's class trip to Spain, where he dressed up as a bull and, right there in the lobby of the hotel in Pamplona, rammed into as many guests as possible. Most recently, about two weeks ago, Damien walked out of the music hall wearing a red lace bra over his navy uniform blazer. His parents, Sir David Kittle and Lady Jane Kingsley-Kittle, had received countless phone calls from Reverend Mother Margaret, but if they ever punished him for his antics, it certainly didn't show. He seemed to be getting crazier each day.

And, of course, there was the added benefit of his looks. He didn't have classically gorgeous features, but his face was interesting in a mischievous sort of way. His eyes possessed a sharp gleam. His lips had a tendency to pucker when he was deep in thought. He had a mop of wavy black hair and a lean, strong swimmer's body that looked equally nice in jeans or a Dior suit. Damien liked to play the part of the average, ordinary guy, but there was no mistaking his aristocracy.

"Well, you won't get away with acting like a kid your whole life," Madison quipped. "But right now it's okay, because I totally love watching you dance."

Damien took the compliment for all it was worth. He shimmied closer to her, turned sideways, and jutted his butt into the air. "Go on, love," he sighed deeply. "Smack it. I know you want to. I know you fancy my bum."

With a grunt, Jessica Paderman slammed shut the book she'd been reading and stormed out of the lounge.

The laugh that shot from Madison's lips echoed way out in the hall.

"I *knew* it!" Damien shouted. "The American avenue girl likes her blokes wild and free!"

Madison suddenly felt her cheeks flush. There was nothing sexier than that thick British accent: it was so-phisticated and steamy and ripe with royalty. She could sit and listen to him talk all day long. "Oh, stop it," she said with a quick wave of her hand. "You're going to get me into *trouble* one of these days."

Damien's face instantly took on a different expres-sion, one that was exaggeratedly serious. He leaned in close to her and said, "Oh, darling, I heard you're already in lots of trouble. I heard you've got yourself a lovely little note from Mother Margaret."

Madison scowled. Great—the word was already out. It hadn't taken more than a few minutes for half the school to know she was on some sort of shit list. She poked him in the shoulder. "Where did you hear that?" she de-manded playfully. "Is that what everyone's saying?"

"Not everyone. Just me." Damien smiled. "I heard that bloody Mother Margaret tell her horrible secretary that you and Lex were expected in her office."

"Lex got a note too?" Madison bit down on her lip. A small piece of the puzzle had just been revealed: anything having to do with her sister Lexington usually spelled trouble. She shot out of the chair, grabbed her bag, and pushed past Damien. "Sorry to cut this short, but I've gotta run."

Damien frowned. The clownish look on his face softened to a genuine smile. He stepped toward her, took her hand, and kissed it gently. Then he stared up at her and said, "I wouldn't worry too much, Madison. A girl as lovely as you can't be in that much trouble."

Madison felt the heat flare in her cheeks again. This was the other side of Damien Kittle she loved—the warmhearted guy who always uttered the sweetest words. She knew he had sensed her fear, and she was suddenly very grateful for his presence. "Thanks," she replied. "I'm glad *someone* around here notices my good side."

Damien kept her hand in his and gestured at the staircase. "I always do," he said with a wink. "May I walk you upstairs?"

Madison hesitated. She really didn't need an escort, but staring down into those ferocious eyes and hearing that sexy accent was enough to make her knees weak. "Okay," she finally said, "but *don't* get me into any trouble."

He gave her a devilish grin. "I'll do my best to make you proud."

They hurried out of the student lounge and into the hall.

And ran smack into trouble.

Well, maybe not *trouble*. But certainly a little bit of unwanted irritation.

Sister Brittany Ignatius was the newest member of the

St. Cecilia's Prep faculty. She was young and pretty and definitely unlike all the other nuns who staffed the school. Tall and thin, she had a graceful walk and a nauseatingly cheerful disposition. She was known for asking tons of questions. She had also managed to invade a number of the otherwise impenetrable student cliques, offering girls her sometimes unholy advice on makeup and fashion. Sister Brittany had appeared suddenly at St. Cecilia's one day back in March, and with any luck, she'd disappear just as quickly.

Madison wasn't her biggest fan. She liked that Sister Brittany wore black Roger Vivier pumps and accented her delicate cheekbones with blush, but all in all, the curious nun had a tendency to be downright annoying.

"Oh, Madison! *Hi!*" Sister Brittany said in her usual jovial tone. "How's your day going? And Damien—what's new with you?"

Inwardly, Madison sighed. She said politely, "Everything's fine, Sister. Thank you for asking."

Damien, of course, couldn't let the moment pass without some sort of crazy behavior. He winked, then stuck his thumbs up and out. "I'm happy as a tray of tea and cake, Sister B."

"Splendid." Sister Brittany smiled. "Oh, Damien, I was wondering if you could stay after school for about an hour today. I'll need some help moving costumes into the theater."

"Sorry, Sis," Damien said, feigning regret. "But I have some important plans this afternoon."

Sister Brittany looked disappointed, then quickly hid her upset. "Okay!" she answered brightly. She turned and stared at Madison. "I just *love* that new shade of lipstick you're wearing, honey. It's so . . . *saucy.*"

Madison nodded. Who used a word like *saucy* outside of a kitchen? "And your blush, as usual, looks wonderful, Sister," she said. "I'd kill for your cheekbones. But if you'll excuse me, I'm late for an appointment."

Sister Brittany beamed at her. "See you later, sweethearts!" she said loudly, turning around and strutting away like a runway model, her black habit swishing around her legs.

Madison continued down the hall, again letting Damien clasp her hand in his.

Once upon a time, St. Cecilia's Prep had been a row of attached town houses on Manhattan's Upper East Side, and while the walls separating them had long ago vanished, many of the original architectural details remained. The crown moldings were on every ceiling. The curving staircases were carpeted. Ornate chandeliers brightened several classrooms and offices. Anyone entering the school for the first time would easily think the building was a hotel or museum. Walking from one floor to another was an exercise in luxury, and the most opulent furnishings could be found on the uppermost level, where the principal's office occupied a large corner.

When Madison reached the fifth–floor staircase landing and hung a sharp right turn, she stopped dead in her tracks. At the end of the hall stood her best friend, Coco McKaid, and her sister Lexington.

"Ahhh," Damien whispered. "The beautiful ladies are already in wait."

Madison took quiet steps toward them, clutching her

bag tightly. She wasn't pleased with Lex's appearance—her skirt was too short, and she had completely redesigned her own version of the school uniform; the customarily plain navy blazer now sparkled with dozens of tiny diamond chips. Her blond hair fell to the middle of her back in wavy tendrils, but the preferred hairdo at St. Cecilia's Prep was far more conservative. Like the French braid that held back Madison's dark locks.

"Hey there!" Lex said, smiling at her sister but offering an even bigger smile to Damien.

Madison shot Lex a disapproving look over the rim of her sunglasses. "Do you have any idea what this is about? I've never been called to the principal's office."

"It's probably nothing," Coco said, looking like her good old messy and tired self. She wore her hair in a cute pixie cut, but several strands were sticking up at the back of her head. "I mean, that's just what I'm assuming. I wasn't called here. I just came along for the walk."

Madison frowned. "Well, this can't be good."

"Just relax," Lex answered. She stepped past Madison and gave Damien's necktie a playful tug. "So, how's my favorite bad boy?"

Damien growled like a hungry dog. "I'm better now that I'm here, with my lips barely two inches away from yours."

Lex snuggled closer to him. "I *love* it when you talk dirty."

Madison rolled her eyes.

"I just want to *ravish* you, Lexington," Damien whispered, sounding more and more like some actor on daytime TV.

"Ravish?" Coco said, confused. "Isn't that a vegetable?"

Madison stared at Lex, who stared at Damien, who stared back at Coco.

*Duh.*

"What?" Coco asked. "Did I hear wrong?"

Madison shook her head. "Damien said *ravish,* not *radish.*"

"Oh." Coco shrugged. It was the defeated gesture of a girl who had never excelled at phonics. "It still sounded . . . tasty." She nudged Lex's arm and winked.

"Anyway, Damien was just leaving," Madison snapped, growing more tense as they stood outside Reverend Mother Margaret's office. "Right, bad boy?"

Damien clucked his tongue. "You getting rid of me so fast, love?" He cupped Lex's hand in his and kissed it.

Lex threw her head back, playing along with the game. "We'll see you tonight, right?"

"A party wouldn't be a party without me." Damien nodded at Madison and Coco. Then he turned around and yelled "Cheerio!" before running back down the hall and out of sight.

"You see?" Coco said. "I know I heard it right that time. He keeps talking about food. He just mentioned Cheerios."

Madison stared hopelessly at her best friend. "Cheerio is a salutation. It's how they say good-bye in England."

"It's *so* hot," Lex added.

"Hot?" Coco wrinkled her nose. "Doesn't make sense to me. Do we all go around saying Cocoa Puffs to each other?"

"Whatever the case, Damien is top on my most

wanted list." Lex reached into her own bag, pulled out a compact, and checked her reflection in the small circular mirror.

"If you're so hot for him, why haven't you hit him up for a date?" Coco asked.

Lex snapped the compact shut. "*I* don't ask guys out. *They* have to ask *me* out. And besides, when it comes to serious relationships, Damien isn't . . . well . . . all that serious. Everybody knows he's a little gay."

"Is he?" Coco raised an eyebrow.

"Only about a quarter gay," Madison said. "Which, when you do the math, comes out to about once every three months. So it's not really a big deal."

Coco nodded in agreement. "Anyway," she said, "I wanted to tell you both that I definitely can't make it tonight. My mom is *still* making me fly out to California with her to some Zen meditation retreat. Three whole days without my cell phone or laptop! I swear, ever since she bought that hotel in Malibu, she's gone crazy."

"Three days without a cell," Lex whispered gravely. "Be brave. Be strong."

"Come *on*," Madison snapped. She grabbed Lex's arm and quickly air-kissed Coco good-bye. "We have to go. We're already late."

Coco glanced at her watch. "*Ugh.* Chemistry in five minutes. See you guys Monday."

Standing shoulder-to-shoulder in front of the closed door of the principal's office, Madison and Lex hesitated. Then Madison said in a low voice, "Do you think Park got one of those notes too?"

Lex sniffed. "Probably not. And it doesn't matter, because she took the day off."

"That's right. I forgot." Madison gritted her teeth. Their sister, Park, had called in sick that morning so that she could join her boyfriend, famed actor Jeremy Bleu, on the set of his newest movie. *Damn you, Park,* Madison thought, *we need you.* And that really was the truth. In Park's calm and reassuring presence, even the most nerve-wracking moments seemed trivial.

"Do you think Reverend Mother already called Dad?" Lex whispered, a hint of panic in her voice.

"There's only one way to find out." Madison curled her fingers around the brass knob and gently opened the door.

The reception area of the principal's office fanned out before them, a rich tapestry of reds, golds, and browns. A long sofa occupied the left-hand corner, two Tiffany lamps perched on either side of it. There was a glass coffee table, a bookshelf, and a tall wall unit made of dark cherry wood. The expensive music system piped out a steady stream of Beethoven.

Seated at the L-shaped desk on the right side of the reception area was the principal's secretary, Mary Grace Burns. A short, wide woman with bright red hair, big owlish glasses, and pale skin, Mary Grace had been a member of the school's administrative team for nearly twenty years. She was one of those quiet and highly efficient assistants who said nothing but knew everything. She glanced up from her desk. "Good afternoon, Madison. Good afternoon, Lexington."

Madison dipped into a proper curtsy. "Good afternoon, Mrs. Burns."

"Hi," Lex said dryly, immediately imparting her I-really-don't-want-to-be-here attitude.

Mary Grace gestured toward the sofa, then got up and disappeared into the small kitchen.

Madison and Lex sat down. They both stared at the closed door ahead of them, where Reverend Mother Margaret was tending to her myriad duties as commander in chief of one of the world's most exclusive prep schools.

"I really hope this doesn't take long," Lex muttered. "We have a lot to do before tonight."

"Be quiet," Madison snapped. "And for God's sake, *don't* mention anything about tonight." But even as she doled out the order, Madison knew that tonight was *exactly* what was on everyone's mind.

Tonight, Manhattan's newest and most exclusive nightclub, Cleopatra, was opening its doors to a select group of invitees—celebrities, fashion designers, actors, directors. Which meant, of course, that most of St. Cecilia's student body would be in attendance. The social event of the season, it had already garnered massive amounts of press all over the world. Cleopatra was being billed as an extraordinary experience in New York nightlife—not necessarily because of its exclusivity, but because it had been erected from scratch on a trendy Lower East Side street, an architectural masterpiece straight out of the ancient Egyptian era. Cleopatra was the latest entrepreneurial brainchild of Trevor Hamilton, mogul and media king, and proud father of the most famous triplets on the planet.

Madison, Park, and Lexington were the club's official guests of honor. In just a few hours, they would be emceeing yet another socially significant party.

Mary Grace emerged from the kitchen holding a tray. She set it down on the coffee table with a nod.

Madison and Lex reached for their complimentary cups of espresso. Madison was already wired, so she took only a few quick sips. Lex, on the other hand, dumped two spoonfuls of sugar into her cup, stirred it quickly, and downed the shot in a single gulp.

Just as the door to the principal's office swung open.

Reverend Mother Margaret John came strolling into the reception area, her long black habit nearly sweeping the floor, her black veil with its ring of white set perfectly over her head. She was a small woman, but she exuded an air of authority. Her blue eyes were deep-set, her thin lips sealed in a perpetual frown. As prioress of the Order of Our Lady of the Avenue, it was Mother Margaret's responsibility to both run the school and manage the student body. The latter was the most challenging aspect of her job.

Madison shifted uncomfortably in her seat. She wanted to say something polite, but the words just didn't come. She focused her gaze on the ivory rosary beads cinched around Mother Margaret's waist and uttered a prayer for mercy.

The nun dropped a manila file and a sheaf of papers onto Mary Grace's desk, then turned around slowly. "Madison, Lexington. You may proceed into my office."

Madison led the way into the spacious room. The three large windows afforded a generous view of Central Park. She and Lex sat in the hardbacked leather chairs and watched as Mother Margaret shut the door and walked around to her side of the desk.

Before sitting down, she shot Madison a long, hard stare.

Madison blanched.

"Miss Hamilton, are you suffering from cataracts?" Mother Margaret asked sarcastically.

"Excuse me? I . . . uh . . . no . . ." As her voice trailed off, Madison realized she was still wearing her sunglasses. She removed them promptly. "I'm sorry," she muttered, mortified that she hadn't taken them off upon entering the office.

"That's quite all right." Mother Margaret sat down. "I'm sure you're both wondering why you've been summoned. I would have called Park as well, but she's apparently . . . not feeling well."

"That's right," Lex responded, quick on cue. "She's been under the weather all week."

"Well, I'm glad to see that *you're* feeling well, Lexington." Mother Margaret folded her hands and leaned forward in the chair. "From the looks of it, you have *a lot* of energy."

"Totally," Lex said. "I've been trying this new macrobiotic diet—but not very strictly. I mean, I still eat chocolate. And I can't resist the burgers at J.G. Mellon. But still—I'm trying."

"That's *not* what I meant." Mother Margaret's voice was sharp. "I'm talking about this new uniform you've invented. Today it's diamond studs, yesterday you were prancing around with bright pink ribbons on your blazer, and the day before you replaced your loafers with stilettos."

"Those weren't actually ribbons," Lex replied, her tone utterly devoid of fear. "They were handmade silk boughs, given to me by Betsey Johnson."

"And they're entirely inappropriate!" Mother Margaret shook her head. "Because of *you*, Lexington, every young woman in the school is demanding uniform updates, and I want it to stop *immediately*."

Madison was shrinking in her chair, unnerved by Mother Margaret's rising voice. She gave Lex a pleading glance, but the glance did no good.

"Excuse me, Mother," Lex shot back, "I don't understand why I'm being held responsible for the behavior of every girl in the school. Instead of demanding that it stop, maybe you should consider what's being said. Our uniforms *aren't* very stylish. They could use an upgrade."

"An upgrade?" Mother Margaret said faintly.

"Yes. Like, well . . . instead of the red and white pattern, why not something a little more eye-catching? Why not pink and black? Or—wait—even better . . . tan blazers and skirts with pink accents? And I'd be happy to redesign your habit too, Mother. I know black is slimming, but don't you want a little splash of color every now and then? And instead of that veil, why not a—"

"Enough!" Mother Margaret shrieked.

Lex frowned. "I'm only trying to help!"

"But you're *not* helping! You're ignoring the rules—*as usual.*" A pause. "As of tomorrow, you will return to wearing the navy blazer. No high heels. No ribbons—"

"Boughs," Lex corrected her, speaking very matter-of-factly. "They were French silk boughs. Ribbons are for wrapping gifts."

"*I don't care!* You will *not* wear them to school again! Is that clear?"

A tense silence fell over the office. Then Lex sighed impatiently and said, "I *guess* so."

Mother Margaret pressed her hands to her temples and closed her eyes, clearly distressed. When she opened them several seconds later, she focused on Madison.

And Madison couldn't stop herself from flinching. *I didn't do anything,* her mind screamed. *I always wear the official St. Cecilia's uniform.*

"Madison," Mother Margaret said in a calmer voice. "I would now like to address the other issue that's concerning me, and I know I can count on you to be agreeable and respectful."

"Yes, Mother." Madison cleared her throat nervously. "Of course."

"Good." Mother Margaret gave her a quick smile. "Now, would you please tell me a little more about this nightclub event that more than half the school seems to be attending this evening?"

*Shit.* Madison felt her stomach knot. She was under strict orders from her father—and everyone at Hamilton Holdings, Inc.—to keep the details about the opening night of Cleopatra private. Rumors about what the nightclub would be like and how much money had gone into its construction had been circulating through the media networks for months, but not a single one of those rumors had ever been confirmed. It seemed the whole world wanted to know what this new extravagant slice of nightlife had in store for its guests.

"Madison?" Mother Margaret said. "Is there something wrong, dear?"

"No, there isn't." Madison straightened in the chair and assumed a businesslike posture, just as her father had taught her to do several years ago. There was no easy way out of this one. Mother Margaret was as curious—and as aggressive—as a tabloid reporter, but she went about collecting her information ambiguously. If sugary tones and bright smiles failed, she often resorted to guilt or holy language. But those tactics wouldn't work today. Madison knew to keep her mouth shut.

She looked Mother Margaret squarely in the eye. "There's not much I can tell you about tonight's event, except that it's very exclusive, and that a lot of planning has gone into it."

"Yes, dear. I've heard that much. But I'm still very concerned."

"About what?" Madison asked her bluntly.

"About the kinds of things that might go on in a nightclub. You must remember that when you are in public, you are representing St. Cecilia's Prep. Antics of an . . . unsavory nature would be terrible publicity for the school."

"Unsavory?" Madison shrugged. "I don't know what you mean, Mother. You'll have to clarify that."

Mother Margaret John shifted uncomfortably in her chair. She was losing her little fight to get the dirt on Cleopatra, and she knew it. "I mean that many young adults—even smart ones like yourself—can sometimes lose themselves in environments that promote sin."

"Where did you get the idea that our father's newest business venture is promoting sin?" Madison asked, a purposeful edge to her tone.

Mother Margaret cleared her throat nervously. "I didn't mean to imply that, dear. I'm just concerned. It's being talked about all over the news, this nightclub opening. I just want to make sure that my students behave themselves. You know how . . . prone young people are to scandal."

Lex clucked her tongue and rolled her eyes.

"Is there a problem, Lexington?" Mother Margaret snapped.

Lex narrowed her eyes at the nun. A playful smirk

tugged at the corners of her mouth. "As a matter of fact, there is. It *smells* in here."

"Smells?" Mother Margaret's voice was instantly alarmed. "Like what?"

"Like . . ." Lex paused and stared at the nun, trying to insinuate the obvious. "Like something *old.*" She jumped when she felt Madison kick her shin.

Sniffing the air, Mother Margaret opened her desk drawer, pulled out a bottle of Chanel No. 5, and sprayed both her wrists. Then she turned her attention back to Madison. "As I was saying, dear . . ."

Madison cleared her throat. "Please don't worry," she said, feigning a smile, her voice at once confident and comforting. "My sisters and I—and all our friends here at St. Cecilia's—will be on our *best* behavior. Nothing wild or out of the ordinary is going to happen tonight. It's going to be a perfectly innocent evening."

In the short silence that followed, Madison wondered what the penance was for lying so blatantly to a nun.

# 2

# Park It on the Set

"Action!"

The director's voice boomed across the set a moment before the cameras started rolling. Park Hamilton stood somewhat aside from the cluster of production assistants gathered at the corner of West Houston Street in Greenwich Village and trained her eyes on the tall, muscular guy hanging from a harness seven stories in the air. The sight made her dizzy. Why on earth would anyone want to perform a stunt *that* dangerous? She listened as gasps fluttered around her, then turned and surveyed the crowd of onlookers: it was thick with ardent fans, all of them pointing up at the actor who looked like a rugged angel suspended in the sky.

Jeremy Bleu was an eighteen-year-old superstar. More importantly, he was Park's boyfriend, and she couldn't keep her eyes off him either. Right now, his black hair was tousled and sweaty and a splatter of fake blood stained the right side of his face. He was in character, playing an ordinary college freshman trying to save the world from a nuclear bomb blast. The movie was titled *Short Fuse*. This particular scene called for Jeremy to dangle from a balcony while a killer attempted to cut off his fingers. Exciting, yes, but Park would have preferred a stunt double up there in the air.

She sighed and shook her head for the millionth time. That was Jeremy—always eager to push the envelope when it came to his work. He was a perfectionist, obsessed with getting every last detail right. He needed to experience his work viscerally. Doing his own stunts was apparently part of the creative process. As much as Park hated it, she couldn't deny that the view from the street was simply delicious. The worn jeans hugging Jeremy's bottom half accentuated all the right parts, and his wet T-shirt clung to his chest like a second skin. It was no wonder all the women were drooling.

She and Jeremy had been dating for nearly seven weeks now. Their romance was headline-making news, a favorite of the tabloids and the paparazzi. They couldn't go out to dinner without someone snapping their pic. They couldn't steal a kiss in private without it ending up in print. Even now, huddled off to the side of the set, she felt several cameras zooming in on her. The next caption, probably beneath a picture in *Star* magazine, would read something like: PARK HAMILTON DOESN'T LET HER MAN OUT OF

SIGHT. The thought made her laugh. It was *so* not true. She enjoyed Jeremy's company, and she was totally hot for him, but she wasn't the type of girl who believed in keeping a leash on a guy. Her life was busy and full and chaotic. She needed her own space—room to concentrate on schoolwork, philanthropic ventures, and the responsibility that came with managing the new Triple Threat clothing line. If anything, it was Jeremy who wouldn't let *her* out of *his* sight.

That was the main reason Park had skipped school today. Last night, Jeremy had called her with one of his customarily dramatic complaints. He'd told her that he was upset, that they didn't see each other enough, that after a long day of filming he wanted to hang out with her at night and just chill. Then came the list of sappy questions that sometimes made Jeremy sound like an infatuated schoolboy: *Why don't you leave me messages on my cell? Did you like the diamond bracelet I sent you? You do love me, don't you?* It had been a long conversation, and in the end Park had decided to surprise Jeremy and spend all of today on the set. This morning, when she arrived, he'd kissed her passionately in front of the entire crew and refused to let go of her hand. He even waved and winked at her between takes. Park often wondered what would happen if the world knew that muscular, macho Jeremy Bleu was really a softhearted pushover.

Now she locked her eyes on the unfolding scene. Jeremy—or, rather, the character he was playing—struggled to maintain his grip on the balcony, emitting a series of grunts. The older man posing as the killer held a knife in his hands. Jeremy swung from left to right, the harness holding him tight, the side camera swerving to catch every last bit of the action. Suddenly, the balcony itself began to collapse in a brilliant display of special effects. The older man gave a believable cry as he dropped the knife, and Park marveled at how well he feigned fear. Jeremy's talents weren't lost in the fray, however: his face registered shock and his muscles tensed and flexed. In what had surely been a well-rehearsed move, he swung onto the crumbling railing and balanced himself against the wall of the building. It all looked so *real*.

Park's heart fluttered for a single instant.

The cameras kept rolling.

Jeremy looked down, then up. There was obviously no escape from the impending disaster. But the heroic main character couldn't die with whispers of a sequel already in the wings, so at the exact moment the balcony collapsed— hundreds of bricks plummeting to the street in a plume of smoke—Jeremy lurched through the air and landed on the next balcony. He stumbled and rolled. He cried out. One end of his T-shirt snagged something jagged, and the flimsy material tore away from his upper body. He looked breathless and pained and exhausted. But that didn't stop him from running a hand across his sweat-soaked chest as the cameras zoomed in for a full-body close-up. He threw a careless glance to his immediate left. And gasped. His eyes had spotted the ticking bomb sitting at the opposite end of the balcony—yet another ruse from the nasty nemesis trying to end the world.

*Ten seconds till it detonates.*

The scene was coming to an end. Park kept her gaze focused upward and thanked God that she wouldn't have to watch the same stunts being shot over and over again. That was the only boring part of moviemaking: the monotony of having to reshoot everything a dozen times. All around her, the onlookers were gasping in panic. She remained calm and cool and braced herself for the finale.

Still in character, looking stunned but determined, Jeremy leaped onto the balcony railing and stared down at the street. Then he threw a last panicked glance over his shoulder. An instant before the staged explosion flashed against the bright blue sky, he jumped—plunging through the air with a guttural scream. The harness did its job and held him tightly.

Park sighed as Jeremy's body landed butt-first onto a huge inflated device that looked a lot like a Macy's Thanksgiving Day parade float.

"That's a wrap!" The director's voice boomed across the set again.

Every onlooker cheered and clapped as Jeremy climbed off the inflated device. He smiled as several production assistants and stunt technicians patted him on the back.

Park finally exhaled. She, for one, didn't feel like cheering. The near anxiety of the last few minutes had probably etched fine lines around her eyes, and she was sure she'd gone pale. It didn't help that she was wearing a black Triple Threat tank top with her Sass & Bide jeans. The contrast would make her look even paler.

"Excuse me, Miss Hamilton?"

Park turned around. The short woman staring at her was holding a clipboard, and the earpiece circling her head was wholly unflattering. "Yes?"

"I'm Jenny Kilmer," the woman said. "Jeremy's waiting for you."

"Oh. Thank you. And you can call me Park, by the way."

The woman smiled and led Park through a maze of street markings, tripods, and blue police barricades. They walked past the pile of bricks and debris caused by the recent explosion, then around the inflated thing that had saved Jeremy from certain death.

"Can I get you anything?" Jenny Kilmer asked. "Coffee? Water?"

"Water would be great," Park said.

"Carbonated or noncarbonated?"

"Non."

"Evian, Poland Spring, Fiuggi, or FIJI?"

"Fiuggi, please."

Jenny Kilmer nodded. "That's my favorite too. It comes straight from Italy, you know."

Park knew. Every July, she, Madison, and Lex traveled to Italy to visit their mother, famed actress Venturina Baci, and were educated in all things Italian. Fiuggi was excellent drinking water. Evian, on the other hand, while basically undrinkable, worked wonders on the hair, sealing split ends like a soothing balm. "At least Fiuggi is bottled in glass," Park said. "Plastic can be so bad for the environment."

They had reached the cordoned-off area reserved for cast members. Three long trailers sat at the corner of MacDougal and West Houston, their entrances manned by security guards. Park accepted the bottle of Fiuggi water, took a long sip, and stepped into the shade. It had to be a hundred degrees. June had come to New York with a vengeance, stifling the air and clogging the streets. Park wasn't a fan of the summer months. She hated the humidity and what it did to her long brown hair. She hated having to constantly pat the beads of sweat from her forehead. As far as she was concerned, there were only two places to be when the temperature soared to ungodly levels: inside an air-conditioned penthouse, or browsing the floor at Henri Bendel.

The door to Jeremy's trailer suddenly burst open, and he smiled down at her from the threshold. "Hey, sweetheart!" he said.

Park might have been angry with him for doing all those stunts himself, but seeing him standing there in nothing but jeans and the white towel slung around his neck was enough to send a chill up her spine. She raced up the steps and into his waiting embrace.

"Did you enjoy watching the scene?" he asked, wrapping his arms around her waist.

"No, I didn't." She shook her head. "I had no idea it was *that* dangerous. You could've gotten yourself killed!"

"Totally not true. I know how to do my own stunts. I'm trained." He winked seductively. "I can do a lot of cool things with my body."

"*That's* certainly the truth." Park tossed her head back and puckered up.

The kiss was long and passionate, and somewhere on the street, a camera flashed in their direction.

Jeremy pulled her into the trailer and shut the door behind them.

Park sighed as a blast of cool air swept over her damp, hot skin. She had been in Jeremy's trailer before, and while it was impressive for something that occupied a gritty street corner, she couldn't get comfortable in so narrow a space. When filming had first started, she'd brought Jeremy several scented candles, and now they were dispersed throughout the trailer, the marble countertops splattered with wax. Crinkled protein-bar wrappers littered the table beside the small refrigerator and water cooler.

"So," Jeremy said, sitting down beside her. "What are we doing tonight? Dinner?"

Park stared back at him as if he had just sprouted a pimple on the tip of his nose. "What are you talking about?" she snapped. "I can't go anywhere tonight. You know that!"

"I do?"

She sighed. "Jeremy, tonight's the opening of Cleopatra, my father's new club. Remember? We had this discussion."

"Oh yeah, I remember." He frowned and pulled the towel off his shoulders. He swiped it across his forehead. "I guess I forgot because I'm not coming."

"Don't sound so disappointed. It's not like you weren't invited."

"I know. I wish I could come. But we're filming all night. I can't get out of it."

"You won't be missing much," Park said, trying to sound offhanded even though she knew Jeremy would be missing the most spectacular event of the year.

"What about later on?" he asked.

"Later on?"

"Yeah, like after the opening. I should finish filming at around two or three a.m."

"We'll see, okay? If not, we'll have dinner tomorrow night. I'm yours for the whole weekend. Or, at least until seven o'clock on Sunday night."

"Why so early on Sunday night?"

"Commencement's on Monday morning. I have to be there to help out. And I have to get a good night's sleep."

He sighed and sulked. Jeremy didn't really understand why Park was so straitlaced when it came to school. She and her sisters were sitting on billions of dollars. They would never be poor. The way he saw it, school was like a hobby for them—the same way it was for him. He had a private tutor who came by the set three times a week, but he didn't really give the woman his undivided attention. He was getting his high school diploma to please his mother back in Iowa. When that neat little piece of paper came, he'd kiss school good-bye. He had no time for college. And what would be the point of it, anyway? He'd just signed four new contracts, which would keep him busy making movies for the next three years.

He stood up and stretched, flexing his thick arms.

In that moment, Park decided that it would be perfectly fine and lovely to just sit in this tiny enclosed space for the next few hours and watch Jeremy walk around shirtless. She might even opt to do that tomorrow night, and for most of Sunday. Big muscles. Thick lips. It was all good.

Jeremy turned around, a pensive look on his face. "I'm actually really glad you decided to spend the day here today, Park. I need to talk to you about something."

She leaned back in the chair. "Okay. What's up?"

Jeremy sat down beside her again. He handed her the towel and indicated the sheen of sweat glistening on his shoulders and back.

Park was happy to oblige. She maneuvered the towel slowly, methodically, over his smooth, tan skin.

"Well, you know how *Short Fuse* has a really big budget behind it," he began. "I mean, it's a formula and it's all there—thriller, action, and the script isn't bad at all. The studio thinks it's gonna be a huge hit when it's released next year."

"All your movies have been huge hits," Park said.

"Yeah, but this one has a big-name cast. Anyway . . . you know how Gabriella DuBois is supposed to play my girlfriend in the movie?"

Park laughed. "Duh. I think I knew that before you did. I saw Gabriella in Paris a few months ago. I think it's going to be her first action film."

Gabriella DuBois was a stunner, probably the most adventurous and opinionated young actress in Hollywood; she had just turned nineteen and already had two Academy Award nominations under her belt. In addition to making movies, Gabriella was noted for her tireless work with several nonprofit organizations benefiting underprivileged children. And when she wasn't in some third world hot spot, Gabriella DuBois was the face of the new Giorgio Armani campaign.

"Well," Jeremy said, "we found out this morning that Gabriella dropped out of the movie. She's got, like, a bunch of political things to do."

"Are you serious?" Park stopped moving the towel across his back. "I can't believe it! She was so excited about this role."

"Yeah, well, it happens. But that's what I wanted to talk to you about. Actually, it's what Gilberto Vitton wants to talk to you about too."

Gilberto Vitton was the director of *Short Fuse*. As it turned out, he had also directed a number of other outstanding movies, one of which had earned him an Academy Award for Best Director.

Park's face registered confusion. "Why would Gilberto want to talk to me?" she asked. "I mean, I love his work, but we really don't know each other."

"Well, he wants to get to know you, and soon." Jeremy stood up. A smile creased his lips as he turned to face her. Then the mildly happy expression went totally ecstatic. He dropped to his knees and grabbed her hands. "Babe, we want you to take on the role that Gabriella DuBois just dropped. We want you to star in this movie."

"*What?*" Park's voice hit a painfully high note. She felt her eyes bug out of her skull.

"You heard me," Jeremy said excitedly. "Gilberto thinks you'd be perfect for the part! It's the role of Lily Zane, and not only is she my love interest, but she's also the girl who helps me counteract a nuclear attack—"

"Jeremy," Park cut in. "That's insane! I . . . I can't just drop everything—"

"—and you wouldn't have to do any of your own stunts. Most of the filming is being done here in New York, and school is about to let out for you—"

"I have to go see my mom in Italy in two weeks! Madison and Lex will kill me if I don't go. Plus all the work we have to do for the clothing line—"

"—and think of the on-screen chemistry we'd have!" Jeremy continued, ignoring her protests. "Think of how great it would be to work together. Babe, this movie's gonna be bigger than anything I've ever done—"

"Jeremy, stop!"

"We'd be the next huge Hollywood power couple. Bigger than Brad and Angelina. Bigger than when Tom and Nicole were powerful."

Park shot to her feet, the towel tumbling to the floor. She clamped her hands on his shoulders and gave him a little shake. "Jeremy, listen to yourself! You're not thinking. And you're not even listening to me."

"What's to think about, Park? This was totally meant to be." He smiled broadly and touched her face. "Who's better than you?"

She rolled her eyes. "How about a *professional* actress? Someone who does this kind of thing for a living."

"You already do it for a living. You've been doing it since the day you were born. You live your whole life in the public eye."

"Yeah, that's true. But I don't *act*. That's a totally different thing."

"Is it?" He sat down again. He looked up at her, his stare hard and serious. "Babe, think about it. You already *are* an actor. When you're out in public, you have to think about every move you make. If you make the wrong one, it'll end up in the papers. If you feel like crying in a room full of people, you have to hold in your tears and act happy. When you do one of your press conferences, you have to act like you're interested in what's going on, even when you couldn't care less. I mean, aside from me and Madison and Lex and your parents and maybe a couple of other people, who knows the *real* you? No one . . . because you have to act the way the public wants you to."

Park felt like she'd been hit in the face with a bucket of ice water. She had never thought of her life in that respect—acting almost every moment, playing a role for the paparazzi and the public. But it was, in fact, true. The little, inane details of life completely eluded her. She had never had the experience of walking down Fifth Avenue in comfortable jogging pants and flip-flops. She had never left her penthouse without makeup. And while the very thought of wearing jogging pants and flip-flops made her want to seek urgent medical care, she understood Jeremy's point. She didn't really *live* the way ordinary people lived. How could she? When you were born a celebutante, life demanded nothing less than perfection.

But that still didn't qualify her to star in a movie. As far as she was concerned, acting was a true art. She had always marveled at the brilliant women and men who graced the stage, who tackled challenging roles and completely transformed themselves for a captive audience. Like Cate Blanchett in *Elizabeth*. Like Johnny Depp in *Pirates of the Caribbean*. And like her own mother, Venturina Baci, in countless European masterpieces. It was a magical talent. Looks, of course, played a big role in the theatrical equation, but you could totally tell the *real* actors from the merely pretty ones. And while Park knew she possessed the beautiful face and hot body for a successful on-screen career, she shivered at the thought of being compared to a sitcom star, or Tara Reid.

She averted her eyes from Jeremy's excited face. The trailer was just too small. She couldn't waltz into another room or hide behind anything. So she sighed and said calmly, "This isn't the kind of decision I can make right now. I mean, I really appreciate the offer and I'd love to work with you, but . . ."

"But what?"

She hesitated.

"Babe?" Jeremy prodded. "What is it?"

"I'm not sure I have the talent," she finally admitted. "And I don't want to look like some bimbo in a movie people can watch over and over again. I mean—did you see *The Dukes of Hazzard*?"

"Oh my God! Park—that's totally twisted!" He threw up his arms, then dropped them back down to his sides. "I know you have the talent. I've seen the way you appreciate film. You feel it. You respect the craft. And, for fuck's sake, it's *in your blood.*"

"Watch your mouth and lower your voice!" she snapped. "There could be kids outside!"

"Sorry," he mumbled. In the strained silence that followed, he reached across the couch and grabbed his Hermès messenger bag. He unzipped it and pulled out a tattered clump of pages.

Park felt a tiny quiver in her stomach.

"This is the script," Jeremy said, holding it out to her. "As far as I'm concerned, it has your name written all over it."

Park laced her fingers around the bulk of pages. She couldn't believe any of this was happening. She couldn't believe she was being offered a major role in a major movie, a movie that could very likely catapult her into an even bigger sphere of fame. It was sheer madness. And yet, something about holding the script in her hands was absolutely thrilling.

"Thank you," she said softly. She drew closer to Jeremy and kissed him. "You and Gilberto . . . you guys haven't mentioned anything about this to anyone, have you?"

"Totally not," Jeremy replied. "But you'll consider it, right? I mean, seriously?"

"Yes, I will." She smiled. "But right now, I have to get going. I'll call you later."

He wrapped his arms around her. "I'll miss you tonight."

"I'll miss you, too," she answered with a smile and another quick kiss. Then Park was climbing out of the trailer and onto the street. She scanned the traffic and spotted her limousine waiting at the corner. She didn't get ten feet before someone called her name.

"Hey, Park!"

She turned and saw Julian Simmons, a fellow St. Cecilia's Prep student, waving at her from across the wide, busy stretch of Houston. "Hey there!" she called back, wondering what the next few minutes would bring.

The son of music mogul Corey Simmons, Julian was himself a hip-hop star in the making. He had spent most of his junior year on tour promoting his first single, aptly titled "I'm a Freaky Funker." It soared up the charts and laid the groundwork for what would undoubtedly be a successful recording career. Julian had the looks and the talent. What was more, he had the attitude—aggressive, confident, sexy. The girls loved him and he loved them right back. He was short and muscular, with a shaved head and piercing green eyes. He held the distinction of being one of only five African American students at St. Cecilia's Prep—and probably the only one who had been caught romancing a fellow senior in the girls' bathroom.

Park approached him with her cheek already poised in the air.

Julian gave her a quick peck, then wrapped his arms around her waist. "God*damn,* girl! You look finer than a Cartier diamond. You here hangin' with your boo?"

"Yes. Jeremy's filming his new movie here for the next few weeks." Park stepped back and gave Julian a quick once-over. "God, you always have the best clothes."

"I'm all about Dolce and Gabbana today." Julian slid his hand down the side of his black blazer. Boot-cut jeans and black leather loafers completed the look.

"Why aren't you in school?" Park asked. "Did you call in sick too?" She pointed to the big brown bag at his side and winked mischievously. "Looks like you spent the day shopping."

"Kind of. I got lots to do, babe. Tomorrow I'm in the studio recording another single."

Park eyed the bag, noting the pink-sequined end of a dress peeking out through a wad of tissue paper and, beside it, the leaves of some sort of plant or bouquet. "A gift for one of your girlfriends?"

Julian glanced down at the bag, then quickly pushed the pink-sequined dress back down into it. "You know me. Always thinking of the ladies." He smiled. "Anyway, I've gotta run. I'll see you tonight."

"You need a lift?" Park pointed to the limo. "I'm going uptown."

"No, no," Julian said, already backing away. He seemed to be rushing the moment, eager to cut it short. "See you tonight! We'll party hearty, girl!"

Park waved and watched as he jogged down the length

of Houston Street. *That* was totally unlike Julian. Usually, he would have jumped at the chance to be in the back of a limo with a girl. Nothing would've happened between them, of course, but it was always fun to flirt.

Right now, though, Park had other issues on her mind. She hugged the movie script tightly to her chest as she walked to her car. *A major motion picture,* she thought. *Lights, cameras, and maybe more action than I really want.*

Most people wouldn't understand her reservations, but there was such a thing as being too famous.

# 3

# The Canoli and the Queen

Concetta Canoli emerged from the Chamber—otherwise known as the basement of her family's town house on East Sixty-fifth Street—and shut the door quietly. She stood there for a moment, listening for a sign. There was only silence around her. She smiled. She had once again succeeded as mistress of the secret court.

Climbing the stairs, she carefully plucked the lightweight crown from her head of curly black hair and stuffed it under her arm. Sweat beaded her cheeks. Her role in the club was no small feat: it required stamina and strength and lots of energy. As she thought back on tonight's meeting, she felt a rush of elation course through her body. Her fellow members had been impressed with her performance. She'd gotten all the little details correct, right down to the bloody finale. Sunday's afternoon session would be even better.

At the top of the staircase landing, Concetta paused and studied herself in the floor-to-ceiling mirror mounted on the wall. Many people would have labeled her heavy or plump or downright fat, but she played herself off as sensual, curvaceous, and pleasantly full-figured. She didn't fit the mold of a typical St. Cecilia's Prep student. She didn't project the image of a celebutante either. While *those* girls swooned at the thought of slipping into anything other than a size-zero dress, Concetta tried her best to project a strong self-image. And she was fully aware that her family name commanded as much power and respect as anyone else's. In an odd and somewhat cruel twist of fate, the Canoli clan had built a global empire creating and selling dietary products—from low-calorie breakfast drinks and frozen dinners to fat-free double-chocolate brownies. But that didn't matter to Concetta. She had abandoned dieting a long time ago. She had given up on drinking a gallon of water a day or smoking cigarettes to curb her appetite. None of it worked for her. It was easier to just hold her head high, act confident, and hope that men everywhere would come to their senses and see that big gals had a lot more lovin' to give.

She pushed open the basement door with her shoulder. The huge kitchen fanned out before her, complete with three professional stainless steel ovens and granite countertops. It was her favorite room of the house. Not because it held hundreds of delectable treats, but because the kitchen was where the Canoli family held their elaborate and very private dinners. From the spotless gleam of the terra-cotta tiles, Concetta could see that the maids had been cleaning today. The thought made her nervous. Had any of them heard her friends screeching and crying? It was unlikely. Concetta had gone to great lengths in sealing the Chamber appropriately. And if the maids *had* heard anything disturbing, they wouldn't say anything. Hell, they were probably too scared to even think about what went on downstairs.

She pranced over to the Sub-Zero and wrestled open the heavy silver door. She shoved aside the frozen squares of her family's fat-free desserts and went straight for the box of DeLafée truffles on the very last shelf. Popping one into her mouth, she hurried past the living room, past the dining room, through the entertainment room, and up the main staircase. At seven o'clock, it was still early. Her parents hadn't arrived home yet from their week at the house in the Grenadines, and her younger brothers were probably out shopping for new lacrosse gear. With luck, Concetta would have the whole house to herself for the rest of the evening. That would give her the chance to pretty herself up without interruption. She had been looking forward to the opening night of Cleopatra for months now. There was a lot she had to do there tonight.

Throwing open the door to her bedroom, Concetta stopped short and let out a gasp. "What are you doing in here?" she said, the words slurred by a mouthful of thick chocolate.

Her best friend, Emmett McQueen, was sitting at the vanity in the corner. Shirtless, his hair wrapped in a

44

towel, he didn't bother turning around as he plucked a few thick hairs from between his eyebrows. "I'm getting ready," he said flatly. "I told y'all I wasn't going home."

"I thought you told me you were going home first to get your clothes, then coming back here." Concetta frowned. "Not that I care. I just hate being scared."

"*You* hate being scared?" Emmett swiveled around in the chair. "Ha! You would never guess that, seein' how you are in the Chamber." His Southern twang echoed through the bedroom. "I swear, my heart nearly stops every time you take a step."

"Oh, be quiet. I'm not *that* scary." Concetta strolled across the room to her walk-in closet and reached for the garment bag hanging from the gown rack. She kicked off her shoes, then shook open the DeLafée box with her free hand and rolled out another truffle.

She was actually glad Emmett had decided to stay. She needed him for backup. Though her family had strong ties to Milan, Concetta sometimes found herself unable to match outfits correctly. Once, at a big Hollywood movie premiere, she'd walked down the carpet in a green gown and red pumps; she had thought it looked fine, but the next day she'd been labeled an olive in the tabloids. Emmett, on the other hand, was a fashion god. He could sweep his eyes across a closet and put together a gorgeous outfit in under two minutes. He could even take a drab brown scarf and turn it into the most dazzling accessory to grace your neck, with the right ensemble. He didn't understand why Concetta always wore oversized shirts and sweaters, especially those frilly Mozart shirts with their dramatic puckered sleeves that nearly covered her hands entirely. She looked like a pirate—and not a sexy one.

They had been best friends for nearly five years. In junior high, Concetta had ballooned—or, as she put it, blossomed—to nearly two hundred and fifty pounds, making her an instant target for cruel jokes and disapproving stares. But Emmett had always come to her defense. With his sharp Southern tongue and unshakeable confidence, he had stood up to the bullies and challenged the mean girls. Both factions had been no match for Emmett: the boys had been put off by his flamboyant ways, and the girls resented him for being such an awesome bitch. But most of the time, Emmett's antics were subterfuge. Concetta knew this. She knew that beneath the flashy, snippy exterior was a simple guy with a big heart and an incredibly high level of intelligence.

It wasn't easy being Emmett McQueen. He was the heir to a massive home-shopping TV empire. He had conservative parents and conservative roots. The paparazzi adored him but he didn't really like being photographed. And, of course, he was totally hot and totally gay, which made him all the more newsworthy.

The last six months had been especially difficult for Emmett. Following an international corporate scandal, his father, Warren McQueen, had been charged with extorting millions of dollars from private investors. The backlash had been downright brutal. For weeks on end, Emmett had watched his family fall apart piece by piece. He had been hounded by reporters outside of school and been the subject of several lurid magazine articles. Then came the final insult—witnessing his beloved dad being marched out of a courtroom in handcuffs, tears streaking the older man's face. Warren McQueen, sentenced to thirty years in a federal penitentiary, had since written countless letters to his son, begging for forgiveness.

In his heart, Emmett had forgiven his father for being such a complete idiot. But Emmett and his mom were still recovering from the damage of the scandal. They had lost over one hundred million dollars. They had been forced to sell their beachfront compound in the Hamptons and their three-hundred-acre ranch in Dallas. As far as Emmett was concerned, the toughest part of the whole mess wasn't really financial; it was the embarrassment that came with being disgraced, the pain of being blacklisted by the elite Manhattan social circles that had always welcomed him.

"Where's your suit?" Concetta asked, dropping the box of truffles onto her desk.

Emmett pointed to the white garment bag on the bed. "All wrapped up and ready to be unveiled."

"Who are you wearing?" She walked over to the bed and inspected the garment bag. "Oh, wait! Did you get Lex Hamilton to design you a Triple Threat menswear piece?"

"I sure did, honey! And it's a masterpiece!" He stood up. He unwrapped the towel from his head and dropped it onto the floor, exposing a shock of thick white-blond hair that fell over his ears in shaggy pieces. Reaching for the garment bag, he unzipped it and held up the one-of-a-kind outfit.

Concetta gasped.

The suit was charcoal, pin-striped, made of the finest materials money could buy, no doubt. A gold handkerchief gleamed in the lapel pocket. The tie was dark and flecked with gold thread. The custom-made cuff links of the crisp white shirt were gold as well.

"It's amazing!" Concetta cried.

"I know. I've never looked so good. I swear, little Lexy knows sexy." He held the suit against his chest and modeled it, shifting his weight from one foot to the other.

Suddenly, Concetta's face registered anger. She bit down on her lips, and a smear of chocolate arced beneath her chin. "You . . . you can't wear that, Emmett!"

He stared at her, shocked. One hand flew to his throat. "And why the hell not? You said yourself it's amazin'."

"It is, but . . ."

"But what?" He laid the suit down on the bed and planted his hands on his hips. "Talk, sister. 'Cause I can't read minds."

Concetta spun around and stomped over to the vanity. She peered into the three-way mirror, giving herself a solid once-over. Her jeans were tight at the waist. Her pink shirt, though oversized, was tight at her boobs. And so her eyes went automatically to her butt, which was big and ample and . . . well . . . as round as a full moon. *She* told herself it looked good. But would the object of her affection like it?

Emmett sighed dramatically. "*Helllllooo?* You gonna talk, or are you gonna stand there like a clove on a baked ham?"

Concetta sighed. "It's just that *you'll* look so good, and *he* might notice *you* instead of *me.*"

"Oh, sister . . . puh-lease!" Emmett waved his hands in the air as if batting away a swarm of bees. "You're gettin' yourself all worked up for nothin'. You'll be the queen of the ball tonight."

"But what if I'm not? What if *he* doesn't think I am?"

"He already likes you. I know it."

"No he doesn't."

"He sure does."

"You really think so?"

With a slow nod, Emmett said, "I *know* so. When it comes to lust, my instincts are never wrong. He's as hot for you as I am for myself."

Concetta laughed. That was certainly the truth. Emmett had every reason to be hot for himself—the lean dancer's body, the blond hair and blue eyes, the perfect features. And all his physical attributes made her panic spike up a notch. "That's what I mean!" she said. "He probably likes you too. Everyone says he swings both ways."

"Well, everyone is crazy. Damien Kittle does not like me. He likes you. And I think we've seen evidence of that these past few months, haven't we?"

"Be quiet!" Concetta rushed to the bedroom door, pulled it open, and glanced up and down the corridor. It was clear. When she turned around again, Emmett was staring at her with wide, questioning eyes.

"What's your problem, Canoli?" he snapped.

Concetta walked back to the closet and began scanning it. "I just don't want anyone knowing that I like Damien Kittle," she said. "It's, like, a secret."

"A secret? What are you talking about? *Everyone* knows you've got a thing for Damien!" Emmett folded his arms over his bare chest. "Where's all that confidence of yours gone?"

"He's British royalty," Concetta said quietly, staring down at the floor. "I'm . . . not."

49

"So?"

"So that makes it really hard for me to even approach him when we're all . . . ya know . . . in the *real* world. In the Chamber things are different—I have no inhibitions. Plus, half the time, I don't even know if he's joking around with me or taking me seriously."

Emmett sniffed. He went back to the vanity and sat down. "You ask me, that boy is fixin' to join some sorta English circus. Did Shakespeare write anything with clowns in it?"

"Come on, Em," Concetta said desperately. "You have to help me tonight. You have to give me advice. I'm not good at attracting guys—even though I can't imagine why." She threw her head back as she shot a glance in the mirror.

Emmett got up and strolled across the bedroom. On the desk was his trademark accessory—a gorgeous Prada bag that acted as his man-purse. It had become somewhat of a running joke at school, but with the multitude of items he used on a daily basis, he saw no point in carrying around some horrible backpack. At least twice a day he needed his hairbrush and ZIRH men's moisturizer. In the event of a fashion emergency, he always carried around a black Polo T-shirt, which matched just about anything. Then there were his sunglasses and scarf, an assortment of Mont Blanc pens, and several sets of Cartier cuff links.

Now Emmett dipped into the man-purse and started shuffling through it. He yanked out a small makeup bag and dumped the rest back inside. "I'm gonna do your makeup. You'll look incredible when I'm finished. But first go into the bathroom and freshen up."

"You're the best!" Concetta threw her arms around him and planted a kiss on both his cheeks. She was in luck: when it came to makeup, Emmett was a genius.

Invigorated, Concetta ran into the master bathroom, slammed the door shut, and jumped into the shower. When she emerged ten minutes later wrapped in a light cashmere robe, the sleeves trailing over her hands, Emmett was standing in front of the mirror studying his reflection.

He looked flat-out gorgeous in the Triple Threat suit; it hugged his silhouette perfectly and even made his chest seem broad and slightly muscular. He had slicked his hair back with gel. He had even applied a fresh coat of skin-firming lotion to his face so that it gleamed in the overhead track lighting, though that could have easily been the gold Nars body cream he'd highlighted his cheekbones with.

"Wow," Concetta said. "If you were straight, Emmett, I'd totally try to seduce you."

He nodded. "I know. So let's get you started. Come over here and sit down."

Concetta did as she was told, all the while imagining what Damien Kittle would say to her tonight. She pictured him walking up to her from his side of the bar with that devilish grin on his face, his eyes undressing her, his hands reaching out to stroke her shoulder. Maybe he'd ask her to dance. Maybe he'd usher her into the very middle of the floor while the shocked crowd looked on. Concetta would handle herself with grace but emote sensuality. Despite her robust frame, she was an excellent dancer. She knew how to rumba. Hell, she knew how to shake like

Shakira *and* Beyoncé. And what better way to get Damien Kittle's attention? Before the night was through, Concetta wanted to make him hers.

And she wouldn't settle for anything less than a kiss.

She closed her eyes as Emmett went to work. She felt herself becoming more and more beautiful with each passing minute. Chiseled brushes glided over her eyelids. Cool cream caressed her cheeks and chin. She tasted lipstick and smelled blush. Then a hair dryer flicked on, the whoosh of noise startling her. Some sort of rich-smelling product was being worked into her thick locks.

When Emmett was done, he pulled her out of the chair and said, "Don't you *dare* look in the mirror yet. Go get dressed first, and then I'll finish up."

Concetta followed his orders. She raced into the bathroom and carefully slipped into her rose-colored silk Missoni gown. Flown in from Milan three days ago, the gown was an extraordinary work of art. Angela Missoni had designed it especially for Concetta, with long sleeves and ruffles that circled her wrists and hands.

Taking a deep, calming breath, she padded out of the bathroom and stared directly at Emmett.

"Beautiful," he whispered. "My heart is a-poundin'. Now come on over here and looky-looky yourself. And don't you *dare* tell me that you ain't gorgeous."

Concetta stepped in front of the mirror—and gasped. Her face was perfect and contoured, as if ready to grace the cover of *Vogue*. Her lips were full and heart-shaped. Her brown eyes looked bigger and brighter than ever. Best of all, her curly hair was now straight and silky as it swept over her shoulders. "I can't believe it!" she cried. "I look amazing! Oh, Emmett, thank you!" She walked into the center of the room. She did a little turn, modeling not only her gown, but also the poise she would be sure to exude tonight. Emmett had schooled her in the ways of projecting full confidence; it meant holding your head high, throwing your shoulders back . . . and drawing attention to the jewelry sparkling around your neck. Every celebutante knew that.

"Will you be wearing emeralds or diamonds tonight?" Emmett asked.

"Emeralds," Concetta said.

"That leaves only one more question." Emmett stared down at Concetta's bare feet—wide, white, big-as-a-pizza-pie feet that no pair of shoes could properly conceal. He tried to smile.

"I know *exactly* which shoes to wear," Concetta said firmly, marching into her closet. "I don't need any advice in that department."

Emmett waited on the threshold, a fearful look on his face.

Shoes were Concetta's fashion passion. Dresses and gowns and designer jeans were certainly a good thing, but every piece of clothing ultimately looked the same on her round body. The sizes only seemed to get larger with each new event. Her shoe size, however, didn't change. In the past five years she had amassed a fabulous collection of footwear. Her personal taste wasn't always of the subtle variety, but she loved spending money on heels, pumps, stilettos, and even comfortable flats to wear around the house.

She walked to the very back of the closet. An entire

wall housed her vast shoe collection, much like a museum exhibit. An array of bright colors and shapes came alive under the overhead track lighting, and she swept her eyes across the rows and columns with practiced ease. There. Right there. She cleared her throat nervously as she reached for the chosen pair, fully aware that Emmett would disapprove.

She slipped them on and walked back out to the bedroom.

Emmett gasped and slapped a hand to his forehead. "*Those?*" he whispered faintly.

Concetta scowled. "Yes—*these*. And wipe that stupid look off your face, okay?" She made a full turn in front of the mirror, liking what she saw, feeling more confident than she ever had. "I swear," she said sharply, "if Damien Kittle doesn't *totally* fall in love with me tonight, I might do something *crazy*."

# 4

# Cleopatra

It was the greatest nightclub ever built.

Rising like a mirage from the gray concrete, Cleopatra stood four stories tall and occupied an entire city block. Impressive stone columns beckoned guests to double doors made of solid gold. The arched plate-glass windows, backlit by spinning strobes, were emblazoned with hieroglyphs and three-dimensional sketches of serpents. A thin red carpet cut down the center of the intricate cobblestone walkway. And high above it all, perched on the rooftop terrace, was a two-hundred-foot-tall replica of the Sphinx. Designed to look like a museum in daylight hours, the club was more Manhattan modern than Vegas tacky. Cleopatra herself would have been impressed.

It was ten o'clock. The streets of the Lower East Side had never been so packed. Blue police barricades blocked oncoming traffic, and groups of private security guards huddled on the sidewalks. Then there were the onlookers— everyone from teenagers and college students to middle-aged couples—pushing as close to the club's entrance as possible to catch glimpses of their favorite celebrities. Up in the sky, two news choppers circled the scene. One limousine stopped to deposit its guests and another pulled right on up. The crowds were so thick, dozens of extra police officers had to be dispatched from their posts all over Manhattan.

It was the marvelous sort of mayhem Lex lived for. As she sat in the back of the Hamilton family limousine, she surveyed the chaos happily. Flashes cut through the shadowy interior like lightning. She had been waiting too long for this night, and now there was only one mission at hand: to party. "Look at how great the club looks!" she said excitedly as the limo drew close to the curb. "I mean—it's incredible! It looks like something from another world! Are you seeing what I'm seeing?"

Park, sitting directly across from her, nodded. "It really is beautiful."

"Is that all you can say?" Lex snapped, turning to face her sister. "It's spectacular! Dad did an incredible job with this one!"

"You're right," Park replied evenly. "It's spectacular. And *we* look downright spectacular too, by the way."

Lex glanced down at her violet dress with its intricate serpentine weavings and pale fringe. It was a show-stopper. It hugged her waist, accentuated her curves, and was perfect for dancing. And it was, of course, one of her own designs, a Triple Threat original.

Park's black silk suit, with its oblong belt and matching leather gloves, was also Triple Threat. In fact, for the next several months, the Hamilton triplets wouldn't be wearing anything *but* Triple Threat designs in public. That was part of the marketing campaign. Whenever they were photographed, the label would be photographed. It didn't matter if they were attending a movie premiere, a stockholders' meeting, or just going out to a simple dinner—the Triple Threat fashion line ruled their closets, with the exception of a few pairs of jeans and shoes.

So far, the plan was working. In just over a month the line had made international fashion news, and Lex was currently in the middle of designing her second collection. Come fall, Barneys and Saks would be among the elite retailers stocking the label.

"Do you think Madison is here already?" Lex asked, reaching for her purse.

"Madison is always on time," Park replied. "She and Theo are probably already on the dance floor."

Lex made a sour face. Mentioning Theodore Aaron West was like hearing a rude burp pierce the air. Despite the fact that the West and Hamilton families were social and corporate rivals, Theo and Madison were totally—and sickeningly—in love. After a year of secret rendezvous, they had finally taken their relationship public. In truth, their relationship had been exposed via a gossip column, but that hadn't mattered to either one of them. They were more than happy to stop sneaking around. And the press was having a day in the park photographing them all over town.

Lex didn't understand it. She knew Theo West was a hottie. She knew he had brains and exuded sexiness, but she didn't agree one bit with Madison's decision to rock the media boat. There were so many guys who adored Madison. Why couldn't she just pucker up to a less threatening affair?

"Stop making faces," Park said suddenly.

"What?"

"You're scowling because I mentioned Theo West. You have to get over it, Lex. They're together, and that's that."

Lex pursed her lips in a disapproving frown. "Fine. But I don't have to like it. And *you* can't make me."

"Is that any way to talk to your older sister?"

"You're only older than me by three minutes!"

Park shrugged. "That still gives me certain rights, and telling you to chill is one of them, okay? I mean, if Dad can handle Madison and Theo being together, so can you."

A dramatic, heavy sigh escaped Lex's lips. She swung the strap of her purse over her left shoulder and winced. It was her all-purpose Louis—the magic purse; beautiful but painfully heavy, it contained everything a girl needed to conquer a difficult moment—or, in her case, the world. "I'll *try* to be on my best behavior," she said. "And while we're talking about attitudes, you should totally curb yours."

"I don't have an attitude," Park replied calmly. "I just have a lot on my mind."

"You're going to star in a blockbuster movie!" Lex screamed excitedly. "You should be thrilled. It'll be the start of a whole new career!"

"I'm *not* starring in that movie. I just have to figure a

way out of it." Park reached for her own purse. "Anyway, let's assume the position. I want to avoid as many reporters as possible."

The limo came to a stop. Lex popped open the door and put one foot on the pavement. Then, counting off five seconds, she emerged into the barrage of camera flashes and screams and took three steps forward. She plastered a broad smile on her lips. A few precise seconds later, she felt Park brush up against her.

"Lexington!"

"Park!"

They stood side by side on the red carpet leading up to the gold front doors of the club. Two beefy security guards rushed toward them, flanking them on either side.

"You're blocking me too much," Lex called out to one of them. Stepping past him, she grabbed Park's hand and made the brisk stride up the carpet. The chorus of voices calling out to them was like a clap of thunder.

"Hurry," Park said loudly into Lex's ear. "I'm not stopping to answer any questions."

On cue, Lex took a few more steps, then turned around to face the crowds again. She counted off five more seconds, giving every photographer a chance to snap flattering pics of her dress.

The chaos of the press and hundreds of screaming fans was instantly replaced by the blare of deafening music as they walked into the club's massive vaulted entrance. Lex spotted Justin, Paris and Nicky, Lindsay, Kanye, and Orlando. She waved warmly. No sign yet of Donatella or Zac yet.

"It's absolutely phenomenal," Park said, looking up at

the four stories that had been constructed in a perfect circle over the wide main dance floor.

"Even better than I expected," Lex agreed. "This will pull in at least twenty mil a year."

"Oh, it'll pull in more than that." Park calculated all of the elaborate space. "Especially when you consider how many special events it'll book, and how many movie studios will want to rent it out for location shoots."

The interior of Cleopatra was customarily dark, but rows of spotlights and crystal chandeliers brightened the long bar areas and little nooks where guests could recline. Dozens of crystal sconces blazed with tapered candles. At the very back of the first floor was a stunning fifty-foot waterfall that spewed sparkling streams of water. But the most astounding corner of the club was the full-service on-site salon that invited guests to freshen up between sets of music and dancing. There were three stylists on hand, as well as two massage therapists and a makeup artist.

It made perfect sense. Lex couldn't remember how many times she had stepped off a dance floor drenched in sweat, her muscles aching. She wouldn't have that problem anymore, and neither would anyone else. Now, when quick primping was in order, or when makeup smudged from too much exertion, the most seasoned Manhattan nightlife-goers would have a place in which to take refuge and freshen up.

Every floor of Cleopatra was teeming. On the main level, guests were enjoying a somewhat relaxed mingling scene, complete with gorgeous waiters and waitresses—probably out-of-work actors and models—passing out champagne and caviar. The second floor was reserved for those who wished to socialize off the dance floor: the décor was decidedly ornate, yet the clean lines suggested a magical translation into modern design. Recalling the magic of the ancient Egyptian era, the space boasted statues of pharaohs, a gilded bar, and rare works of art purchased directly from Sotheby's. The third and fourth floors were strict dancing zones. Madison had hired the MisShapes kids to DJ, and the huge speakers pumped out their mix of old and new while strobe lights flashed over suspended cages.

It was this last sight that worried Park. She had never liked those big iron cages that lifted dancers almost to the ceiling and allowed them to boogie in the air. Looking at them now, she was reminded of Jeremy's stunt earlier today. Too dangerous. What kind of birdbrain would risk her life just to dance in a suspended cage?

"I *love* the cages!" Lex suddenly exclaimed, staring upward. "I can't wait to get in one." She fell in synch with the beat of the music and began gyrating her hips.

Park rolled her eyes. "Figures you'd say something like that."

Just then, Madison came powering toward them, pushing her way through the pockets of guests with both her arms. She was wearing a stunning red silk dress that stopped just above her knees; it was shorter and more daring than anything she'd worn in the recent past, but her trim body filled the dress out perfectly. She looked beautiful. But she didn't look happy.

"You're *not* going to believe this!" she snapped, stepping in between Park and Lex.

"What's wrong?" Park asked.

Madison bit down on her lower lip and pointed toward the upper floors. "I just found out that the floral arrangements on the fourth floor are . . ." Her voice trailed away, and she clamped her eyes shut. "Oh, God. I can't even say it."

"What?" Lex grabbed ahold of Madison's arm.

Madison shook her head.

"For God's sake, just spill it," Park urged.

"The floral arrangements are . . . *completely out of date.*"

"*What?*" Lex screeched. "Are you kidding me? Have you lost your mind? Like the eighties' 1-800-FLOWERS? Or more like seventies-*Scarface*—that could be kind of cool."

"No—it's worse. They aren't even like River Nile or baby Moses—and I don't know how it happened!" Madison said. "I saw them out of the corner of my eye—this weird reddish-purplish color and big prehistoric leaves—and then I went up to them and looked closely and that's when I nearly died!"

"*Prehistoric leaves!*" Lex shrieked. "As in Paleolithic? Did you pull them off the tables? Did you get rid of them?"

"No. I couldn't. I can't even stand to touch them!" Madison brought a hand to her forehead and started breathing heavily.

"It serves you right!" Lex said coldly. "You were responsible for most of the décor in here! Do you have any idea what will happen if word gets out that we have ugly florals, instead of the arrangements that were supposed to be flown in from Morocco? They were supposed to be era-appropriate!"

"Both of you, calm down." Park grabbed her sisters by their hands.

"I can't calm down!" Lex answered back sharply. She pointed at Madison. "This dimwit screwed up the flowers!"

"I'm sorry," Madison choked out. "Oh, if I even see those things again, I'll vomit."

"Both of you, listen to me." Park threw her head back and did a quick sweep of their immediate surroundings to make sure no one important was in earshot. "We're going to casually make our way upstairs and collect the ugly contraband, and that will be the end of it. Okay? Now just follow me."

And with that, Park led the cool, easy march up the glass-and-metal staircase. When people reached out to greet them, she made certain to nod and smile, but she kept moving. Madison and Lex did the same. They made it to the fourth level, where the ghastly arrangements sat in vases on three glass tables.

"Horrendous," Lex seethed. "Those aren't even flowers. They're plants!"

Park coolly approached the first table and wrapped her hands around the green stems. She made a pretense of holding them to her nose and inhaling a sweet scent. If a curious passerby took notice, he or she would see nothing odd about the little gesture. She walked over to Lex and said, "Open the magic purse."

In one fast, fluid movement, Lex unzipped the purse and held it open. The first clump of stems and leaves barely fit, but she shoved them down with her fist. "Ugh," she said, flexing her fingers. "They feel like dirty wax." She held the purse out to Madison. "Go ahead, feel them.

I want you to know how dangerous mismatched floral arrangements can be at an exclusive event."

Madison wrinkled her nose. She extended her hand and lowered it into the magic purse as if she were about to make contact with a poisonous, exotic viper. When her fingers finally grazed one of the green leaves, she gasped. Then she scanned a nearby table and found what she was looking for: a champagne flute filled to the rim with Dom Perignon. She took three long gulps.

There were two more vases to empty. Park collected them swiftly and easily. But with no more room in the magic purse, Lex had to resign herself to holding the ugly bunch of fernlike leaves and stems. Her mouth fell open in a silent scream. She stared at Park, who had already turned around and begun waving at a number of their St. Cecilia's Prep friends. Madison was still swaying from the floral infraction.

"Here comes trouble," Park suddenly said over the music.

Lex and Madison turned and saw Damien Kittle walking toward them.

"Good evening, ladies!" he purred, instantly rubbing up against Lex. "You're looking smashing." He grabbed her hand, brought it to his lips, and kissed it.

"Oh, Damien, you're such a charmer!" Lex laughed and planted a kiss on his cheek.

"A snake charmer, maybe," he replied with a grin.

"That's a great suit," Madison said. "Who are you wearing?"

"Zegna. His suits make me look innocent, don't they?" He made an angelic face, rolling his eyes heavenward.

"It's totally impossible for you to look innocent," Lex said. "You're too much of a devil."

"Hey, Damien, you look pale." Park stepped toward him and gave one end of his sleeve a tug. "Have you been partying too much already?"

He shrugged. "It's possible, I suppose." He wiped a trail of sweat from his forehead and coughed. "I'm extremely tired. Long day."

Staring at him intently now, Lex noticed the unusual pallor of his skin and the bright blotches on his forehead. "Have you been sneaking drinks from the bar, Damien? You *know* high school students aren't supposed to be drinking."

"Ha! That's a good one! I'm probably just tired because all the ladies keep begging me to dance." He shot a glance at Madison. "How 'bout you, Mads? Take a spin with me on the floor?"

"I can't," she replied. "My boyfriend's here."

"And speak of the devil," Damien said, gesturing his head over her shoulder.

Madison turned and saw Theo West climbing the stairs. The moment their eyes met, she smiled.

Theo was tall and handsome, an all-American playboy. The Hugo Boss suit Madison had picked out for him last week accentuated his long, firm physique. His hair was combed neatly and parted to one side. "Hey," he said, wrapping his arms around her and planting a kiss on her lips. "I was looking for you downstairs. Why'd you disappear?"

Madison shook her head. "We had some . . . business to take care of up here." She cleared her throat. "Anyway, are you having a good time?"

"The best." Theo nodded at Damien, then set his eyes on Park and Lex.

"Hi, Theo," Park said cordially. "Glad you could make it." She air-kissed his cheek.

Lex kept her expression stony but, remembering Park's earlier admonishment, allowed the barest hint of a smile to shine through. "Hi," she murmured, and then steered her gaze over Damien's shoulder.

"You girls look beautiful," Theo said.

Lex nodded. "We know."

"I think what Lex *meant* to say was thank you," Park said, an edge in her tone. She shot Lex her sternest stare.

"So come on then," Damien shouted. "Let's party!" Spinning around, throwing his arms out wide, he shook his chest like a female stripper and purposely shimmied toward Theo.

Theo's eyes widened in stunned surprise.

"You ever dance with another man, Mr. West?" Damien whispered. "Could be brilliant between us."

"Uh . . . no . . . I don't think so," Theo answered, his cheeks flushing a vibrant red.

Lex burst out laughing.

"Hey, look. Here come Concetta and Emmett," Madison said excitedly. "Lex, the suit you did for him looks *amazing*!"

Emmett McQueen didn't just walk toward them—he strutted as though he were commandeering a catwalk during Fashion Week. His hips swayed, one foot crossed directly over another, and his right hand sat firmly on his waist while his left swung in the air. He got to within two feet of Lex and came to a sudden stop. Then, keeping his eyes cast downward, he pivoted ninety degrees. He repeated the well-rehearsed move until he had modeled the suit front and back. His Prada man-purse hung from the fingers of his left hand.

Lex thrust the ugly florals at Madison and broke out in applause. "You're *awesome*! Where are the damn photographers when you need them?"

"My whole body feels like gold," Emmett said. "I swear, sister, you should be livin' in Mee-lann and designing with the rest of those eye-talians."

Madison sighed a bit too loudly. "Those *Italians*, Emmett, happen to be artists. And Lex is a New York girl. *Milan* is much too far away."

Emmett sniffed, not bothering to hide his distaste for Madison. They had never liked each other. The highbrow, straitlaced Madison and the snippy, catty Emmett just didn't get along. She thought he lacked discretion; he thought she lacked personality. It was a relationship best kept at bay.

Now Emmett dropped his eyes to the pseudobouquet nestled in the crook of her left arm and said, "Those look like plastic flowers. Were you runnin' late, sweetheart? Couldn't stop and get yourself some real ones?"

"They're *not* plastic," Madison shot back coldly. "They're . . . they're . . ." Her voice faded as she clamored for an excuse.

Park instantly came to her rescue. "They're actually pieces of a new headdress we're thinking of producing," she said seriously. She plucked three of the green stems from the pseudobouquet and slipped them into Madison's hair. She pretended to arrange them, but the end result was a wilted mess that made Madison look like a flower girl on crack.

"Yes, they are," Lex chimed in, using her best bluffing voice. "It's a new style just coming out of Paris. Very trendy. Oh—look at how they catch the highlights in your hair, Madison. Don't you think so, Theo?"

"Uh . . . yeah. Totally." Theo coughed. "Breathtaking."

Madison had gone paler than a jar of Crème de la Mer. Tearing the stems from her hair, she scowled at her sisters and put a hand on Concetta's arm. "Darling, you look fabulous. Is that Missoni?"

Concetta nodded and smiled. Then she tossed her head from side to side, showcasing her silky, straight locks. "I wear it well, don't I?"

"Beautiful," Park said.

"You should be on a catwalk too," Lex commented.

Concetta giggled.

Julian Simmons suddenly burst into the group. "What's up, bitches?"

"Can't you address us more politely?" Madison snapped.

Julian laughed, then ground himself suggestively against Park. "As long as I get to dance with this here beauty, I'll undress you any way you want."

"I said *address,* not *undress.*" Madison turned away from him.

"Catch you later, baby," Julian said, winking at Park as he walked away.

"Well," Park said, sighing. "He really is a charmer."

Concetta trained her eyes directly on Damien Kittle. The lusty stare was so apparent, so painstakingly obvious, that everyone else in the group went silent.

Damien, thankfully, didn't make a snide remark.

Concetta inched her way closer to him. "So, um . . . how's it going?"

"Fine, love. I'm preparing to dance up a storm."

"So am I!" Concetta giggled again. She twirled a strand of hair in her finger and bounced up and down on her left leg. "Feel like . . . going out there with me?"

Damien shrugged. "Well, certainly. Let's get to it." He nodded at Madison, Park, Lex, Theo, and Emmett. "Cheerio!"

As he and Concetta headed for a spin, Madison turned to Park and Lex. "Well, we have to get to the main floor stage. It's about time to make our opening speech."

"I guess it is," Park said. "Dad's probably waiting for us."

"Yeah. Let's get this party started!" Lex bumped Emmett with her hip. "You owe me a dance, McQueen!"

"My body's on fire for you, sweet pea." Emmett winked, but the wink was aimed straight at Theo.

◇   ◇   ◇

Back on the main level, the traffic had grown thicker. Cameras flashed like lightning. Champagne bottles were being popped open and more than half the St. Cecilia's Prep student body had shown up. Cheers went up as Madison, Park, and Lex sifted through the crowds. Hand in hand, they walked to the large stage just beside the waterfall, where their father, Trevor Hamilton, was immersed in conversation with Donald and Ivanka.

Trevor was a tall, debonair, solidly built man. His gray hair was pushed back from his angular face. His blue eyes twinkled when he smiled. He had turned fifty in January, and his skin showed the subtle signs of aging—delicate lines on his forehead and around his mouth, a slight puffiness to his cheeks. He was a tireless entrepreneur, jetting from one continent to another on an almost weekly basis. It was no wonder he looked tired. And, unlike most famous men of his years, he refused to undergo plastic surgery of any kind.

When he saw Madison, Park, and Lex step onto the stage, he smiled and indicated the microphone that had been set up for them.

Madison walked into the spotlight smiling. "Welcome to Cleopatra!" she said, her voice booming across all four floors. "On behalf of Hamilton Holdings, Inc., and my sisters, Park and Lexington, I would like to welcome you to the hottest new club in the *world*!"

Raucous cheering shook the air. The ten photographers who had been permitted access to the event were snapping one pic after another.

Madison raised her hand in a perfect windshield wiper wave. Then she casually began unfolding a smooth sheet of paper—the speech she had prepared. But before she could launch into her intellectual spiel about the myths and legends of Egypt and the dangerous glamour of the great queen Cleopatra, she felt Lex bump her from the spotlight.

"Hey, everybody!" Lex said into the microphone. "Let's party! Let's get freakin' wild!" She let out an ear-piercing scream that prompted the DJs to take it to the next level.

Music exploded over the speakers and the crowd surged onto the dance floors, a wave of gyrating bodies.

Lex threw her arms up, flung her head back and forth, and launched into a carefree dance.

"You stole my spotlight!" Madison screamed over the music. "I worked on this speech for days! *Days!*" She shook the sheet of paper at Lex, slapping her with it.

"Honey, we'll all listen to your speech at home, okay? I promise." Park's voice, though barely audible, was reassuring. "Right now, though, why don't you just hit the dance floor? Theo's waiting for you."

Madison bared her teeth at Lex before disappearing down the stairs.

Park shoved Lex out of the spotlight and into a darker corner of the stage. "So now what?"

"Whataya mean?" Lex asked, coming off her dance high.

"Neither one of us has a date," Park said. "I guess that means we're destined to be wallflowers tonight."

"Never!" Lex screamed. "Not having dates is *way* better than having them! It means we can do whatever we want! Come on!" She clasped Park's wrist and dragged her back onto the floor.

And so in the middle of the crowd, strobes spinning and music thumping, Lex and Park danced the night away. They managed to steal Madison from Theo's grasp for a few minutes, long enough to form a triplet-power triangle in the shadow of the great waterfall. It went on for nearly two hours—nonstop dancing, one set after another, bodies packing every level of the club.

But it all came to a crashing halt shortly after midnight.

Madison, Park, and Lex were swaying to a beat when the overhead lights suddenly dimmed. People paused to glance up. Confusion registered everywhere. Then came the whine of the speakers—a loud screech that quickly burst into an eerie classical tune set to chanting.

Madison recognized it at once. "It's a Mozart Requiem," she said, instinctively reaching for Lex's hand.

"What's going on?" someone called out.

"Hey, look!" another voice shrieked.

The Requiem grew louder as one of the suspended cages glided down from the vaulted ceiling. It descended slowly, almost gracefully, stopping only three feet from the floor. A spotlight illuminated what lay inside the wrought iron bars.

It was Park who saw the trail of blood dripping from one end of the cage. It was Madison who screamed.

And it was Lex who instantly recognized the body of Damien Kittle.

# 5

## Stiletto

Even as chaos erupted around her, Lex kept her cool and darted for the cage. She shoved through the crowd like a bulldozer and didn't stop until her hands were firmly wrapped around the cold iron bars. Her heart was thudding in her chest. Her ears were ringing. And the spooky Requiem echoing throughout the club was sending shivers up her spine.

"Damien?" she called out. "Damien, is this one of your jokes? Damien? Answer me!" Her words were swallowed up by a chorus of other sounds—the music, several high-pitched screams and cries. Finally, in sheer desperation, she hoisted herself up, using the bars for leverage, and knocked open the cage's door. The whole box swayed from side to side as she tried to maintain her balance. Then, holding her breath, she forced herself to stare down at the ugly picture sprawled out before her.

There was no doubt that Damien was dead. His body was motionless, lying facedown, his left arm flung over his opposite shoulder. And there was blood—lots of it: little splatters and specks and a solid, oily stream oozing from his head. A thin trail of crimson spilled over one side of the cage, tiny drops hitting the dance floor below.

The breath shot from her lungs.

"Lex!" Madison was staring up at her, a panicked look on her face. "Oh my God! What's going on? Is he okay?"

Theo was beside Madison, his hands clasped protectively around her shoulders. "Lex, you should get down from there!"

"Is he okay?" Madison asked again.

"He's dead," Lex said flatly. The shock of her own words made her feel dizzy.

"Dead?" Madison wailed. "Are you sure?"

Lex glanced down at her sister and Theo. "I'm sure. He's totally dead."

"No!" Madison cried. "That can't be!"

"Jesus Christ," Theo whispered.

Madison broke from his hold. "Maybe Damien's just unconscious! Maybe he needs help—"

"Madison!" Lex snapped. "I'm looking at him right now, and he's, like, graveyard dead."

A flurry of whispers shot through the crowd. Several security guards rushed across the dance floor. The eerie music suddenly stopped.

"Theo," Madison ordered, "go make sure the police and an ambulance are coming. Now!"

With a nod, Theo pushed past the crowd and disappeared through the entryway.

"Somebody up there, lower that cage to the ground!" Madison yelled. She was staring at the ceiling, talking to the invisible technicians. "Hello? Does anyone hear me? *Lower that cage!*" Her voice echoed like thunder, and a few seconds later, the cage creaked as it came to a complete rest on the floor.

A new round of screams pierced the air. Now everyone in the club had a bird's-eye view of Damien Kittle's corpse, and the harsh end it had met.

"Okay, everybody please stay calm." Somehow, Park had made her way back to the stage. She was standing at its brightest end, a wireless microphone in her hand. "Let's all take a deep breath and start moving toward the exits." She motioned left and right, her arms outstretched and crisscrossing. She looked like a stewardess performing an evacuation demonstration. "There," she said, pointing to the left. "An emergency-exit light is blinking above the side doors. Please exit the club promptly, thank you." Despite the even tone of her voice, the instructions went unheeded.

People were scrambling around the cage, eager to get a look at the carnage. Cell phone cameras flashed. In a matter of moments, there were at least two dozen St. Cecilia's Prep students standing there, gasping, shaking their heads, crying openly.

Lex was trembling. She couldn't tear her eyes from the sight of Damien's unmoving body. Everything around her disappeared—the music, the crowd, the club itself. She was rooted to the spot, and yet a part of her wanted to bolt from the building and pretend this was all a nightmare.

"He was bludgeoned."

Lex nearly jumped out of her skin. She turned and saw Madison standing beside her. "What?"

Another wave of protests erupted from the crowds as security guards began pulling people outside.

"The wound on his head," Madison said quietly, "that's where all that blood's coming from. Someone popped him right behind the temple."

"It's so . . . *gross*." Lex cupped a hand over her mouth.

"Ladies and gentlemen, please prepare to exit the building immediately." Park's voice again, echoing through the speakers. "The highly attractive security guards are now directing you toward the exits. There's really nothing to see here. It's better if everyone just meets outside. Thank you!"

Madison waved her hands in the air to get Park's attention, motioning her over to the middle of the floor. That was when she locked eyes with several of her classmates. The faces staring back at her were all pale, sweaty, and scared.

"The cops will be here soon," Lex said. "I guess . . . we should . . ." She looked at Madison, waiting for instruction.

But the panic was evident on Madison's face. "I don't know what to do! We all *know* what'll happen once the cops get here. I mean, for God's sake, all they need is our name and a body and *poof*—instant slander."

Park had made it through the crowd. She climbed into

the cage quickly. She threw a glance at the body, gulped, and then trained her eyes on Madison and Lex. "Okay, first things first. Where's Dad?"

"I saw him leave over an hour ago," Madison said. "He has a meeting in Miami in the morning."

"Shit. I forgot." Park ran a hand through her hair. Short, steady movements. Matter-of-fact tone. Not a trace of fear on her face. "So," she said, "what've we got?"

"He was bludgeoned." Madison's voice broke. Tears welled up in her eyes.

"And just to think how much fun we were all having," Lex whispered. Her own eyes had gone glassy.

"I know," Park said. She put her hands on both of their shoulders. "This is shocking and insane and totally twisted, but now's not the time to fall apart. We're standing here doing nothing, but we have to do *something*."

"I don't want to go anywhere near poor Damien's body," Madison cried. "I don't think I have the courage."

Park tightened her grip on their shoulders. "Of course you do. We all do. When you get right down to it, this club belongs to us, and that's the first thing everyone will be blabbing about. Now come on—let's get ready. We have to inspect the body."

Lex nodded.

After a beat, so did Madison.

Park led the pre-investigatory procedures. She opened her purse, pulled out her compact, and flipped it open. She immediately applied a fresh sheen of blush to her cheeks.

Madison, her hands still trembling, winced at her own reflection. She was pale, and the corners of her mouth looked dry. She ran a light pink gloss over her lips, then smoothed out the edges with a wad of tissue.

It took Lex a little longer to sift through her magic purse. When she finally found her compact, she reached for her eyeliner and quickly worked some color around her eyes.

"Okay," Madison said. "I think I feel a little better."

"That's because you look beautiful." Lex pointed to Madison's lips. "I love that shade. It totally highlights your cheekbones."

"It's a new variation on pink berry." Madison sniffed, holding back her tears. "I have an extra one. I'll give it to you when we get home."

Park took slow, careful steps across the huge cage. It was at least twenty feet long. She circled Damien's body, stopping only a few inches from his twisted arm. She leaned over and, holding tight to her purse, swept her eyes over the trail of blood.

"Wait," Madison said. "You're never supposed to disturb a crime scene."

Lex nodded. "I know, I know. The smallest movement can contaminate forensic evidence. I've been reading all about it."

"We're not disturbing the crime scene," Park said nonchalantly. "We're . . . checking to make sure that Damien isn't actually still breathing. I mean, what if he needs CPR or something?"

"Okay, that works." Madison drew closer to the body.

Park squatted down and gently pressed her right hand to the side of Damien's neck. "Well, he definitely doesn't need CPR." She shook her head sadly. "He's dead. And this wound on his head . . ."

"What about it?" Madison asked.

"It looks . . . *ugh*. It's all matted with blood and . . . other stuff."

"What other stuff?" Lex walked around to Park's side. She squatted down and leaned in even closer. "Look at the strands of hair around the wound. There's, like, a weird glitter to them."

"Did Damien use any special kind of hair gel?" Park asked them both.

It was Madison who answered. "How would we know? But I would guess that he didn't. I've never seen a glittery shine to his hair before."

"Neither have I." Lex stood up. "But I don't get it. What was he killed with? Where's the weapon?"

"Good question." Park shifted her weight onto her knees as she continued her close inspection of the body. Unable to find a comfortable position, she swung her purse off her shoulder and handed it to Madison. Then she ran her hands through her hair and knotted it into a bun at the back of her neck.

"You *don't* want to be photographed like that," Madison warned.

"I know. But it'll only be a minute. I think . . ." She rested both her hands on one side of the body and gave it a little shove. "I think he's lying on something. His back is arched, like there's something pressing into his stomach." She glanced up, a determined look in her eyes. "I'm gonna roll him over."

"Be careful!" Madison whispered fiercely.

Using all her weight, Park managed to lift Damien's body a few inches off the floor of the cage—just enough to catch a glimpse of what he was lying on top of. She couldn't help but gasp. "Oh, my God."

Madison took a step back. "What is it?"

"Lex, honey," Park said quietly. "I don't think you should look. It's . . ."

"It's what?" Lex asked.

"It's something really, *really* gross." Park closed her eyes and shook her head in a gesture of complete horror. She gave the body a final, hard push, grunting as it rolled over.

Damien's back hit the bars of the cage. The side of his face came into view.

And so did the object he had been lying on top of.

It was a large, garish hot pink stiletto; its straps looked like they were made of vinyl, and the blue rhinestones studding both sides were unmistakably plastic. By all accounts, the ugliest piece of footwear on the planet had just been discovered.

The moment Lex saw the stiletto, her eyes began rolling into the back of her head. She dropped her magic purse and grabbed on to the sides of the cage for support.

"Catch her!" Park shouted.

Madison's arms bolted out and encircled Lex.

"I'm feeling . . . faint," Lex whispered. "Please tell me I'm hallucinating."

But she wasn't. Her disdain was echoed by the crowd of onlookers.

Madison pulled Lex into a tight embrace, cradling Lex's head against her shoulder. "Don't look," she whispered into her ear. "It's not something anyone should see."

"The final insult," Park said angrily. "That's the murder weapon. There's blood on the stem of the heel."

Madison gasped. "Is it . . . ?"

Park looked up and closed her eyes as she nodded. "It's a steel-tip stiletto," she said quietly.

Her face still buried in Madison's shoulder, Lex let out a horrified wail.

"Come on now," Madison said. "Be strong. Think of what poor Damien had to endure."

Lex lifted her head. "*That's* the most awful part of all," she sobbed. "To think that Damien's last moments were spent struggling against . . . against . . ." She mustered her strength and stared down at the stiletto. "Against *that*! I can't accept it!"

Park was still kneeling beside the body. She leaned over it again, trying to inspect the wound. "Lex," she said. "I think you should see this."

"I mean, who on earth would be that sick?" Lex ranted. "What kind of a killer would use such an appalling weapon?"

"Lex?" Park tugged on the hem of her sister's dress.

"And where would you even get something so ugly?" Lex continued. "What reputable retailer would sell something like that? I—"

"*Lex!*" Park's voice was sharp.

"What?" Lex drew a tissue from her purse and dabbed at the corners of her eyes.

"I know you don't want to do this, but you have to. I need your expertise." Park waved her down to the floor. "Look at the wound on Damien's head, then look at the stiletto."

"Why?"

"You're the one who knows about shoes. Just do it!"

With a reluctant sigh, Lex squatted down again. "How

much can I possibly take in one night?" she sighed. And then all thoughts dissolved as her eyes swept from the gaping, bloody wound to the steel tip of the stiletto. She studied the shoe intently, taking in every last detail, from its mammoth size to the high arch.

"Well?" Madison asked.

"It's the murder weapon," Lex said. Her voice was firm and confident, all traces of fear gone. "The wound is about three inches wide. It's circular, just like the stiletto's tip. The tip is only about a quarter of an inch wide, but that means the killer popped Damien in the head with it and dragged it, creating a gash. But . . ."

"But what?" Madison's voice rose.

"The stiletto's straps are vinyl and very weak," Lex said. "Not at all the same tensile strength as leather or snakeskin. The killer obviously held the shoe from the front end and then struck, but there isn't any damage to the front end at all. That's pretty weird. I would've expected at least some minor stress in the vinyl."

"And what exactly does that mean?" Madison asked, growing impatient.

"It means that I'm ninety-nine percent sure this was the murder weapon." Lex pointed at it. "But I'm still a little confused. I know it has a steel tip and everything, but is that really enough to kill a person? Maybe at the right angle it could do a lot of damage, but actually cause *death*?"

"It's called blunt impact trauma," Park said. "We've been reading the same books, Lex. I'm sure you've got it right. I *knew* you'd pick it up faster than any autopsy person."

"You're right," Madison agreed. "That has more to do with fashion than anything medical. That stiletto has to be a size twelve."

Still squatting, Lex swept her eyes over Damien Kittle's body, stopping when her gaze found his face. His eyes were open but unseeing. His lips were parted in a grimace. The hives on his forehead dotted his face now, looking more like bright red welts. Lex couldn't stop herself from letting a fresh wave of tears spill over her cheeks. For the first time in her life, she didn't bother wiping away the black streaks of mascara swirling almost to her chin.

Madison kneeled down beside her. "I know," she whispered, her own voice breaking. "Our crazy English bad boy. What are we gonna do without him?" Then, forgetting about the onlookers and the continuous stream of whispers—forgetting about any stray paparazzi—she reached out and tenderly stroked Damien's cheek. It was ice cold.

"All those ugly welts on his skin," Lex said. "Where'd they come from?"

Madison shook her head. "I don't know. But there were blotches on his forehead the last time we saw him. I remember that."

Park leaned over them. "I think I hear sirens outside," she said gently.

Lex stood up.

Madison, however, stayed kneeling. As she stared down the length of Damien Kittle's body, something caught her eye. There, in the palm of his right hand, was a dark mark, clearly visible through his splayed fingers.

She leaned in closer to inspect it. "Damien had a tattoo?" she asked, confused. "I don't remember seeing that before."

Park hunched over, pulling her hair out of the bun as she did so. "That's weird. But it doesn't look like a tattoo. It looks like a . . . stamp of some kind. Like ink. The edges are smeared a little."

"Like it's fading," Madison said. Slowly, carefully, she grasped the wrist of Damien's right hand and drew it forward. The stamp was a perfect circle, and in it was a small but clearly defined human profile.

"What is it?" Lex asked.

"It looks like a Roman coin." Madison leaned over until her face was less than two inches from Damien's palm. "I've seen this image before, in one of the Roman collections at the Met. Yes, it's definitely a Roman coin. The human profile in the stamp—it's wearing a Corinthian helmet."

"What the hell does it mean?" Lex sounded impatient.

"I don't know," Madison said. "But why would he have a stamp like that on his palm? I didn't notice it when I saw him today in the student lounge."

The question hung on the air as a burst of noise echoed across the main floor of the club. A line of uniformed police officers stormed in through the entryway, all of them ordering guests outside. In minutes, the upper levels were being cleared as well.

Madison, Park, and Lex stepped out of the cage but remained standing beside it. They didn't budge as a tall, well-dressed man came striding toward them. He looked to be in his forties, with thinning blond hair and stylish rectangular glasses. He wore a navy suit and tie.

"Detective Aaron Connelly," he said as he approached them. He reached into the pocket of his blazer and pulled out his badge. "Homicide."

"We assumed as much." Park offered him a cool smile. "Our father, Trevor Hamilton, owns this club."

"Yeah, I know," Aaron Connelly said. "It's been all over the news for weeks." He stared up at the high ceiling, at the waterfall, at the elaborately decorated levels. "Never thought I'd be in here tonight—or ever, for that matter. This is one amazing piece of architecture."

Madison cleared her throat. "Thank you. All the marble was imported from Europe."

"And most of the art on the second level is priceless," Lex added. "You should totally see it. You like Egyptian art?"

"Yeah, actually, I do. My wife and I went to Egypt last year." Connelly flipped open a small notepad, then reached into his blazer pocket again, this time pulling out a pen.

"You must've had a great trip," Lex said. "The sunsets in Cairo are *so* romantic."

"My wife is actually a professor of Egyptology," Connelly said proudly.

"Really?" Madison tried to sound totally interested. "If only I'd known. I could have employed her as a consultant."

"Eh, maybe next time." Connelly smirked. He turned and stared through the bars of the cage at the body of Damien Kittle. "So what happened here?"

Park gave him a synopsis of the morbid events.

Connelly took notes furiously, turning one page after another. Several minutes passed before he looked up. "Tell me about Damien Kittle," he said.

"There's not much to tell," Madison replied. "He was a wonderful guy. Everybody loved him."

"Well, not *everybody*," Connelly said. He gestured his head at the trail of blood. "Were most of the guests here tonight from your school? St. Cecilia's Prep on the Upper East Side?"

"No," Madison said. "There were a lot of students here from St. Cecilia's, but the guest list was long. Why?"

Connelly cut her a wry stare. "Pretty pricey school you got there. All you famous kids can't have everything in common."

Madison cut him an equally sharp stare. "What's that supposed to mean?"

"Just that there are a lot of suspects to consider," Connelly said.

"You don't actually think anyone from *our* school is guilty of this crime, Detective?" Park's tone was incredulous.

"It's possible, isn't it?" Connelly asked. "So many of your fellow classmates were here tonight. Maybe one of them who hated Damien Kittle took the right moment and killed him."

Madison gasped. "That's completely impossible. We're a united student body at St. Cecilia's Prep."

"It's a family environment," Park added.

Lex shook her head at the detective. "Our uniforms are even color-coordinated. There's no way Damien was killed by one of our own. He was too well liked. He was fun and fun-loving."

"Yeah, well, it's been my experience that even the fun-loving types have their enemies." Connelly stepped into the cage and squatted over the body. He began taking more notes. He waved at one of the younger men standing by the club's main entrance, a crime scene photographer who approached the cage and immediately began snapping pictures.

"I can't think of a single enemy Damien might have had," Lex whispered to Madison and Park. "Can either of you?"

They both shook their heads.

"So, now, I guess none of you girls saw who was in this cage dancing with Damien, huh?" Connelly asked.

"No," Park replied. "We were all here on the main level. The cages were suspended way up in the air. And the strobes were spinning and the music was really, really loud."

Connelly shook his head. He slipped on a pair of latex gloves and reached for the stiletto. Turning it over to stare at the steel-tip bottom, he said, "Poor guy got clocked in the head pretty hard." He stood up. "I'll need a list of the people you invited to tonight's event—and I mean the *full* list, before RSVPs."

"I have that at home," Madison said, sniffling again. "But I can totally assure you, Detective, that none of our guests did this."

"So you're telling me you think someone—the killer— got past the door guy, got around security, snuck in here, got into the cage, killed Mr. Kittle, and just *left*?" Connelly twisted his mouth in a bemused expression.

"It's possible, isn't it?" Park said.

"You tell me," Connelly snapped. "I was under the impression that security was tight here. A stranger couldn't have just waltzed in unnoticed. The killer is someone who knew Damien Kittle. And probably someone who knows all of *you*."

"We don't know *anyone* who would own a pair of stilettos that ugly." Lex's voice was adamant, sharp. "The fact that you would even try to tie us to this whole thing is offensive."

"It's *sickening*," Madison whispered.

"I mean, really, Detective," Park said calmly. "Do we look like we'd condone a piece of footwear like that? Something so . . . plastic?"

There was a brief silence as Connelly looked at the huge ceiling of the club, at the other suspended cages and the long catwalk leading to them. The staccato murmuring of voices echoed from outside as more chaos ensued. The reporters were obviously going crazy, clamoring for dirt.

Then Connelly nodded to the team of forensic technicians and said, "Okay, boys. Wrap the vic up and transport him to the morgue. We'll have him autopsied first thing in the morning."

"The *morgue*?" Madison snapped. "You're not just going to take Damien Kittle's body to a city morgue, are you?"

"What the hell is that supposed to mean?" Connelly asked. "It's procedure."

Park stepped forward. "Detective, are you sure you know what you're doing? Damien Kittle is the fifth duke of Asherton. He's—or at least he was—English royalty. As in blue blood."

"Like, related to the queen of England," Lex chimed in.

Connelly shrugged. "So?"

"So you can't just bring him to some smelly old morgue!" Madison screeched. "There has to be some sort of official procedure to follow when English royalty is murdered in the United States!"

"Oh, really?" Connelly sniffed. "Whataya want me to do—find a crown to put on his head?"

"Well, maybe not a crown," Park replied. "But you can't just drape a white sheet over his body. Maybe something more . . ."

"For God's sake—something more royal!" Madison ranted.

"That's enough!" Connelly shouted, his voice echoing across the main floor and the empty upper levels. "I'm not gonna stand here and listen to your craziness! All of you, go on outside and let us do our jobs! You're on the verge of interfering with justice. In case you didn't notice, I have a killer to catch!"

At that precise moment, a ruckus erupted from the long, dimly lit hallway beside the cascading waterfall—two arguing voices, two bodies seemingly locked in mortal combat. A male uniformed police officer was tugging a reluctant female onto the main floor; their arms were entwined as they stumbled into the light.

"I found this little lady hiding in one of the bathrooms!" the officer said, shoving the girl forward.

"Concetta!" Lex cried. "Oh my God! What happened to you?"

Concetta Canoli looked totally wrecked. Her face was streaked with wet mascara. The left side of her Missoni gown was torn. Her hair was matted to her forehead in a ring of sweat. Instead of answering Lex's question, she heaved a sigh and began sobbing. Her whole body trembled, and the gown lifted and fell with her heavy breaths.

That was when Madison and Park noticed her feet—her right one was tucked into a hot pink stiletto, and her left one was bare.

Detective Connelly's jaw dropped.

"Oh, heavens to Saks," Madison whispered.

Park simply stared, unable to believe what she was seeing.

And Lex, seeing the second half of the hideous pair of shoes, let out an ear-shattering scream.

"Your—your shoe," Park stammered. "Concetta, did you . . . ?"

Concetta's swollen eyes shifted to the cage. To Damien Kittle's body. Her sobs grew louder and more strained. "I . . . I don't know what happened," she cried. "I don't know what's going on."

"What's going on is pretty obvious," Detective Connelly said, walking over to Concetta. He pointed at her bare foot. Then he pointed to the hot pink stiletto beside the body. "Do you remember taking off your shoe, young lady?"

Slowly, she shook her head.

"Do you remember maybe arguing with Damien Kittle? Getting mad at him?"

"No."

"Do you remember whacking him in the head and *killing* him?" Connelly yelled, the question a clear accusation.

"No! I didn't do it!" Concetta cried. She looked pleadingly

at Madison, Park, and Lex. "Tell him I'm innocent. Tell him! Please—*tell him I didn't kill Damien!*"

But as Detective Connelly snapped handcuffs on Concetta Canoli's wrists and led her out of the club a few minutes later, Madison, Park, and Lex could only watch.

# 6

# Where Smart Girls Keep
# Their Secrets

They dove into the waiting limo. Heads bent. Backs hunched. Arms thrust out like swimmers racing across a pool. It was the only way to avoid a sudden media backlash.

The short walk from the club's front doors to the side-walk had been totally hazardous. Police officers and extra security guards had managed to keep the screaming re-porters at bay, but the barrage of camera flashes had per-sisted, cutting through the night with blinding force.

Madison was the first to fly into the limo. Her butt hit one end of the cushioned leather seat, and she had to steady herself to keep from slamming against the side door. She dropped her purse and reached out her arms, yanking Park in beside her. Lex, agile and quick as a cat, didn't need any help: she did a little tuck-and-roll move, using the magic purse as a pillow, slamming into the seat and simultaneously pulling the door closed.

"Monsters!" Madison screeched, waving her fist at the tinted windows. Cameras couldn't penetrate the dark glass, but the flashes continued.

Park and Lex leaned their heads back and sighed.

Their new chauffeur, Donnie Halstrom, was a twenty-seven-year-old medical school dropout from Virginia. Tall, beefy, and painfully introverted, he had paid his way through college as a racecar driver. Speed was in his blood. He'd been working for the Hamilton family for less than two months, but he already knew the routine.

Everything was about making a fast getaway.

Donnie didn't wait for Madison, Park, or Lex to tell him to slam down on the accelerator. The moment the back door clicked shut, he took off.

"The beginning of a nightmare," Lex said quietly. She reached into her purse, found a lavender velvet eye pillow, and slapped it over her forehead.

"I can't take any more," Madison cried. "My nerves are totally shot! We've probably aged five years in the last hour!" She turned toward the bar and mini-refrigerator beside her and frantically searched for the small bottle of champagne. She found it, and then began looking crazily for a carton of milk. Her special—and very strange—antistress concoction was completely in order right now.

But Park leaned forward, snapped her fingers to get

Madison's attention, and said, "You won't find milk in there. I got rid of it."

"You *what*?" Madison yelled.

Park shook her head. "That disgusting little brew you mix isn't healthy. It's full of fat and empty calories. And I won't have you burping up the limo all night."

"You had no right to do that!"

"Listen to yourself, Madison," Park told her calmly. "You're hysterical. And what's the point of that? Nothing good comes out of it. Just sit back, take a few deep breaths, and maintain."

Unwilling to give up, Madison stared at Lex—and at the bottomless magic purse.

"No milk in there," Lex murmured. "The last time you made me carry around a pint, it spoiled."

Madison dropped her face into her hands. "I just want to go home," she sobbed. "I want to forget that this happened and wait until someone tells me Damien isn't dead."

"You'll need a Ouija board if you wanna talk to him," Lex snapped. "He's gone. And his murder is only the *beginning* of the story. Can you imagine what's gonna happen at school when word gets out that Concetta Canoli killed him? St. Cecilia's Prep will never live this down."

Madison stole a glance through her fingers. "You don't really think Concetta killed him," she said.

"I don't *want* to think that," Lex replied, exasperated. "But what other choice is there? The evidence stared us right in the face. And who knew, by the way, that Concetta had such horrible taste?"

"An open-and-shut case," Park said. "And for the

record, I've known about Concetta and her shoe thing for a long time, but a pair that ugly really is scary."

"But how did she do it?" Madison asked, finally sitting back and taking a deep breath.

"Maybe she didn't." Park shrugged. "Like Detective Connelly said before Concetta was brought out of the bathroom—anyone there could've killed him. The club was filled with people."

"Will you please make up your mind?" Lex shook her head. "You just said it's an open-and-shut case!"

"It could be," Park said. "I'm just posing theories. Concetta was supposedly dancing in the cage with Damien, and plenty of people probably saw them in there. But did anyone maybe see her exit the cage at some point? Think about it. The spinning strobes, the craziness of the dance floors—it was pretty wild. I mean, aside from Theo, who else did *we* see dancing close to *us*? The only person I remember is Julian Simmons."

"Theo!" Madison suddenly wailed. "Oh my God— I completely forgot about him." She reached into her purse, pulled out her cell phone, and tapped out a text message.

Lex crinkled her nose. "Theo probably ran back home to avoid negative publicity. That loser wouldn't want anything to do with this."

"Shut up!" Madison waved the cell phone at her. "He was nothing but nice to you tonight."

"Both of you, be quiet." Park clapped her hands. "Can either one of you answer my question? Who else did you notice dancing close to us on the main floor?"

It was silent for a few seconds. Then Lex said, "I saw

Emmett with Rebecca Franklin. And Chloe Marx and Penelope Renton."

"And I saw Billy Wright," Madison added.

"So that leaves six St. Cecilia's Prep students out of the equation," Park said. "No one who was dancing with us on the main floor could've killed Damien."

"Yeah, but there were about fifty other kids from school at the opening tonight." Lex threw up her hands. "And how would we know where any of them were when Damien got clocked in the head? I mean . . . the evidence against Concetta is circumstantial right now, but maybe it *is* as simple as it looks. Maybe she did kill him."

"A crime of passion," Park whispered.

"Or maybe even something more than that," Madison offered. "I mean, Damien was our friend, and so is Concetta. But when you think about it, how much do we really know about either one of them? We all have secrets. I just can't bring myself to believe that Concetta would be *that* stupid—stupid enough to kill him right then and there."

"When you think about it, though . . . it wasn't a sudden violent act," Park said. "It wasn't a homicidal impulse. Planning went into this. Think about the Mozart Requiem—that didn't come from one of the DJs. Which makes me think—the DJs must know something, or they must've seen someone suspicious. I *so* wish we could've stayed at the club and questioned them ourselves. The Requiem was all part of the production."

"That's *totally* true," Madison said. "I hadn't even thought of that. Everyone knew Damien had a passion for classical music, especially Mozart. So it *was* premeditated."

Lex ran both her hands through her hair, then reached up and turned one of the air-conditioning vents toward her. "People do pretty sick things in the heat of passion," she said. "Concetta had probably been burning up about this for months. Maybe she told Damien she had the hots for him and he kept turning her away. And Damien was always flirting with everyone. It probably drove Concetta nuts. What if she finally just snapped? She seemed happy to see him tonight, but what if that was all part of her plan? We were witnesses to that—how giddy she acted when we were all standing together. So then they go into the cage and start dancing, and at the right moment she takes off the stiletto and *wham*. Turns his head into meatloaf."

Madison placed both hands on her stomach. "Please, don't mention food. Especially meatloaf."

"You pretty much constructed a good crime there, Lex." Park gave a nod of approval. "It's absolutely plausible. But if it was so planned out, why would Concetta leave the shoe in that cage for everyone to see?"

"Because she panicked," Lex said. "Because in that awful moment, she freaked out and went into shock herself. Or maybe she just got dizzy and ran. I don't know, but she obviously doesn't have a brilliant criminal mind. So what it really all boils down to is a botched crime of passion."

The possibility, while all too sad and shocking, couldn't be discounted. Concetta Canoli was a well-liked member of the St. Cecilia's Prep student body, but she'd had a very public crush on Damien Kittle. *Everyone* knew that much.

Suddenly, Donnie Halstrom cleared his throat. "Uh, girls? I'm taking you home, right?"

"No." Park's voice was firm. "Take us to school, Donnie."

Madison sat up straight. "What?"

"Whatever you say," Donnie said. The limo picked up speed as he steered it onto the FDR Drive.

Park looked at Madison and Lex. "Personally, I think there's more to this crime than meets the eye," she told them. "I don't know if I believe Concetta killed Damien just because he might've rejected her. For all we know, they could've been having a little relationship already. Concetta obviously has some secrets, and there's only one place a smart girl keeps her secrets."

"Her locker," Madison and Lex said in unison.

"Exactly." Park clutched her purse tightly to her stomach. "Donnie, step on it a little, will you? I want to get to school before the cops do."

The limo smoothly picked up speed.

Lex sighed. "I *hate* breaking into school after hours."

◇   ◇   ◇

Ten minutes later, the limo came to a stop on the west side of Fifth Avenue and Seventy-ninth Street. The Gothic façade of St. Cecilia's Prep glowed like a jewel in the night. Madison, Park, and Lex reached into their purses and pulled out black silk scarves; reserved for emergency purposes, the scarves were long and wide and fringed, perfect for avoiding the press at a moment's notice or, in this case, for breaking into a building. They tied the scarves around their heads and across their chins.

Park leaned forward and stretched her arm over the limo's partition. She tapped Donnie on the shoulder and said, "Wait here. If Dad calls, tell him we're safe, and that we're trying to comfort our friends."

Donnie nodded in his usual, quiet way.

Park popped the door and stepped out onto the pavement. Traffic was blessedly light. She led the way across the street, past the front entrance of the school and along the side of the building. Trees shadowed them as they stared up at the zigzagging fire escape that spiraled up to the roof.

"You're both *insane*," Madison said. "I can't climb up there! I'll get sick if I look down."

"Then *don't* look down," Lex replied sharply. "And stop being such a baby."

Madison pursed her lips and shivered.

"Hurry," Park said. "Give me a boost."

Lex cupped her hands together and gestured her head at Park's feet.

"Wait!" Madison cried. "What floor are we climbing to? How are we gonna get in?"

Lex sighed. "The same way we've all snuck *out*— through the science lab window. It's been broken for centuries, and it's only two stories up. Now be quiet!"

Park slipped out of her shoes and dropped one of them into the magic purse, holding the other under her arm. Then she stepped into Lex's cupped hands as Madison supported her from behind.

"Nice and easy," Lex said.

Park hoisted herself high, looking like a ballerina as her right leg stood rigid and her left leg kicked up behind her to balance herself. She stretched as much as she could. The ladder to the fire escape was still a few inches out of her grasp. Carefully, quickly, she grabbed the shoe from under her arm, held it up and out, and hooked the heel around the first rung of the ladder. She gave a hard tug; the ladder creaked once, then slipped down and locked into place.

"That's it!" Madison said happily. "See? You can totally do your own stunts when you start filming the movie!"

Her weight unsteady in Lex's hands, Park eased herself onto the ladder and climbed up to the first landing. The steel was cold beneath her bare feet. She waited until Madison and Lex were beside her before mounting the stairs to the second level.

They took fast, quiet steps, ignoring the few cars that drove by the building. But when one of the cars slowed suspiciously, headlights gleaming, they each froze in place and struck statuelike poses.

Lex put her left hand on her waist and lifted her right one into the air, looking like a mannequin.

Park assumed the rigid posture of a soldier in salute.

Madison, panicking for a split second, went down on one knee and folded her hands as if in prayer.

The car kept moving.

"That was close," Madison said. "What if someone calls the police on us?"

Park shrugged. "The three of us forgot our homework and didn't want to wake the nuns by ringing the bell of the convent," she said, again using her nonchalant, unaffected tone. "Who could blame us for wanting to be good students?"

"Okay," Madison whispered. "I guess that could work—if we're unbelievably lucky."

At the landing to the second level, Park ignored the secured door and went instead to the window a few feet to the left. She placed her palms flat against the glass pane and pushed it up.

One by one, they climbed over the sill and eased themselves into the science lab. Lex lowered the window back into place.

The room was nearly pitch-black. A scant ray of light from the hallway cut into the darkness, outlining the long marble tables and microscopes, the cabinets that held various test tubes and chemicals used for chemistry lessons. The air-conditioning had been turned off. It smelled musty.

Park moved to the door and opened it completely. She stepped into the threshold, poking her head out to scan the long second-floor hallway. It was empty. She waved Madison and Park forward, and together they began the long, dangerous trek down to the main level. Only two of the overhead chandeliers were on. Long shadows stretched along the walls and spilled into the other classrooms. They had to move silently: the convent of the Order of Our Lady of the Avenue was attached to the school, accessible through several adjoining corridors. One loud bang or misstep, and Mother Margaret would come flying out to greet them.

"This is so creepy," Lex whispered. "I feel like we're totally being watched."

"Well, we're not," Park said. "So just lose the fear."

"That's easy for you to say." Madison reached out and slugged Park's shoulder. "Do you have any idea how much trouble we'll get into if we're caught?"

Park dismissed the suggestion with a wave of her hand.

They made it to the end of the hallway. Next came the staircase; though it was carpeted, the wood beneath was old and creaky. Park pressed a finger to her lips, then gestured with her fingers, indicating that they take the steps in synchronization.

Lex hooked her hands around Park's waist, and Madison hooked her hands around Lex's. They descended the staircase in a tightly linked chain, freezing whenever a creak pierced the silence. Lex, stuck in the middle, nearly lost her balance twice as the weight of the magic purse strained on her shoulder.

All the lockers at St. Cecilia's Prep were located on the first floor, in the west wing of the building. The wing also housed a small theater, two indoor tennis courts, and a master chess room. It took Madison, Park, and Lex nearly two minutes to make it across the east wing and into the lavish student court, where the lockers stood in neat, gleaming rows. Nearly six feet tall and made of solid cherry wood, each locker held enough space for two school uniforms, several pairs of shoes, a tennis racket, two coats or jackets, and one or two shoulder bags; a built-in jewelry case was attached to the back of each door, and the uppermost shelf was wide enough to store an array of cosmetic products.

Concetta Canoli's locker was smack in the middle of the court. Her initials were etched into a gold placard that hung over the top.

Lex reached into the magic purse and found her penlight. She flicked it on and aimed the small straight beam directly ahead, sweeping it once across the floor to make certain they were safe.

"Wait a minute," Madison said as they reached the locker. She pinched her fingers around the thick steel padlock sealing the door shut. "How are we going to open *that*?"

Park paused and blinked, as if weighing the question.

"Jeez, Madison, sometimes you're a total Kmart-for-brains," Lex snapped. "Think about it. A confident, full-figured girl like Concetta Canoli? What do you think her locker combination would be?"

Madison scowled. "I don't know. But don't *ever* attach my name to a retail chain that sells man-made fibers exclusively!"

"Oh!" Park snapped her fingers. "Lex, you're *totally* right. The combination would be Concetta's body measurements. And there's no way Kmart doesn't sell cotton fabrics."

"Bingo." Lex trained the flashlight on the padlock, ignoring her sisters' bickering. She closed her eyes in concentration. "Now, let me see," she muttered, trying to deduce Concetta Canoli's robust body measurements from a mere mental image.

"Come on," Park said. "You can do it."

Lex took a deep breath. "Thirty-nine chest, thirty-five waist, thirty-seven hips. Try it."

Park went to work on the padlock, spinning the dial carefully but quickly.

The combination failed.

"Try these measurements," Lex offered. "Forty, thirty-six, thirty-eight."

Again Park tried, and again the numbers bombed.

Madison's eyes suddenly brightened. "I have an idea," she told them quietly. "How about *this* combination? Twelve, fifteen, ninety-two."

"What's that?" Lex asked, her tone scornful.

"Just try it!" Madison snapped.

Park spun the numbers through the dial.

The lock opened.

Lex gasped, a hand flying to her mouth.

"Madison, how the hell did you know that?" Park asked, shocked.

Madison shook her head. The expression on her face was one of disappointment and fear. "It's pretty freaky, but those numbers are Damien Kittle's birthday—December fifteenth, nineteen ninety-two. Last year he invited us to celebrate it in Vegas that weekend, but we were in Copenhagen with Mom. Remember?"

"Shit, that really *is* freaky," Park said. "Who knew Concetta was *that* obsessed with Damien."

"Gives me the creeps." Lex shivered. "I mean, her feelings for Damien were obviously deeper than anyone knew."

"Well, let's hope Concetta's locker isn't as creepy." Park had already begun shifting through the coats and blazers and bags. She patted her hand over the top shelf and found a notebook, which she handed over to Madison for perusal.

Lex swiped the penlight along the inside of the locker. She bent down and inspected the shoes—they were all huge, but not hideous. A small leather box caught her attention a few seconds later. She popped open the lid and blasted it with light. Inside were several small folded pieces of paper, along with pictures of Damien Kittle. "Look at this," she said breathlessly.

The pictures were actually snapshots, and they had very obviously been taken without Damien's knowledge. In one, he was sitting in the music room reaching for a violin. In another, he was walking out of a classroom lugging an armful of books. There were a number of profile shots as well. He wasn't smiling in any of them.

"Evidence of a total lovesick psycho," Park whispered.

Lex dropped the stack of pictures back into the box and reached for one of the pieces of paper. She unfolded it. She traced her eyes over the scrawl and made out three words: *in my house.* Another read: *It's our secret.* And yet another: *We stand in the shadows.* Lex said, "What the hell?" and glanced up at Park.

"Beats me," Park replied. "Her coat pockets are all empty. And then there's her gym bag, which is totally rank."

"I knew I smelled wet wool." Lex crinkled her nose. "Don't go near it."

That was when Madison stepped in between them and said, "I found something pretty strange." Her head was bent, her eyes trained on the pages of the notebook in her hands. Finally, she turned it around, holding it by its spine so that Park and Lex could see what she was talking about.

The first page of the notebook had four words scrawled across it in neat script:

This was followed by an inky symbol—the same Roman coin symbol that had been stamped on Damien's palm. Then came the list: several familiar names and their odd, corresponding titles.

Concetta Canoli—Mistress of the Court
Damien Kittle—Prince of Illusions
Emmett McQueen—Knight of Daggers
Jessica Paderman—Princess of Shadows
Julian Simmons—Sage of Magic

The following pages were diary entries, complete with dates, times, and detailed descriptions written in Concetta's hand.

April 5: Tonight, the Black Cry Affair delved into the realm of King Arthur's court. We had a blast. Damien played a drunken servant, and Emmett played a wealthy scoundrel. I reigned as a queen, of course, and the rest of the group couldn't get enough of our scuffling. For nearly two hours, I totally forgot the real world and lost myself in the game. I didn't want it to end. Neither did Julian.

April 19: The Black Cry Affair should really go public. We're all so amazing at playing our roles. Tonight we transformed the Chamber into the Coliseum and left New York for ancient Rome. Damien was awesome as Marcus Aurelius. He and Emmett got into a gladiator duel while I played the role of a damsel in distress. They had an amazing sword battle. Damien totally won.

May 10: It's obvious that being in the club means a lot to everyone. There was a crazy storm tonight, but all members of the Black Cry Affair braved the weather for one of our games. With the thunder booming and all that scary lightning, we decided to assume complete fantasy roles. I was a fairy princess. Damien was a dragon-slayer. We got so into our roles. At one point I thought we were even going to kiss, but it didn't happen. Maybe next week?

Park lifted the notebook from Madison's hands and continued flipping through the pages. "This is the craziest thing I've ever seen," she whispered. "Who knew that any of this was even going on?"

"I still don't get it," Lex said, tugging her arm. "What's all that writing about?"

"I think the Black Cry Affair is a role-playing club," Madison explained. "Obviously, Concetta and Damien and Emmett are the main role-players, but Jessica Paderman and Julian Simmons are also members."

"There could be five or ten more members, for all we

know." Park kept scanning the pages. "And this stamp—the one of the Roman coin—it's the same one we saw on Damien's hand tonight."

"Yes." Madison nodded. "I guess that's what they do whenever they have one of their little club meetings—the stamp is a symbol of admittance into the club. Of recognition."

"But you said you didn't see the stamp on Damien's hand today in the student lounge," Lex said to Madison. "Does that mean these Black Cry Affair weirdos met before coming to the opening of Cleopatra?"

"I would say so." Madison turned and gave the locker another quick scan.

"Yes, that's exactly what it means." Park held the notebook out, pointing to the top of a folded page. "Look. It says right here that the Black Cry Affair had a meeting today at six o'clock. Concetta keeps mentioning this Chamber thing. I wonder where it is." She went back to perusing the entries.

"Wait a minute." Lex held up a hand. "You honestly think this whole role-playing thing has something to do with Damien's murder? I mean, I think it's totally weird, but it could also be totally innocent."

"You're right," Madison admitted. "It could be."

"But it isn't." Park looked up. Again, she held the notebook out to her sisters. "Check out this entry."

They lowered their eyes as Park shined the flashlight onto the page.

May 24: I'm not happy. Tonight, the members of the club had a great time visiting medieval Europe, but I noticed a lot of tension in the Chamber. I feel like there are secrets being kept from me. Why do Damien and Emmett seem so tense with each other? Why does Jessica keep smiling at Damien? Julian's been weird too. I feel like something bad is going to happen, something that just can't be stopped. . . .

Madison gasped.

Lex's eyes widened.

"Doesn't sound so innocent," Park said. "Maybe things got a little out of hand in the club—and maybe it all led up to Damien being killed."

Before Madison or Lex could reply, a huge bang sounded from the floor above.

Then came the footsteps—soft, swift, steady. There was definitely someone else in the school.

"Shit." Park slammed the notebook closed and placed it back on the top shelf of the locker. She shut the door silently and slid the padlock back into place.

Madison and Lex grabbed on to each other, panic lighting up their faces.

"Stay calm," Park whispered.

They were standing at the very end of the hall. They had only two escape routes: the main entrance of the school, or the staircase that led back up to the science lab. The front doors weren't really an option—alarms would sound and pull the sisters from their beds—but the thought of facing someone upstairs was terrifying. Standing still, their backs pressed to the lockers, they waited in silence.

Another round of footsteps sounded above them.

Several tense minutes passed, and then Lex broke out of her position and began tiptoeing back down the hall to the staircase. She looked over her shoulder and motioned for Madison and Park to follow her. They assumed the human chain again, taking the steps one at a time. Now the footsteps sounded like they were moving across to the east wing of the school.

"It can't be one of the nuns," Madison whispered. "Not at this hour of the night."

"So then there's an intruder," Park whispered back. She gestured her head at the magic purse. "Lex, what've you got for protection?"

Lex reached into the purse and pulled out a nail file with a razor-sharp tip. She held it up and out like a blade. "I can totally shred someone with this," she said quietly.

They continued to the second-floor staircase landing.

And that was when they saw the shadow.

It was like a flash of black lightning across their faces.

Madison shrieked as Lex and Park tumbled into each other.

But where they expected to see a knife-wielding murderer, they saw only a mass of black clothing flip through the air. The long, lean, elegant figure was clearly a nun. She did three cartwheels in rapid succession, drawing closer to them, then expertly knocking the nail file from Lex's outstretched arm.

"Oh!" Lex screamed, more stunned now than frightened. Her eyes went wide as she watched the acrobatics unfold.

With the last cartwheel, the nun landed firmly on her

feet. Her hands shot out in a defensive karate-chop position and her black veil settled like a mop around her head.

"Sister Brittany!" Madison exclaimed.

There was a tense silence before Sister Brittany's expression softened into its usual cheerful mask. "Girls!" she shouted. "Oh my Lord! *What* are you doing here?"

The question hung in the air for several moments.

Then Lex sighed and looked at Madison and Park and said, "Shit. We're *busted.*"

# 7

# Good Girl Gone Bad

Jessica Paderman rushed through the private side entrance of the St. Regis Hotel on East Fifty-fifth Street. Reserved for penthouse residents, the small double doors led directly to a bank of elevators far away from the busyness of the lobby. Her shoulders were slumped. Her eyes were cast downward. Anyone spotting her disheveled appearance would know there was something terribly wrong.

Ordinarily, Jessica liked passing by the front desk and waving to the lobby attendants. She liked eyeing the excited tourists too. In the past, she had even stopped to chat with many of them, happily offering pointers on what sites to visit. She generally instructed first-time visitors to avoid the Statue of Liberty and the Empire State Building, especially during the summer months. Why deal with stinky elevators and crowded observation decks? There were far better places to visit in Manhattan. Her favorite was the American Museum of Natural History on the Upper West Side. After that, she loved Carnegie Hall and Lincoln Center and the Central Park Zoo. That was Jessica: brainy, reserved, proper to a fault. And always eager to please.

But right now, she didn't even want to *think* about anything remotely cerebral. Certainly not classical music. Not Beethoven or Tchaikovsky or Vivaldi. And definitely not Mozart.

The eerie notes of the Requiem were still playing in her mind. She heard them as she stepped into the elevator and jammed her fingers against the penthouse button. She saw that frightening image flash through her mind—the cage descending from the ceiling, the trail of blood dripping from one end. She squeezed her eyes against it and tried to steady her breaths.

*Damien is dead.*

A sob shot past her lips. When the elevator yawned open, she stepped out into the antechamber of her family's penthouse, dug into her purse for her key, and jammed it into the lock. She threw open the door. All was blessedly quiet. Her mother was asleep upstairs, and her older brother wouldn't be home till morning. As tears blurred her vision, Jessica bolted for her bedroom. She didn't turn on the lights. She didn't kick off her shoes or get undressed. She simply stumbled through the darkness and collapsed onto her bed.

The night, at last, was over. But as that realization dawned on her, so did everything else.

She felt a surge of guilt so powerful, her entire body trembled.

She was lying flat on her back. Thin streams of light cut through the window blinds and played across the ceiling. She let her eyes trace over them until they all converged into a single square. Almost like an exit sign. The irony of the image wasn't lost on her. She wanted to find a way out of this whole unexpected mess, a doorway that would lead her into a safe world where there weren't any dead bodies or ugly big shoes.

A world where there weren't any secrets.

The minutes continued to tick by, and Jessica had to wrestle herself out of her stupor. She was sure she was experiencing a classic state of shock. She had seen it on TV—people witnessed horrible events and then went totally still, like mannequins in a store window. Their minds just . . . shut down. Sometimes they even picked up and ran away because they forgot who they were. That had happened countless times on *All My Children.* A case of temporary amnesia. It would certainly make life easier right now. If she could play the role of forgetful victim, maybe the cops wouldn't come knocking on her door.

But as Jessica rose unsteadily to her feet, she knew it was an impossibility. She didn't fit the psychological profile of someone who collapsed under pressure. Her whole life, she had been the strong, determined, intelligent girl who got things done. She was an outstanding student. She had won many academic awards. She didn't abuse her connections or her clout as a celebutante like most of the kids at St. Cecilia's Prep. In fact, she couldn't remember the last time she had actually made a mistake. When she got that ugly B— in history last term, she worked insanely to memorize all the complex dates and historical facts and in a matter of weeks became the best student in the class. When she scored 2200 on her SATs, she reviewed her notes obsessively, not sleeping, walking into school every day exhausted and pale; the second time around, she upped her score to a near-perfect 2350. Last month, determined to outrank even the most seasoned players at the annual school chess tournament, she walked away with not one but two trophies. And she had accomplished all these feats while counseling her parents through a messy divorce and trying to steer her brother off his addiction to Wite-Out and superglue.

People had only one image of Jessica Paderman: strait-laced and capable. There wasn't anything she couldn't do. And when it came to the silly, immature antics that so often got teenagers into trouble—drinking, smoking, partying all night with the wrong crowd—Jessica was never mentioned. She didn't partake in frivolous activities. She saw no point in acting seventeen just because she *was* seventeen. Her mind was focused on more serious ventures.

Or, at least, it always *had* been.

*My fault,* she thought. *It's all my fault.*

She didn't know what instinct had led her to join the Black Cry Affair. It had been an uncommonly rash decision, and now she realized that it was the worst decision of her life. If she'd stuck to her one-track ways, she would never have gotten so close to Damien Kittle. She would never have gone to the damn opening of Cleopatra either. And she obviously wouldn't be in so much trouble right now.

Kicking off her shoes, Jessica cursed that day six months ago when she'd inadvertently caught a glimpse of Concetta Canoli's hand and noticed the Roman coin stamp on her palm. Jessica's curiosity had led to several questions. Concetta had been evasive but still a little too giddy, saying things like: *It's nothing you'd be interested in, Jess. It's not for girls like you. You don't have the time for fun anyway.* Jessica, both hurt and offended, had challenged Concetta's mysterious response. *I can have fun,* she said. *I'm not as nerdy as you think. Tell me, what is it?* Later that afternoon, Concetta invited Jessica into the Chamber, and Jessica had been blown away by the elaborate town house basement. Dozens of colored lightbulbs, chests filled with costumes and sparkling jewelry, long antique swords. Standing there in the thick of it, Jessica hadn't been able to speak. She'd felt like she'd stepped into another world.

And then came Concetta's scintillating question: *Who do you really want to be, Jessica? I mean, in your heart of hearts, what kind of a person do you wish you were?*

Jessica's initial response had been perfunctory and typical: *I like who I am. I'm happy being me.* But her eyes had belied the confidence in her voice. She shrank away from Concetta's knowing stare, not wanting to admit the truth—that deep down inside, she had always fantasized about being a bad girl, about exploring the wild side of life. Let her hair down. Kiss whomever she wanted to kiss and laugh out loud without worrying about who might cast her a scornful glance. What would that be like?

In the end, Concetta had seen right through Jessica's steel wall. *I know there's a lot of you that you keep hidden,*

*Jess,* she'd said. *You can't always like being the one to do everything right. Even the smart girls need to cut loose every now and then. Do you want to be a member? Do you want to enter the universe of the Black Cry Affair?*

Despite the goody-goody instinct telling her to walk away, Jessica smiled. She'd thought: *I can come here and live out my fantasies. I can be a Greek goddess or slutty princess. I won't have to live by the rules once I enter the Chamber. No one except the other role-players will ever know about it.*

And up until tonight, that had been absolutely true.

Being a member of the secret club had taken the edge off her otherwise rigid personality. It had even boosted her confidence a little. Prancing around in those elaborate costumes, forgetting herself for the space of a couple hours, just plain *cutting loose* from the tensions of everyday life . . . it had given her a sense of freedom unlike any she had ever known. That was why she had accepted the Hamilton triplets' invitation to attend the opening of Cleopatra. That was why she'd worn a tight-fitting silk dress instead of a typical—and more conservative—floor-sweeping gown. Before the Black Cry Affair, Jessica would never have ventured to a nightclub, much less onto a dance floor. Hours spent bumping bodies with a bunch of drunken, sweaty classmates? Of course not. The old Jessica would have opted to spend the night doing homework or perfecting her college application essays.

*The old Jessica wouldn't have lost control.*

Another sigh broke from her lips. *I'm an idiot,* she thought. *A moron and a jackass. Why did I let myself get involved with that stupid group? Now look at what's happened.*

She tore off her dress and kicked it across the floor. She stomped into the bathroom, flicked on the light, and stared at herself in the mirror. She looked worse than ever. Dark circles rimmed her eyes. Her cheeks were puffy and damp. Every last stitch of makeup had disappeared from her face. And yet, when she studied her reflection, she saw a faint glimmer of coolness in it, an edgy poise that hadn't been there several months ago. Maybe what Damien had told her was true—that when you go a little crazy and have a little fun, everything else falls into place. That had certainly been her experience when in his company. She could see it now in the way she stood, in the way her shoulders fell back in a relaxed posture. She could feel it in her heart too.

But when the police and the reporters and the public all caught wind of the club, her own stellar reputation would be as cheap as last season's wardrobe. *Jessica Paderman was involved in something so silly and immature? Good, smart Jessica? What on earth got into her?* She could already hear the slanderous comments, the disappointment, the shock. There had to be a way to stop it from happening.

Tonight, seeing Damien's body on the floor of that cage, she had thought only of that. Of herself and the embarrassment she would face *after* the fact.

Soon enough, everyone would know. She wouldn't be able to keep the secret.

She leaned over the sink and took several deep breaths.

*I'm sorry, Damien. I'm so sorry. But I did what I had to do.*

"Jessica?"

She jumped as her mother's voice echoed from the

dining room. She slammed the bathroom door closed. "Yeah, Mom?" she yelled out. "What is it?"

Abigail Paderman's heavy footsteps clunked on the hardwood floors. "Oh, thank God you're home! I've been calling your cell! Come out here!"

"I can't, Mom," Jessica said. "Give me a minute."

"It's all over the news!" Abigail shrieked. "The night-club! Damien Kittle! Is it true? My God!"

*Yes, it's true.*

"I'm okay. I'll be right there," Jessica called out. And then she swept her long red hair into a ponytail, turned on the faucet, and began washing the blood from beneath her fingernails.

# 8

## Secretive Sisters

"Detention for one month!"

Mother Margaret John's outraged voice echoed through the principal's office and out into the empty fifth-floor hall. At nearly three o'clock in the morning, she looked like a penguin that hadn't slept in decades. Her habit was wrinkled and uneven. Her veil was crooked. She kept pacing the same length of floor while wringing her hands.

Madison, Park, and Lex were sitting side by side in front of the huge L-shaped oak desk. For the past five minutes, they had listened to Mother Margaret scream on and on about school policies and procedures, about what happened to people who committed felonies, and about a particularly nasty prison upstate where young rich girls wore polyester jumpsuits and were denied manicures. It was all nonsense, of course. Nothing more than the ramblings of a distraught woman. Mother Margaret wasn't handling the news of Damien Kittle's murder well.

Madison had expected this sort of hysterical display of emotion. In just a few short hours, Mother Margaret had been forced to accept a scandal that would rock the foundation upon which St. Cecilia's Prep had been built. One student was dead. Another was in police custody. The media storm would descend on the uppity principal like an avalanche.

"Bad signs!" Mother Margaret shouted, pointing at the triplets. "These are bad signs about what will become of you girls! Breaking and entering! Sneaking around private property! What's next? A gambling ring? A drug cartel in the gymnasium? I *won't* have it!"

Madison sighed. "Reverend Mother, please calm down."

"Don't speak until I give you permission to speak, young lady!" Another wag of her long, bananalike finger.

"Madison is right, Mother." Park straightened in her chair. Her voice was firm. "We get the picture, okay? What we did was wrong and we apologize. But we didn't break into the school just for fun. We obviously have a very good reason for doing it."

"I don't care about your reasons!" Mother Margaret went on. "When school starts up again in September, you will each be spending *every day* in detention. September first to the thirtieth. Monday through Friday. Three o'clock to five-thirty."

"Like hell!" Lex shot back.

In a far corner of the office, standing beside a bookshelf, Sister Brittany gasped.

Mother Margaret's jaw dropped. *"What did you just say?"*

"There's no *way* we're spending the whole month in detention," Lex told her. "And if you even *try* to pull that punishment off, there'll be *huge* consequences."

"There really will be," Madison agreed quietly.

"Huge," Park echoed. "Like, as huge as Bloomingdale's and Saks put together."

Mother Margaret, her eyes softening slightly, pulled out her chair and sat down slowly. "What are you girls trying to say? And why do I feel as though I'm being threatened?"

"You're not being threatened," Park said offhandedly. "You're just being . . . informed."

"Informed of what?" Sister Brittany asked, stepping forward.

"Well, July is usually when our dad makes his annual donation to the Order of Our Lady of the Avenue recreation fund." Madison crossed her legs and leaned back in the chair, assuming a relaxed position. "If he's upset about any kind of cruel and unusual punishment being inflicted on us, there's no telling what he might do."

"And let's not forget," Lex jumped in, "that the Hamilton donation is always the biggest, Reverend Mother. Three commas in that check. Count 'em. One. Two. Three."

"So much money, in fact, that the convent usually finds itself flush with more cash than it knows what to do with." Park frowned. "If I'm not mistaken, Mother, last year you and the other sisters took a two-week vacation to Biarritz right after our dad dropped his annual check."

"That's *right*," Lex said. "You haven't forgotten, have you, Mother? Last year I bumped into you in Barneys. You were buying a vat of Kiehl's moisturizer. And you had a slammin' tan."

"Enough." Mother Margaret held up her hands, but she did it calmly. The fury had left her face. "There won't be any detention. But you girls *will* tell me and Sister Brittany everything you know about what happened tonight." She lowered her eyes. Tears spilled onto her cheeks. "Because I still can't believe it."

Thankfully, Madison, Park, and Lex hadn't had the awful task of breaking the news to Mother Margaret and Sister Brittany. All the nuns had been awakened long before the news aired on television. A phone call from the British embassy had informed them of Damien Kittle's murder.

Park didn't want to revisit those frightening moments again, so she doled out a brief synopsis of what had happened inside Cleopatra, right down to Concetta Canoli's bare foot and the horrid pink stiletto that should have been on it.

"You've told me what I already know," Mother Margaret said. "But what I want are the details—the ones you girls aren't sharing with anybody. And don't play foolish. I know how you triplets operate."

"All one brain," Sister Brittany commented, smoothing her hands down the length of her habit. "But really, girls, you *should* tell us everything you know."

Park stared at Lex. Lex stared at Madison. Then they

all stared at one another. Although no one would have known it, they were, in fact, beginning a conversation. Albeit a strange and silent one.

Park asked the first question. She did this by swinging the strap of her purse over her left shoulder as she stared intently at Madison and Lex. The slight gesture, in Hamilton triplet code, meant: *Should we tell them?*

Lex answered immediately. She opened the magic purse, pulled out a lip gloss, and quickly ran it over her lips. This was a clear and adamant *no.*

Just as swiftly, Madison reached for the pearls around her neck and gave them a hard shake. *Yes.*

Lex didn't appreciate that at all. She pursed her lips, threw her head back, and shook out her long locks. She had just asked another question: *Why should we?*

Park lifted her right arm, rattling the bracelets on her wrist. This meant *I think we have to* or *It's the right thing to do.*

Lex went into the magic purse and pulled from it a small custom-mixed bottle of perfume. Then she carefully and very clearly spritzed some onto the left side of her neck. Translation: *You're both wrong. It's a mistake.*

Using her right hand, Madison slipped several strands of hair behind her ears. *I say we do it.*

Park stretched out her left leg and extended her foot, as if modeling her shoe. *Whatever is fine with me.*

Growing more agitated, Lex pulled at the spaghetti strap on her right shoulder. *Let's keep our mouths shut.*

"Oh, my!" Sister Brittany said, watching the odd exchange, her head bouncing from Madison to Park to Lex and back again. "It's some sort of code."

"Yes, I've seen them do it before." Mother Margaret sighed. "To the ordinary observer it looks like an innocent primping session. All we can do is wait until the conversation is over."

In response to Lex's last gesture, Madison yanked a tube of lipstick from her purse and ran it over her lips in counterclockwise motion. *Don't argue with me.*

Lex dabbed moisturizer onto the back side of her right hand and rubbed it in. *I know what I'm saying.*

Madison flicked her left earring. *I'm warning you . . .*

Park lifted her hands up and out, then splayed her fingers apart as if studying her nails. *Both of you, stop it. I'm getting a headache.*

Lex crossed her right leg over her left. *It's not my fault. I'm not the bonehead.*

Park rattled the bracelets on her left wrist. *That's not nice.*

Lex yanked on a bra strap. *I'm tired of being nice.*

Madison scowled. It was time to end the conversation. She reached back into her purse, pulled out her sunglasses, and slipped them on. She looked to the left. She looked to the right. Then she removed the shades and pushed them onto the top of her head. *What I say goes. Don't challenge me.*

It was the final, decisive gesture. As the eldest and firstborn, Madison had the power to overrule her sisters, and she had just used it.

Lex sighed, disappointed and defeated.

Madison said, "Okay, Mother, we'll tell you everything we know."

"But only on one condition," Park said coolly.

Mother Margaret raised her eyebrows. "And what would that be?"

"That you don't tell our dad we broke into the school," Lex said. "Will you accept the deal?"

Mother Margaret leaned back in her swivel chair. "I'll accept it fifty percent."

"Impossible." Park shook her head. "That doesn't give us any return on our investment. And, mind you, we're giving you this deal interest-free."

"Sixty percent," Mother Margaret offered.

"In this market?" Lex's voice shot up. "We could easily take our information elsewhere, Mother. What we know is worth a lot."

Madison nodded. "We really would need you to accept our terms one hundred percent, Mother. I think we're being very nice here. We're basically giving you a chance to buy a lot of stock before the shares rise and split."

Mother Margaret remained silent for several long moments. She looked at Sister Brittany, then nodded. "Okay. Deal." She raised the pinky finger of her right hand and traced a big letter *C* in the air; short for *Cecilia*, it was the sign of an oath taken in the strictest confidence. All St. Cecilia's Prep students made promises this way.

"Deal," Madison, Park, and Lex replied in unison. In synchronization, they repeated the gesture, each tracing a letter *C* in the air.

"Now tell us what you know," Sister Brittany said.

Madison cleared her throat. "It looks like the pink stiletto really is the murder weapon. We inspected Damien's body before the police arrived, and Lex deduced that the wound was consistent with the size of the shoe's steel tip."

"We also noticed some kind of glitter around the wound," Park said. "Glitter is used in a number of hair gels and sprays, but none of us has ever known Damien to use anything with it."

"So you think the glitter could have been left there by the killer," Sister Brittany stated.

Park nodded. "Probably. Especially if the killer sprayed or styled his or her hair and didn't wash his or her hands."

"Does Concetta use this glittery product?" Mother Margaret asked.

"Not that I've ever noticed," Park replied.

"Me neither," Park said.

Lex shook her head. "Same here."

Park shifted in her chair, leaning her tired body against the armrest. "So the way it looks now, Damien died as a result of blunt impact trauma. The stiletto slammed into his skull at a totally twisted speed, and with lots of force. And Concetta's really the only logical suspect."

Mother Margaret sighed and ran a hand over her face.

Sister Brittany said, "What about other evidence? Did you girls notice anything else in or around the cage?"

"We didn't have time to collect trace evidence, Sister," Park said. "If there was anything suspicious in the cage, the forensic techs hopefully found it."

"One of my students is dead, and another is being charged with his murder." Mother Margaret wiped more tears from her eyes. "Can it get any worse?"

"We also found a strange . . . symbol on Damien's palm," Madison said. "It's a stamp of a Roman coin—a male head wearing a Corinthian helmet. And that pretty much leads us to why we broke in here."

Both Mother Margaret and Sister Brittany leaned closer to them.

"We wanted to break into Concetta's locker and see what we could find," Lex explained. "And we found a lot. We matched the symbol on Damien's palm to something in Concetta's locker. We actually found a whole lot in Concetta's locker."

Mother Margaret swiveled her chair to the left and stared out the dark window. "The Black Cry Affair," she said. "Right?"

Madison and Park gasped.

Lex flung her hand in the air in a gesture of disbelief. "Excuse me? You *know* about this secret club, Mother? Hello?"

"I've known about it for some time," Mother Margaret said gravely.

"How?" Lex waved her hand again.

"I once overheard Concetta talking about it," Mother Margaret explained. "It was a few months ago, and Concetta was in the first-floor parlor waiting for her mother to come pick her up. I heard Concetta talking on her cell phone. She was trying to be as quiet as possible, but I was walking by and couldn't help overhearing her. She must've been chatting with one of the other members of the club, because she was mentioning some of their . . . practices."

"So you were eavesdropping," Lex said flatly.

"I was, yes. Concetta never saw me. But I heard her talk about a few things, mainly about how they apparently play different roles." Mother Margaret shot a glance at Sister Brittany. "It seemed very . . . innocent. But maybe it's not."

"Is that all you heard?" Park asked. "Did you hear her mention any names?"

"Yes. I had already assumed immediately that Emmett McQueen was a member of the club," Mother Margaret said. "But I was shocked to learn that Damien was a part of it. And Julian Simmons."

"*And* Jessica Paderman," Sister Brittany blurted out.

"Jessica Paderman!" Mother Margaret's voice shot up like a rocket. "That can't be!"

"It is," Park informed her. "We just saw Jessica's name in the diary Concetta keeps about the club."

Madison shot Sister Brittany a sharp stare. "How did *you* know that?" she asked, her tone blatantly suspicious.

"It was an assumption," Sister Brittany replied quickly. "I've seen Jessica and Concetta together a lot. I've even tried to talk to Jessica, to get her to open up to me the way so many of the other girls do, but she never has."

Mother Margaret shook her head. "I really hadn't given that club much thought until a few weeks after I overheard Concetta's conversation."

Park leaned forward. "What happened then?"

A pause. Then Mother Margaret sighed. "I believe you girls have told me the truth. I believe you've told me what you know and that you genuinely want to help, so I'll be very honest with each of you. But what I tell you must remain private. You cannot go around school blabbing it to your friends."

Madison, Park, and Lex glanced at one another. Then Madison said, "You have our word. Please tell us what you know."

"Several months ago, back in March, we had a theft

here at the school," Mother Margaret began. "It was the weekend of March eighteenth. I remember it distinctly because the very next day, Sister Brittany came to join us. Anyway, that weekend, someone broke into the school, and the intruder didn't try to be neat about it. Whoever it was had the audacity to leave a mess right here in my office. That's why it was easy for us to see almost immediately that a number of the school's highly confidential financial documents had been invaded, and several were stolen."

Lex's face registered confusion. "Who would want that stuff? Are there a lot of secrets in those documents?"

"Not necessarily secrets," Mother Margaret said. "But things—information—that are best kept private. But the theft really wasn't what disturbed us the most. It's what the police found in here after they came to investigate."

"What did they find?" Park asked.

Mother Margaret and Sister Brittany again exchanged worried glances. "The police found traces of nitroglycerin, sodium carbonate, and diatomaceous earth," Mother Margaret said gravely.

"You'll have to clarify what that means," Madison told her. "Unfortunately, none of us is that great at chemistry."

Sister Brittany sat down on the edge of the big desk. "Those substances are used to make dynamite, girls. As in, explosives."

"Explosives!" Lex cried. "Are you kidding me?"

"Unfortunately, we're not." Mother Margaret shook her head. "The investigation has been ongoing since then—privately, of course. We didn't want to worry students and parents."

"That's understandable," Park said. "But I still think the student body and our parents have a right to know."

"Federal agents from the Bureau of Alcohol, Tobacco, Firearms, and Explosives have been in here repeatedly, and they requested that we keep it quiet," Mother Margaret replied. "And I've respected their wishes. There's also no immediate threat to the school or my students. Right now it's just . . . a disturbing fact."

"Does this mean someone was trying to blow up the school?" Madison's voice broke. She reached out and grabbed Lex's hand.

"We don't know," Sister Brittany replied. "Right now it means that the person who broke into the school back in March had traces of those chemicals on his or her clothes or shoes."

Park nodded firmly, then held up her hand. "Okay. This is all totally crazy news, but what does it have to do with Damien's murder or the Black Cry Affair?"

"Well, first of all, the members of that little exclusive club—Concetta Canoli, Emmett McQueen, Julian Simmons, and now Jessica Paderman—are all outstanding chemistry students," Mother Margaret said. "Damien was a good chemistry student too, but not an *outstanding* one."

"But you're making a very big assumption here," Park said. "Lots of students are outstanding in chemistry. What you're saying is very, very circumstantial. Besides, what motive would any of them have?"

Mother Margaret shrugged slowly. "I can't think of one. I'm merely making the connection between the break-in here at the school and Damien's murder."

"That would never hold up in court," Lex continued. "Did you mention your suspicions to the ATF?"

"Yes," Mother Margaret answered. "I gave them a list of all our top chemistry students, but they said what you've just said. And that weekend, every locker in the school was thoroughly searched."

Madison's eyes widened. "You mean, federal agents went rifling through our lockers without our permission?"

"I'm afraid so." Mother Margaret replied. "What other choice did they have, dear? Possession of dynamite is a felony directly related to terrorism. They couldn't take any chances."

"But the Feds didn't find anything suspicious in Concetta Canoli's locker," Park said. "Or any member of the Black Cry Affair's locker?"

"No. Nothing." Sister Brittany shook her head. "But there's still reason to believe the Black Cry Affair might have had something to do with the theft and the dynamite . . . and with Damien's murder."

"Forgive me for saying this, Sister," Lex said. "But you sound totally twisted. The club is a group of role-players. Why would they be interested in making dynamite, or stealing documents?"

Another exchange of glances between the two nuns.

"The night of the theft, police found something else— a little detail I hadn't given much thought to, until now," Sister Brittany told them. She pointed to the black steel file cabinets on the opposite side of the office. "There was a smattering of glitter on the cabinets. Probably the same glitter you girls saw tonight on Damien's hair."

"Oh, crap," Park said as Madison and Lex gasped.

Sister Brittany leaned over. She put her right hand on Park's knee and her left one on Lex's. Her bright, cheerful face went dark and serious. "No one really knows what goes on in those role-playing sessions. No one—certainly not any of us—has been able to penetrate the Black Cry Affair. It's a very secretive club. Everything you found in Concetta's locker—the notebook—could all be a ruse for what might really be going on."

"And we think Damien was about to blow the whistle on the club," Mother Margaret added. "He came and made an appointment with me earlier today. He was supposed to come speak with me on Monday morning, before the graduation ceremony. But now, of course . . . he won't."

"So that's why he was in your office today," Madison said. "When I saw him in the student lounge, he told me he'd overheard you telling Mrs. Burns that Lex and I were expected in your office."

"Damien was probably still standing out in the hall when I told Mary Grace you and Lex were expected in here," Mother Margaret replied.

Park shook her head. "Wait a sec. If the Black Cry Affair really is a group that's doing bad things—like engineering dynamite—and Damien wanted to blow the whistle on them, why would he wait for an appointment to speak with you? Why wouldn't he just bust in here and tell you there are psychos walking these halls?"

"True." Lex nodded. "I don't get that either."

"I'm assuming he wanted to do it quietly, without creating a ruckus or arousing too much suspicion." Mother Margaret stood up and began pacing the floor again. "Damien was also the only person who knew about the secret surprise guest coming to Monday's graduation ceremony."

"Who's coming?" Lex asked.

"As you girls know, it's St. Cecilia's tradition to have a surprise guest at every graduation ceremony," Mother Margaret said. She sighed and clenched her hands together. "On Monday, specifically because Damien was supposed to graduate, David Gordon, the prime minister of England, will be here to address our graduates."

"I *love* David!" Lex bounced up and down in the chair. "He's always so sweet to us when we visit London."

"Make sure you have blueberry scones on the menu," Park said to Mother Margaret and Sister Brittany. "He loves those."

"The way things look now, the prime minister most likely won't be coming!" Mother Margaret wailed. "Damien was himself English royalty. The news has already sent shock waves throughout England."

"David will *absolutely* still come," Madison said confidently. "It would be a bad publicity move if he didn't show up. Foreign relations between Britain and the United States are very strong. And you'll be doing some sort of memorial service for Damien, won't you?"

"Of course!" Sister Brittany gasped.

"When does David arrive?" Lex asked.

"Tomorrow," Mother Margaret answered. "I'm expecting a call from him any minute now. This is disastrous, just . . . disastrous. The prime minister will have the worst time of his life here—the press, the shame."

Park reached into her purse, pulled out a tissue, and wiped a trail of sweat from her forehead. "Listen, Mother. I know you have a lot on your plate right now, but as it stands, Concetta Canoli has been arrested for killing

Damien. I don't want to believe it either, but the evidence fits. She was completely obsessed with Damien, and she was wearing the weapon."

"Unless you girls figure out otherwise," Mother Margaret said quietly.

Park raised an eyebrow. "What's that supposed to mean?"

Sister Brittany stood up. Her eyes squinted into a hard gleam. "We can't penetrate the Black Cry Affair because we're adults. But you girls *can*. Concetta is a friend of yours. So is Emmett McQueen. You could—"

Lex's right hand shot into the air. "I am *not* joining some role-playing club. I refuse to prance around in bad clothing. If my wardrobe ever gets a little overdramatic and costume-ish, it's only because Jean Paul Gaultier or John Galliano designed something for me."

"You don't understand," Mother Margaret said, coming around the desk. "In just a few hours, every newspaper will be running the story of Damien's murder and Concetta's alleged guilt. It's going to wreak havoc on the school. And then the news of the chemical traces will be made known. It's more scandal than we can handle. There are already countless people out there who hate St. Cecilia's Prep for being such a powerful private school— just imagine how much ammo this will give them!"

"It could very well ruin the school forever," Sister Brittany whispered.

Park didn't know what to say. Neither did Lex. They both stared at Madison, silently waiting for her advice.

"I just don't know," Madison said quietly. "What makes you think we can even penetrate the club?"

"Because you girls are *excellent* when it comes to getting your own way," Mother Margaret replied. She shot them a pleading look. "Please, help us. Monday's commencement ceremony will be ruined. The prime minister will be mortified. And I don't know who else will end up *dead*!"

# 9

## Hey, Mr. DJ!

The penthouse slumbered in the cool darkness. Madison opened her bedroom door as quietly as possible and tip-toed out into the corridor. She took careful, silent steps as she bypassed Park's room and then continued into the kitchen. It was nearly dawn. She felt wired and edgy and tense, images from the night flashing before her eyes like snapshots.

She knew sleep wouldn't touch her. And even if it did, she feared her dreams would be vivid with splotches of blood and garish stilettos. Or, worse, they would be old memories of Damien Kittle playing out against her subconscious—his smile, his laugh, the feel of his lips against the back of her hand. As she stepped through the darkness and into the kitchen, she fought to hold back another flow of tears, knowing that her sobs would wake Park, Lex, and their housekeeper, Lupe. She needed to be alone for a while. And she needed the company of old, familiar friends.

Reaching the refrigerator, Madison yanked the door open and immediately spotted a carton of milk. She pulled it out and set it down on the island. Next came the chocolate sauce from the lowermost cabinet. She felt her muscles loosening by the second, but where the hell was the champagne? There was none on ice, nor was there a spare bottle in the pantry. Several minutes went by before she finally turned on the lights and climbed onto the counter beside the sink. She stretched her arms up to the two cabinets usually reserved for emergency baking products and many of Lupe's odd South American herbal remedies. Finally, Madison found a bottle of Dom Perignon hidden behind a jar of pickled celery and pig's feet—a secret age-defying mixture, Lupe once told her, that rivaled Botox. The very thought of it made Madison dizzy, so she grabbed the champagne and hopped back onto the floor.

She smiled happily as she filled a glass halfway with milk and shot it with the chocolate syrup. The bottle of champagne wouldn't be so easy: it wasn't as much fun if you didn't pop the cork, but she knew how important it was to be quiet. If her sisters found out, they'd forbid her to drink the dangerous concoction. She bit her lip as she searched for something to mask the sound. She found a damp dish towel, but just as she was about to twist the cork out, a strange feeling seized her.

She was being watched.

Throwing a quick glance over her shoulder, she scanned the kitchen and even peered through the shadowy web of the dining room. Nothing. Then, dropping her gaze slowly to the floor, she spotted Champagne, Lex's teacup Chihuahua, staring up at her. The dog's small, shiny eyes were disapproving and accusatory, as if he were saying: *You know you're not supposed to drink that. Now put the damn bottle down.*

"Shoo!" Madison whispered. She waved her hand over him, hoping the gesture would get him moving, but Champagne stayed put. Maybe Champagne wanted some champagne? She sighed and went back to the dish towel.

The dog started growling.

"Be quiet," Madison pleaded. "If you wake them up . . . oh . . . I'll burn every last piece of doggie couture Lex bought you. Now hush!"

In response to her threat, Champagne barked.

Madison swiftly opened the cabinet under the sink, pulled out a box of dog biscuits, and tossed one across the kitchen.

Champagne skittered after it, settling down beside the stove.

Madison sighed. Why did everything have to be so difficult? Determined to mix her favorite stress-relieving drink, she wrapped the dish towel around the mouth of the bottle and gave it a twist. The cork moved but didn't pop. She pressed the bottle against the edge of the counter, trapping it between her stomach and the solid marble. But as she pulled back again with her right hand, the cork shot out and up like a rocket, cutting across the kitchen, slamming into the toaster with a clang, and ricocheting off the refrigerator door before finding its target: Champagne's little head.

"Oh!" Madison gasped. "Oh, no—" She jumped back as the frothy contents of the bottle spewed into her face like a geyser, a bubbly stream of it rushing into her nostrils. She shook her head, trying to ward off a second spray, but in three seconds flat her cheeks, chin, and forehead were dripping wet.

The dog emitted a low, weak groan.

Madison set the bottle on the counter and quickly wiped the wetness from her eyes. "Oh my God!" she screamed, dropping to her knees and scooping Champagne up in her arms. "Oh, you poor little thing! I'm so sorry! Auntie Madison didn't mean it! I swear! Oh, Champagne, please don't die!" She held the dog up and stared into his cloudy eyes; he looked as though he were going to pass out any second. Unable to control her panic, Madison cradled him in her arms and began fanning him with the dish towel. Was there some sort of procedure to follow when it came to canine trauma? Were you supposed to perform CPR on a dog? She would have gone on asking herself questions if Park hadn't suddenly stepped into the kitchen.

"Oh! Thank God!" Madison cried. She set a wobbly Champagne on the counter. Then she turned around, slid across the puddle on the floor, and landed flat on her butt. "Ouch," she whispered.

Park was staring down at her with a calm, bemused expression.

"I guess I woke you up," Madison said. She sniffled to free her nostrils of the bubbly booze.

Park shook her head. "Look at what you've become—a desperate alkie who'll do anything for her fix of milk and champagne."

"And speaking of Champagne . . . I think I killed the dog!" Madison heaved a sigh as she scrambled to her knees.

"I don't even want to know how this happened," Park said, reaching out and scooping Champagne into the crook of her left arm. She went to the refrigerator, grabbed ice from the freezer, and dropped several cubes into a paper towel. Then she applied the little ice pack to the knot on the dog's head and stared at Madison. "You have Dom Perignon all over your face, up your nose, and all over your head."

Madison stuck her chin up and ran a hand through her damp hair. "In some countries, Dom Perignon is known for its medicinal purposes. It'll probably make my hair shinier and fuller."

Park sighed. "Go ahead and fix yourself the stupid drink. You've gone to enough trouble already."

"Is the dog okay?" Madison asked as she reached for the bottle and her glass again.

"He'll be fine. He just needs some rest. I won't tell Lex you tried to kill him." Park smoothed her hand over his ears.

Madison scowled and finally, blessedly, filled her glass with what was left of the Dom. She gave the drink a quick stir and then took a long, sweet gulp. "God, that feels good! I can already feel my anxiety melting away." She held the glass out to Park.

Crinkling her nose in disgust, Park stuck her hand

out. "*Ugh*. If we were marooned on a desert island and that was the only drink we had, I'd *still* opt for seaweed juice."

"I'm sorry I woke you up," Madison said quietly.

"You didn't. I was already awake. I've been watching the news since we got home." Park set Champagne down and watched him skitter into the pantry. "The news is tearing us apart again, as usual, and I can't bring myself to believe that Damien is dead and that traces of dynamite were found at school. I can't believe any of it."

"What are they saying about us?" Madison asked, taking another long gulp.

"The same crap. Scandal, too much partying. You'd think these reporters would remember that we caught a killer not so very long ago."

"That's *good* news about us. The media doesn't want to report the good stuff."

"And Concetta? They're already calling her the Mozart Murderer." Park sighed. She walked over to a flat-screen built into the counter and flicked it on.

A picture filled the screen: a male reporter standing in front of Cleopatra while sirens flashed behind him and yellow tape sealed off the front entrance of the club. ". . . where the body of Damien Kittle was discovered," the man was saying. And a moment later: ". . . the Hamilton triplets—Madison, Park, and Lexington Hamilton—were inside the club but have not given any statements to the media regarding . . ."

Park shook her head. "See? Same crap. What the hell are we supposed to say? It's obvious that we're upset."

"Has Jeremy called you yet?" Madison asked.

"Yeah, he left me two messages, and we finally spoke

about an hour ago." Park yawned. "I had to convince him not to come over. He thinks we're in danger with a killer on the loose."

Madison rolled her eyes. "Like we haven't been in *that* predicament before. But . . . you know . . ." Her voice trailed off.

"What?" Park said.

Madison opened her mouth to speak, but no words emerged. Instead, a gargantuan, earsplitting burp shot out of her and rocked the air around them. She stared at the floor.

Park closed her eyes and shook her head. "Put down that glass, Madison. *Now.*"

Madison set the glass on the counter and shoved it away.

"What were you going to say?" Park asked.

"I was going to say that, technically speaking, Jeremy *does* have a point. I mean, a killer *might* still be out there."

"So then you don't believe Concetta's guilty."

"I don't know what I believe," Madison answered quietly. "Was this really a crime of passion, or does the whole secret club Concetta runs have something to do with it? And what about all that stuff that was found in Mother Margaret's office? If it *is* all tied together somehow, then we have a lot to worry about."

"I have a bad feeling about the Black Cry Affair," Park said. She took a bottle of Pellegrino from the fridge and poured herself a glass.

"Meaning?"

"Meaning that I don't think it's just an innocent role-playing club. I think there's a lot more that goes on in that

Chamber thing than anyone might imagine. Let's say the group *does* have something to do with the break-in back in March and the traces of explosives—what are the members of the group planning? Why play around with deadly stuff like that?"

Madison frowned. "The glittery stuff we saw on Damien's head and the glitter that was found on Mother Margaret's cabinet pretty much link both crimes."

"Yeah—but why would Concetta break into the office?"

"Maybe she didn't," Madison offered. "Maybe another member of the group did. We don't know why yet, but it could've been someone else. And every member of the Black Cry Affair was at Cleopatra tonight."

"We have to consider the obvious facts first." Park held up a hand, as if to keep speculation away. "First off, Concetta was wearing the murder weapon—it belongs to her. Second of all, we all saw her going toward the cages with Damien. Third, she was obsessed with him. Fourth—"

"She has an intense shoe fetish." Madison nodded sadly. "Talk about a clear picture. But, you know, stranger things have happened."

Park narrowed her eyes and stared across the kitchen, rapt in thought. "Talking about strange—did you notice anything strange about our little meeting in Mother Margaret's office tonight?"

"Duh," Madison said. "I think you're referring to Sister Brittany—I don't buy her explanation of how she knew Jessica Paderman is a member of the club."

"Totally right."

Madison patted her chin and cheeks with a napkin. "So what are we saying now? That Sister Brittany is up to no good? We can't keep digging holes here. And no matter what—she *is* a nun. An annoying and nosy nun, but still a nun."

"If we're going to link the break-in and Damien's murder, we have to believe he was killed for some very specific reason, and not that this was a crime of passion," Park deduced.

"We don't know enough yet," Madison said quietly. "It's all just a big blur."

Park sighed and ran a hand through her hair. "There are too many freaking questions to consider! I *hate* this!"

A silence descended over the kitchen as they both leaned against the counter. The television was still on, and now the reporter's voice circled them.

". . . another development that has just been released by NYPD officials," the man was saying. "According to one source close to the investigation, detectives are ruling out as suspects the two DJs who were working the opening night at Cleopatra. Apparently, those two DJs—Christopher Mellin and Frank Kellerman—were found *unconscious* in their music booth above the dance floor at Cleopatra. Both of them were rushed to Saint Luke's—Roosevelt Hospital, where they're apparently undergoing treatment for what appears to be . . . uh . . . some kind of respiratory distress. Now, this distress looks like it might have been the result of inhaling some sort of toxic chemical. . . ."

"What?" Madison screamed. "Holy shit!"

Park's jaw dropped as she stared at the television.

The screen flashed from the live shot of a male reporter standing in front of Cleopatra to a bright news studio where Diane Sawyer was sitting at the anchor desk.

"Now, John, have the police given any word as to *why* Concetta Canoli might have committed this truly horrendous crime?"

The screen jumped back to the male reporter. He frowned and shook his head. "The police have not made an official statement yet, Diane," he said. "All we know is that teen heiress and celebutante Concetta Canoli is the main suspect in the murder of Damien Kittle, and that she's being interrogated right now and will very likely be arraigned in court in just a few hours."

Back to Diane. She shook her head gravely. "A tragic story creating shock waves on both sides of the Atlantic . . . and made all the more shocking by the horrendous piece of footwear that is apparently the murder weapon. We turn now to our top fashion expert . . ."

Park flicked off the television. "The DJs were unconscious," she whispered. "So *that's* how the Mozart Requiem was played. Concetta actually went into the tech booth where the DJs were working and . . ."

"And what?" Madison threw up her arms in frustration. "Sprayed them with anesthesia? Suffocated them with her other shoe? What the hell led to 'respiratory distress'?"

"Some sort of . . . chemical, I guess?" Park said, insinuating the obvious.

*Nitroglycerin. Diatomaceous earth. Sodium carbonate.* The chemistry terms rang through Madison's brain. Was that it? Had Concetta actually plotted this whole crime? Was she some sort of chemical-mixing psycho? The very thought of it sent a chill up her spine. She thought of all the times they had hung out together in school, and how

Concetta had seemed so . . . normal. Had it all been fake? "So now we know the DJs couldn't have seen much," she said evenly. "I guess Concetta—or, I mean, the killer?—obviously knew what she was doing."

Park started pacing the floor. "But it *still* doesn't make sense. If she went through all this to kill Damien in such a public way, why would she allow herself to get caught so easily? She left her damn shoe in the cage!"

Madison folded her arms over her chest and gritted her teeth. "I don't like this at all. I'm getting *totally* annoyed here, Park. All the evidence points to Concetta but the crime itself doesn't make sense. There's something we're not seeing."

"Like what?"

"If I could tell you that, I'd be able to see it!" Madison snapped.

Park stared at her. "You don't have to get so testy. Answers will become more available if we stay calm and investigate things without rushing."

"How can we not rush? Commencement is Monday morning. Prime Minister Gordon is supposed to be there, and how will this whole mess look for everyone involved—including us—if it isn't solved?"

Park took a deep breath. "Let's start with an obvious question: is there anyone at school who hated Damien enough to kill him?"

"No one I can think of. His life was pretty normal."

"Except for being a member of the Black Cry Affair."

"True."

"Okay. So then we agree that the secret club is somehow linked to all this. But we can't really go any further with that thought because we don't know what the club really does behind closed doors. So I guess we have to find that out first."

Madison looked down. She hadn't really wanted to consider that possibility.

"Well, I, for one, am pissed off."

Madison jumped at the sound of the voice.

Park whirled around.

Lex was standing just outside the kitchen, her shorts and tank top wrinkled, her fluffy slippers planted firmly on the floor.

"Jesus, Lex. Did you have to scare us like that?" Madison snapped.

Lex marched toward them. She threw her head back as she opened up the fridge and grabbed a carton of orange juice. "I don't appreciate the two of you having an investigative meeting without me," she said coldly. "You don't *really* think you'll be able to solve this case sans my fashion expertise, do you?"

"Of course not." Park reached for a glass and handed it to her.

Madison rolled her eyes. "Have you heard the newest bit of information? We're way beyond fashion here."

"I've been watching the news in my bedroom," Lex said. "I haven't been able to sleep at all. And to tell you the truth, I'm not surprised the DJs were knocked out. How else would Concetta have played the Mozart Requiem?"

"So then you definitely think Concetta's the killer," Park stated firmly.

"Yes," Lex said without a moment's hesitation. "I do."

Madison grimaced. She clenched her hands into fists

and shot a quick glance at Park. "Well . . . *I* don't! I think there are other possibilities. And I'm not giving in that easily. There's more to this than meets the eye."

"Fine," Lex replied offhandedly, happy to play devil's advocate. "I totally hope you prove me wrong. But we won't know unless we get to work." She poured three glasses of orange juice, spiked them with the remaining champagne, and then handed one each to Madison and Park.

There was definitely time for mimosas before heading off to their laptops.

# 10

# The Queen's Court

Just after dawn on Saturday morning, Emmett McQueen threw on jeans and a plain blue T-shirt and slipped his feet into his favorite pair of pink leopard-print slippers. It was an uncommonly sloppy outfit. He usually never left his bedroom without coordinating his clothes to make sure the color scheme he was wearing accentuated his eyes and hair. Although he and his mother lived in a secure doorman building in midtown Manhattan, paparazzi and smart reporters had been known to sneak their way into the stately corridors. One pic of him dressed so garishly would wreak havoc on his social life.

Not that he had much of a social life to speak of

anymore. Ever since the scandal that had ruined his family and kicked his father into prison, Emmett's partying days had dwindled considerably. He still had a lot to be thankful for—neither he nor his mother would ever be poor—but the media storm was what Emmett thought about every morning when he woke up. Those ugly gray courthouse hallways were engraved in his memory, as was the sound of his father's weeping and that ugly image of his mother nearly overdosing on sleeping pills. They had collapsed under the weight of the trial, and Emmett had found himself playing the role of parent to both of them. It hadn't been fun. No seventeen-year-old dreamed of coming home to see his mother passed out in front of Maury Povich reruns or watching his father smuggle Valium out of the bathroom.

Bypassing his mirror, Emmett opened his bedroom door and walked down the long corridor into the kitchen. He grabbed his sunglasses from the counter and slipped them on. A pot of coffee was already brewing. His mother, Tammy Lynn, was awake and probably showering. *Great,* Emmett thought, annoyed. *Just when I need her to be drugged up and sleeping, she's operating on cruise control.* He stepped out of the apartment and hurried into the elevator. A minute later he was strolling through the main lobby, throwing glances over his shoulder to make sure no one was milling around. Only the doorman, Ken Smith, spotted him. Ken waved and smiled, and Emmett nodded a curt hello. Then he saw the stack of newspapers beside the front desk and lunged for them. He picked up copies of the *New York Times,* the *Post,* and the *Daily News.* They belonged to other residents, but this was a total emergency.

Before Ken Smith could say anything, Emmett dashed into the elevator and rode it back up to his apartment.

*Please, don't let the news be that bad,* he prayed. *I can't stand it.*

Rushing to the kitchen, he threw the papers down onto the table and flipped them open.

They all had similar, scathing headlines: MURDER AT CLEOPATRA—BRIT ROYAL KILLED, one read. Another: HIGH-SOCIETY SLAYING. The last one: CANOLI KILLER—YOUNG CELEBUTANTE CHARGED WITH MURDER.

Emmett took off his sunglasses and dropped them onto the table. The shock of the headlines made him dizzy. On the cover of the last newspaper was a picture of Concetta being led out of the nightclub clad in her gown and handcuffs, her left foot bare, her right one encased in the pink stiletto.

She had never photographed well.

And now, with his eyes locked on the newspapers, he remembered the words Concetta had uttered yesterday as she'd stood in front of her closet.

*If Damien Kittle doesn't totally fall in love with me, I might do something crazy.*

"Damn," Emmett whispered.

It *almost* made him laugh. Talk about all the pieces falling into place. Was there even a reason to complete an investigation? Everyone knew the cold hard facts, and the coldest fact of all was that Concetta had been insanely in love with Damien. The cops were probably digging into that juicy little nugget of info right now.

"Emmett."

He spun around. "Mornin', Mama."

Once upon a time, Tammy Lynn McQueen had been a great beauty, the proverbial Southern belle. Naturally tall and lean, she had refined features, elegant posture, and a beautiful smile. But, even after multiple surgeries, very little of that was visible anymore. Her blond hair was streaked with gray. Her skin was parched. And, saddest of all, she had the droopy-eyed look of a well-medicated patient. She had aged about ten years since her husband had been sent to jail. She didn't even have the motivation to get her roots done anymore, much less keep up her Botox appointments.

Emmett no longer felt a pang of sorrow when he saw his mother. What he felt was much more powerful—a deep, boiling rage that knew no limits. It just wasn't fair. Why the hell had his family been singled out for ruin? God knew, there were hundreds of CEOs breaking the law when it came to how they handled money—why had *his* father been caught? The answer, Emmett knew, was both simple and complex. Someone had squealed on his dad, tipped off the Internal Revenue Service, and got the jailball rolling. And because of that, Emmett's distrust and dislike of people was growing.

"How are you, honey bear?" Tammy Lynn asked, her voice low, her speech slurred.

"I'm fine, Mama. How're you feelin' today?"

"Oh, a little tired," Tammy Lynn replied. She had one hand in the side pocket of her pink silk robe; the other was holding the countertop for support. "I didn't sleep well last night."

Emmett walked around to the coffeepot and poured himself a cup. He knew his mother had actually slept like a log, courtesy of a mixture of two or three pills. She didn't ask about Damien's murder or Concetta's arrest because she probably hadn't seen the news yet. He dropped a spoonful of sugar into his coffee and stirred it. "You shouldn't be takin' showers when you're feelin' so tired," he said. "Want me to fix you up a nice bowl of oatmeal?"

Tammy Lynn wasn't listening. She had pulled a prescription bottle out of her robe pocket, and now she was trying to twist the cap off.

Emmett reached out and snatched the bottle from her hands. He read the label and sighed. "Mama, how many times have I told you that you can't go fixin' yourself up these prescription cocktails?" He waved the bottle in the air.

"I just need one of those," Tammy Lynn whispered. "My back is knotted worse than a pine tree."

"No." Emmett shook his head. "This is Percocet. Did you take Ambien last night?"

"I . . . I don't remember." Tammy Lynn ran a hand through her damp hair.

"Of course you did! You take 'em every night! And you *can't* take these today!"

"But my pain . . ."

"Forget it, Mama. No Percocet today. My nerves are gonna go crazy with you."

Tammy Lynn took slow, careful steps to Emmett's side. She cradled his face in her hands as tears welled up in her eyes. "Your daddy woulda been so proud of you, sugar. Takin' care of your crazy mama the way you do." She tried to smile, but it seemed too great an effort. "I just . . . I just wish he was here. I wish he could see you grow up and go off to college."

Emmett stared at her, swallowing his rage. He wished more than anything that time would transport him back to the days when he and his parents had lived in Dallas. He missed the mansion, with its high ceilings and big, sunny windows. He missed watching the horses being exercised early in the morning. But most of all, he missed the parties Tammy Lynn used to throw for her friends and business associates—elegant, spectacular events that had turned the mansion into a country club. White lights twinkling on the veranda, guests arriving in droves, the air thick with the scent of the dogwood trees that lined the expansive property. Sometimes, when he closed his eyes, Emmett could still see his mother standing in the great hall of the mansion, all beautiful and perfumed and dolled up, a drink in her hand. His father would entertain guests with cigars and tours of the beautifully decorated rooms.

Emmett missed those days more than he wanted to admit. He hadn't been happy when McQueen and Crux, the television home-shopping empire his father had built twenty years ago, moved their executive offices to New York. Life here had been spectacular up until a few months ago, but Emmett would have given anything to have things the way they'd once been.

He cleared his throat and threw his arms around his mother. "I promise you, Mama—one day I'm gonna find the person who ratted Daddy out, and then all hell's gonna break loose. But right now, go on and lie down. I got lots of things to do today."

"Maybe I will take a little nap," Tammy Lynn said. She patted Emmett's face and quietly disappeared down the corridor.

Emmett went to the table and folded up the newspapers. He took three long gulps of the coffee. Then he rushed back into his bedroom, jumped out of his clothes, and stepped into the shower. He emerged less than five minutes later. He knew he had to move quickly. From his bureau drawer he pulled out a pair of black YSL jeans and a matching shirt. He ran gel through his hair, applied a little eyeliner to his eyes, and scanned his jewelry box. The chunky silver Celtic cross would look good against the black outfit he was wearing; he fastened it to the left side of his shirt and slipped into a pair of Bruno Magli loafers. Then he reached for his Prada man-purse and bolted out of the apartment.

◇  ◇  ◇

It was a muggy Manhattan morning. Emmett ran up Park Avenue and hailed a cab at the corner of Forty-ninth Street. He climbed in and said, "Eighty-fourth and West End Avenue. And put that pedal to the metal!"

As the cab sped up Park Avenue and then across Central Park, Emmett stared out the grimy windows, mentally reviewing his facts. If his calculations were correct—and his calculations were generally correct—the police would come knocking on his door soon. By then, Concetta would have been arraigned. No matter the amount of money, her family would post bail and bring her back home. And that was when the real trouble would begin.

Emmett knew Concetta well. They had been best friends all these years, sharing secrets and slumber parties and clothes. Sharing fears and hopes and fantasies.

He was the only person who had been allowed to see Concetta's insecurities up close. He was also a good judge of character, and he couldn't imagine Concetta holding up strongly in a dingy police interrogation room, being slammed with questions and accusations. Though physically you might think so, she wasn't made of steely stock. She played the role of a confident and self-assured heiress, but beneath it was an insecure girl who had never taken care of herself. Concetta cried easily. She panicked when the going got rough. In the hands of demanding cops, she'd very likely buckle and spill her guts.

*And she probably told them everything about the club. About what we do.*

Emmett nodded to himself. Yes, he was sure that had happened. He was sure that overnight, after being photographed and fingerprinted, Concetta had given the cops more information than they had needed. And that information would undoubtedly point fingers at the members of the Black Cry Affair. Bloody stiletto or not, they would all look guilty of something.

At the corner of West End and Eighty-fourth, Emmett chucked a twenty-dollar bill at the driver and climbed out of the cab. The town house at the very end of the street, the one with the glorious view of the Hudson River, was his first stop. He mounted the steep stairs and rang the bell.

Less than a minute later, Julian Simmons opened the front door, looking exactly as Emmett had expected him to look—shirtless and sweaty from a grueling early-morning workout, his trademark gold rope chain sparkling around his neck.

"What the hell are you doing here?" Julian said, his

eyes bugging out of his head. He yanked Emmett into the foyer and shut the door. "Did anyone see you come here, McQueen?"

Emmett sniffed. "You that afraid people will find out we know each other? And what's with callin' me by my last name? Just 'cause you act like a drill sergeant doesn't mean I'm gonna listen."

Julian clenched his fists at his sides. "You can't come in here. My—my parents don't like it when I have guests over on the weekends."

"Cut the bullshit, *Simmons*. I know your parents are out in L.A. for the new MTV show they're producing." Emmett raised his hand, traced a circle in the air, and snapped twice. "We got business to talk. So shut up and listen." He pushed past Julian and walked into the sprawling first floor of the town house.

Music blared from the massive sound system— Julian's own music, to be exact. Emmett recognized his voice cutting through the air, recognized the rhyming, stylized rap that would probably be playing on radio stations all over the country in a few weeks. The single was typical of Julian: explicit, macho, and a wee bit scary. In fact, everything in the town house was exaggeratedly masculine, from the black shag carpets and ebony wood to the life-sized posters of near-naked women hanging on the walls.

But the girl sitting on the couch wasn't naked. In fact, Jessica Paderman looked like hell. Her flaming red hair was swept up in a bun. Tears smudged the makeup around her eyes. She was puffing on a cigarette and flicking ashes everywhere.

"Well," Emmett said. "Looky what the cat dragged in."

"Don't start with me, Emmett," Jessica snapped. "I'm really upset. I'm not in the mood for a fight."

Julian stepped in front of Emmett. "You still didn't answer my question," he said angrily. "What are you doing here?"

Emmett shook his head and flung his man-purse onto the leather sofa. "Are you really *that* stupid, Julian? You haven't put two and two together yet?"

Julian's sweaty face went dark. "If I've told you once, I've told you a thousand times—outside of the Chamber, I'm just myself. So the answer to your question is *no*—I don't know what you're talking about."

"I see," Emmett replied with a smirk. "So I guess when the cops come a-knockin' at your door in a few hours, you're gonna deny everything that Concetta told them, huh?"

Jessica heaved a sigh and hung her head down. "Oh, God," she whispered.

Julian started as though he'd been pricked by an electrical current. He raced across the living room and pulled the plug on the music. Then he whirled around and stared at Emmett, a crazed and nervous look on his face. "What are you talking about?" he screamed. "What did Concetta tell the cops?"

"Aren't you even gonna offer me some tea?" Emmett asked, sounding purposely nonchalant. He sat down on the edge of the sofa and crossed his legs.

"Cut the crap, McQueen, and *don't* piss me off!" The huge muscles in Julian's forearms flexed. He had begun sweating again, despite the fact that he'd long since stopped exercising. "Tell me!" he shouted.

"Concetta probably spilled the beans about our whole

little club," Emmett said. "Why, I wouldn't be surprised if she told the police everything about what goes on in the Chamber."

"You don't really believe that," Jessica said desperately. She ground the cigarette into an ashtray and reached for another one.

"That's just stupid!" Julian fired back. "Everyone already knows she's guilty. All the papers are saying it. So are the news channels. Why would the cops give a shit about us?"

"A girl will probably say anything to muscle her way out of going to prison," Emmett said. "And that would include dirt about us."

Jessica shot to her feet and started pacing the floor. "Dangerous dirt. Stuff that could get us into a lot of trouble."

"Uh-huh," Emmett said as he took the cigarette from Jessica's fingers. He inhaled, blew out a trail of smoke, and handed it back to her.

Julian folded his arms across his pumped-up chest. "I'm completely innocent, and that's what I'll tell the cops. It's as simple as that."

"That's all sweet and pretty, but how about when certain *details* get out into the public?" Emmett flashed a quick look at his nails, then slowly raised his eyes. He glanced at Jessica. He glanced at Julian. "Won't be very flattering."

"It's true," Jessica said quietly, not bothering to hold back her tears. "And you know what? I wouldn't blame Concetta for dropping the bomb. We all ran out of Cleopatra last night like a bunch of wimps."

"What were we supposed to do?" Julian shouted. "The cops came and started hustling us out!"

"But she's probably mad at us. She's probably *furious*." Jessica puffed hard on the cigarette, her whole body shaking.

"Holy shit," Julian whispered. He smoothed both his hands over his bare scalp and began pacing the floor. He looked like an animal narrowing for a midnight kill. He set his eyes on Emmett. "You and Concetta said something like this would never happen! You both *promised*!"

"Well, how the hell was I supposed to know that she was gonna up and kill Damien!" Emmett yelled back. "Until now, the whole club's been a secret, so we kept to our side of the promise."

"We swore an oath!" Julian said desperately. "A *sacred* oath that what goes on in the Chamber would remain secret. No one is ever supposed to know. That's what you and Concetta said when I joined."

"When I joined too," Jessica cut in.

"—and that's what I've always believed!" Julian flung his arms up. "I swear, from here on out, I'm done with it—done with the whole club! Screw you *and* the Black Cry Affair."

"Hush up, Simmons." Emmett waved his hand in the air. "You're losing control, and that's the first thing the coppers wanna see."

"Well, maybe Julian's right," Jessica said. "Maybe we should all just forget it and move on. Maybe we should—"

"Is that what you really want?" Emmett's voice was flat and sharp. "Is that what either of you really want? You want to give up the power and control of being in the club?"

The question was like a double-edged sword. And Emmett knew it.

"Of course not," Jessica admitted. "But it's inevitable. If Concetta blabbed to the cops about everything, we'll be forced to confess, and that'll be the end of it anyway."

"I don't *know* that Concetta blabbed to the cops," Emmett said. "I'm just assuming she did. And if that's the case, we have to be prepared. I don't want stuff about the club made public either. But maybe if we play our cards right, we can stop it from happening. That's why I'm here, kitty cats."

"Concetta's the one who's guilty!" Julian yelled. "And that's the first thing I'll tell the cops. She should've known from the beginning that Damien didn't like her. It's her own damn fault."

"Julian, *please.*" Jessica shook her head. "Concetta's still a member of the club. And I hate that she did this—that she killed Damien—but I still feel bad for her. She just lost control. She didn't mean for it to happen."

"That's not my problem!" Julian answered. "*I'm* not gonna lose everything I've worked for just because *she* couldn't keep her mouth shut! I'm gonna tell the cops everything about her—how obsessed she was with Damien, how she resented that he didn't like her—"

"Watch your mouth, muscle boy." Emmett fixed Julian with a hard, unforgiving stare. The comment was meant as a threat, and Julian knew it.

Silence descended over the room.

"We could *all* turn the tables on each other if we wanted to," Emmett said. "But I'm not about to let you go and disgrace Concetta more than she already has been.

All those newspapers. All those stories calling her fat and cherubic and everything else. You best keep your mouth shut and play the game right."

As the words settled over him, Julian looked at the ground and took another deep breath. He sat down on the opposite side of the sofa, clearly defeated. "Okay," he said quietly. "Fine. What do you think the cops are gonna ask me about?"

"For starters, they're probably gonna ask you why you don't look a shred upset that Damien's dead," Emmett snapped. "Workin' out with the music blastin' and the plasma on like you're in some Vegas hotel! Doesn't look to me like you're upset Damien's gone."

Julian's brows knitted together. His muscles flexed again. "That's probably because I'm *not* so upset that Damien's dead," he whispered. "And you know exactly what I'm talking about."

"Oh no I don't!" Emmett said. "All I know is what Concetta knows."

"What's that supposed to mean?"

Jessica let out a strangled sob.

Emmett leaned into the plush cushion supporting his back. He said, "Yesterday, after the club finished up with our usual Friday-afternoon session, Concetta and I heard you and Damien arguing. Loudly. Some might even say dangerously."

"Yeah, that's right," Julian said. "So what are you trying to say? That I'm the one who killed him?"

Emmett shrugged. "You might've had the motive. At least that's what the cops will be thinking."

"Well, screw that!" Julian shouted. "Concetta and

Jessica and you *all* had the same motive! You know damn well why I was arguing with Damien. You would've argued with him too. That little prick was starting to get on my nerves!"

"And is *that* what you're gonna tell the cops, Einstein?" Emmett sniffed. "They'll be snappin' cuffs on you like a pit bull in a playground."

"Well, what else am I supposed to say?" Julian screamed. "That I was Damien's best friend? That I liked the way he'd been acting lately?"

"Hush *up*," Emmett snapped. He leaned forward and cut Julian a serious stare. "You be angry all you want with Damien, but the truth is the truth—he was an important part of the club, and we got a whole hell of a lot done because of him. The Black Cry Affair has given us all a lot."

Jessica sat down again. "It's true. I'll be the first one to admit that."

"I know," Julian replied, his voice softening. "I love being a part of the club. You know that. But none of us expected it to get to this point."

"Sometimes bad things happen," Emmett said. "That's just life. You have to accept it and deal with it and, if you can, figure a way out of it."

Julian stood up, walked across the wide living room, and threw on a tattered black T-shirt. He stood there for a long moment, staring out the window with his arms folded across his chest like a beefy bodyguard on the lookout.

The pose almost made Emmett laugh. It never ceased to amaze him how much of a meathead Julian Simmons really was. "There's nothing to do now but continue," he said. "My nerves are fried, but now's not the time to start going crazy on each other. We have to stick together. It's the only way to protect our own asses." Emmett stood up and swung the man-purse over his shoulder.

"You mean meet in the Chamber tomorrow, like usual?" Jessica asked, panic-stricken.

Emmett nodded. "I'm pretty sure that's what Concetta will want. And it's what we all have to do anyway. In case we need to get our stories straight about our little club."

Jessica shook her head. "But . . . Concetta's a killer! I'm—I'm scared! And there's no way in hell my mother will let me out of the house—especially if she knew I was heading over to *Concetta's.*"

"Stop being an idiot," Emmett snapped. "Y'all know Concetta's not gonna kill anyone else. It'll look worse if we all start to disband. Just swallow your fear and get on with it. And why does your mama have to know you'll be going to Concetta's? Tell her you're goin' someplace else."

"My mother knows me better than that," Jessica choked out. "She'll know I'm lying. She'll see right through me and then we'll end up fighting."

"Well, how'd you get away from her to come on over *here*?"

"She went for her usual spa appointment," Jessica explained. "She doesn't know I'm here. She thinks I'm in my bedroom reading."

Emmett gave her a devilish smirk. "Well, you've been lying to her for months already, Paderman. Why stop now? Julian's parents are away, and my mama will be too drugged up to know anything. But *you'll* have to find a way there."

Julian didn't move from his place at the window. "In the club?" he whispered. He turned around and stared at them. Wiped a line of sweat from his forehead.

"In the club," Emmett and Jessica responded in unison.

# 11

# Dynamite News

It was a Saturday ritual: massages at noon.

Once a week, the library of the Hamilton penthouse was transformed into something of a spa. The huge mahogany desk was pushed back against the windows, the leather chairs were moved into the front hall, and three padded massage tables were assembled in the very center of the room.

Madison, as usual, made the appointment on time. She walked into the library wrapped in a towel and smiled at three female masseuses. She set her cell down on the windowsill, then climbed onto the first table.

A minute later, Park and Lex came strolling in. Park

had a manila file folder in one hand, and Lex was cradling Champagne in the crook of her left arm and a bunch of newspapers in her right.

"*Must* you bring the dog?" Madison snapped.

"My baby was alone for half the night," Lex said, kissing Champagne and setting him down to run freely though the library.

Park dimmed the lights as one of the masseuses lit several scented votive candles. The room immediately filled with the aroma of lavender and eucalyptus.

Lex climbed onto her table, still clutching the newspapers.

When they were each settled and the massages began, Madison sighed. "Okay, what've we got? Give me the news first."

"All the stories basically have the same facts," Lex began, "and they all end up going into detail about Damien's life and the fact that he was a duke. Thankfully, we're only mentioned briefly, so at least this time it doesn't look like we'll have to fight off being suspects."

"Thank God for that." Madison moaned as warm hands kneaded the muscles in her shoulders. "Is that all? Nothing about Concetta's arraignment?"

"According to one of the papers, she should have been arraigned at nine o'clock this morning." Lex stretched her neck out and up, giving the masseuse a clear signal of where she was hurting.

"What was her bail set at?" Park asked.

Lex sighed loudly. "The newspapers say her bail was set at three million. Oh, right there. My muscles are sore from dancing so much." A pleasurable pause. And then she said, "But I did find one thing strange."

"What's that?" Madison asked.

"All the newspapers said Damien's body would be autopsied this morning, but they didn't allude to the cause of death being blunt impact trauma, even though Concetta's stiletto is mentioned as the weapon."

Park's head popped up. "That's bizarre."

"It is," Madison agreed. "It looks like we have to prepare ourselves for a short road trip. Concetta should be released from police custody in about an hour or so. We'll have to pay her a visit."

"Do you think she'll see us?" Lex asked.

"She'll have to. We won't go away unless she does." Park stretched her left arm out and the masseuse gave it a gentle circular tug.

"What did your research uncover, Park?" Madison let out a series of happy moans as her masseuse's hands worked down to her lower back.

Park reached for the manila file folder sitting on the edge of her padded table. She flipped it open. "According to the ATF Web site, the chemicals found in Mother Margaret's office aren't necessarily difficult to come by, but they're mostly confined to offshore rigs and fairly remote areas. You can have it trafficked if you pay enough money. In most cases, dynamite is used to blast through mountains or for demolition purposes, for mining and underwater blasting. Like when a bridge needs to come down. That's all legal, so the dynamite is purchased through proper channels."

"What else?" Madison held on to the table as the masseuse gave her right leg a tug.

"Nitroglycerin is the main ingredient in dynamite," Park continued. "It's three parts nitroglycerin, one part diatomaceous earth, and a little bit of sodium carbonate. But the nitroglycerin by itself is totally strong—it's what they call shock sensitive, which means that physical shock can cause it to explode. So, like, if it's transported, it can blow up."

"Who the hell would have that kind of stuff that *we* know of?" Lex asked.

"Someone who has a clandestine laboratory," Park answered. "And like Mother Margaret said—they'd have to be pretty good at chemistry. But the funny thing is that these days, the use of dynamite has been eclipsed by the use of water gel explosives, which are safer to handle."

Madison sighed again as the masseuse applied pressure to the center of her back. "Oh, wow . . . that feels good. I didn't realize how tense I've been." She took a deep breath. "So now we're supposed to believe that Concetta Canoli has some sort of laboratory in her house? That traces of nitroglycerin ended up in Mother Margaret's office when Concetta broke in there to steal confidential documents that may or may not be related to Damien's murder?"

"That pretty much sums it up," Park said.

"And Concetta certainly has enough money to buy off the black market." Lex's voice sounded like a series of trembling burps as her masseuse did a number of karate-chop movements across her back. "Is there any chance that some of those chemicals used in the making of dynamite could look like glitter?"

"No, there isn't," Park replied. "The glitter is really the only thing that ties the theft and the murder together.

*I* still think it was plain old glitter that we saw—either from a hair product or an arts-and-crafts kind of thing. Possibly a horrible eye shadow, but glitter that large would be dangerous to use around the eye—it could scratch a cornea."

"Could've also been from cheap clothing," Lex said. "And from the looks of those stilettos, we know Concetta owns some of that. Otherwise, we're looking for a killer who makes dynamite and uses glittery hair products or wears cheap clothes."

"That describes half the population of Greenwich Village." Park stretched her other arm out. "Madison, what did you come up with?"

"I found the blueprints of Cleopatra," Madison told them. "There are five suspended dancing cages in the club. Damien was killed in cage number one, which is closest to the catwalk that links all the cages. So if you want to believe Concetta is guilty, she would have easily been able to kill him and then make a fast exit. The staircase is only a few feet from where the catwalk begins. It's staircase B, which, when you take it downstairs, ends right at the corridor that leads to the first-floor restrooms." She yelped as the masseuse squeezed down on her shoulders. "I also found the guest list for Detective Connelly. We only had three no-shows. It would've been a spectacular event . . . if not for the murder."

The three masseuses exchanged worried glances but kept quiet.

Park said, "I went through a lot of my new criminal psychology books, and I found some interesting things on this whole phenomenon of role-playing. It's actually pretty common. But, from a psychological perspective, it differs entirely from acting or anything theatrical. Actors act a part or play a role creatively, and while they're doing it they know that they're ultimately doing a job— performing for an audience. Acting is also a creative process. Role-playing, on the other hand, springs out of a deeper psychological need. Role-players actually believe in the worlds they've thought up, and those worlds or the roles they choose to play are usually manifestations of deep, private fantasies. People who belong to role-playing groups have reported feelings of euphoria and pleasure and total freedom—most role-players love the whole process. But it *has* been known to go a little far. There've been a few killers who were into role-playing."

"So then, what's our profile of the killer?" Lex asked. "Assuming it's not Concetta."

Park folded her arms under her chin. "Someone very intelligent. Someone who's pretty fearless and thinks she or he is above getting caught. Someone with control issues. And someone with a very creepy side, as evidenced by the Mozart Requiem."

"And someone who doesn't have an eye for fashion," Madison added.

"I don't really see how that's relevant," Park said.

Lex gasped. "The hell it isn't! A killer with any shred of fashion awareness would *not* have killed using that shoe. The killer would've been totally repulsed by it."

"Ya know, Concetta has never had an eye for fashion, even though she has a shoe fetish," Madison pointed out. "Remember how she was dressed at commencement last year? She wore a black dress with those hideous white Minnie Mouse shoes."

Park sighed. "Here we are doing all this work when the real killer has probably already been caught."

"But the motive," Lex said. "I'm not sure if I buy the crime-of-passion thing. We really do have to find out what goes on in those Black Cry Affair meetings to figure out the whole truth."

"Then let's get to it." Madison checked her watch, then glanced up at the masseuse. "A little firming lotion on my back, please. I don't want to look eighty years old while I'm on the beach in Capri in two weeks."

For the next fifteen minutes, the library sounded like a pleasure palace: high-pitched squeals and moans of delight, low groans of ecstasy as the masseuses worked their magic. Lex turned onto her back and assumed a yoga position, stretching her right leg up while her masseuse pulled both her arms. Park arched her neck as high as it would go, feeling every last bit of tension drain out of her muscles. Madison nearly slid off her table with a yelp when the masseuse applied too much pressure to her lower back.

Exiting the library, towels tied firmly around their bodies, Madison, Park, and Lex fixed themselves warm cups of green tea in the kitchen. Then Madison stood up and said, "We'll meet in the living room in ten minutes. Hurry."

Ten minutes later, dressed casually in Triple Threat clothing, they grabbed their purses from the hall table and started for the front door of the penthouse. That was when Lupe walked in, trailing several plastic shopping bags behind her.

"Nobody go nowhere!" she screamed, dropping the grocery bags to the floor.

"We have to, Lupe," Madison said. "We're late for an appointment. Sort of."

Lupe shook her head. "No, no. Before he left, you father said you stay home this today, and you mother already call *three* times since last night."

"We'll call them later," Park assured her, planting a kiss on her cheek. "Now go on into my bedroom and relax. They're reairing the first season of *Sex and the City* on HBO, and there's gourmet popcorn in the kitchen."

Lupe frowned. "What I tell your father when he calls?"

"Tell him we're out running errands," Lex said. "And if Mom calls again, tell her we went bikini shopping for our trip to Italy."

"Okay," Lupe replied, sighing. She looked at Madison and pointed to one of the grocery bags. "I buy milk and champagne and chocolate syrup for you."

Madison's eyes widened. "Oh! Wait—let me fix myself a drink before we leave. Please!"

*"Absolutely not,"* Park snapped. She ran a hand through her hair. "You drink that and you'll have gas for the rest of the day. The answer is no."

Madison grunted as they walked out to the foyer and into the elevator.

◇　◇　◇

Donnie Halstrom was sitting in the lobby. When he looked up from his newspaper and saw the triplets, he shot to his feet. "Hi, girls," he said.

"We're only going a few blocks, Donnie, but we'll still need a ride." Lex smiled at him, then watched as he ran outside to the limo and held open the back door for them.

It took all of five minutes to reach the Canoli town house on East Sixty-fifth Street. There were two police cars parked out front and several news vans scattered along the block. Donnie cut the engine, then turned around and said, "Looks pretty bad here. You girls want me to walk you to the front door?"

"No, thanks," Park answered him, already climbing out. "But wait for us, okay? I don't know how long we'll be."

"Okay," Donnie said.

Madison led the way to the town house, Park and Lex close at her heels.

A female reporter with short blond hair dashed out of one of the news vans and came bounding toward them, trailed by a cameraman. "Madison!" she called, already holding out her microphone.

"Damn," Madison muttered. She threw a glance at Park and Lex. "I'll handle this one."

"Are you friends of the accused, Concetta Canoli?" the reporter asked.

Madison kept her eyes trained on the woman even as she felt the camera zooming in on her for a close-up. "We're friends of Concetta's, and we were also friends of Damien Kittle. We're distraught by this tragedy and our condolences go out to Damien's family, and to the citizens of England, who have lost an incredible young man."

"Do you think Concetta's guilty of the crime?"

"We cannot make any statements regarding the crime until a full investigation has been completed."

"Are you girls investigating this one?" the reporter asked excitedly. "We can't forget that you all solved the murder of legendary fashion editor Zahara Bell."

Madison cleared her throat. "We are doing all we can to aid in the investigation," she said simply. But as she started to turn around, instructing Park and Lex to do the same, the reporter stepped in front of her.

"There are people claiming that St. Cecilia's Prep is a school with a lot of secrets and a lot of strange academic practices." The microphone hung in the air like a giant, hairy fly. "Do you think the school will try to cover up certain secrets to avoid more scandal?"

"Absolutely not," Madison replied sharply. "St. Cecilia's Preparatory High School is an educational institution of the highest caliber. The work is demanding and challenging, and records show that nearly ninety percent of graduates go on to attend Ivy League colleges and universities."

"One last question," the reporter pressed. "How do you feel about the *other* charges being filed against Concetta Canoli?"

Madison glanced at Park and Lex. "What other charges?"

The reporter held the microphone a little higher. "It was leaked to the media about ten minutes ago that forensic analysis of the Canoli town house revealed traces of nitroglycerin and sodium carbonate—chemicals used to engineer explosives—in one of the rooms."

"*What?*" Lex cried.

Park nudged her shoulder, indicating the rolling camera.

It took every ounce of strength for Madison to maintain her composure. She licked her lips and cleared her throat even as her stomach knotted painfully. "I'm afraid we don't know anything about those charges," she said firmly. Then she grabbed Park and Lex by their hands and made the quick dash up the front staircase.

"Do you think Concetta Canoli is involved with a terrorist ring operating out of St. Cecilia's Prep?" the reporter called out.

Madison ignored the question and banged on the front door of the town house.

"Holy shit," Lex said quietly. "I can't believe what I just heard. See? I'm right."

"I can't believe it either." Park kept her head held high, aware that cameras were still rolling behind them.

"Well, I, for one, am *furious,*" Madison whispered. "We're going to find out what the hell is going on here— and then we might have to kick Concetta's ass." She banged on the door again.

When a small, impish maid appeared on the threshold, Madison literally shoved her to the side and stepped into the foyer of the town house.

"Oh!" the woman yelled. "Wait! You can't—"

Park closed the door behind them. "Where the hell is Concetta?" she demanded.

The short maid stared at them with wide-eyed horror. "You Hamilton girls can't just come barging in here! I'll call the police! Get out!"

"Cut the crap!" Madison screamed back. "Where is Concetta?"

"Concetta is not receiving guests, and Mr. and Mrs.

Canoli are out speaking with their attorneys." The maid pointed to the closed front door. "Now you have to get out of here! I'm not telling you anything—and I'm not letting you move one step further."

"You have to!" Lex cried. "Please!"

"Out!" the maid shouted. "You little bitches have no right to be in here."

Madison bared her teeth and emitted a low, wolflike growl.

"Oh, great," Park whispered, taking a step back. She shot a glance at the maid. "Now you've really done it."

"Madison, please stay calm." Lex plunged a hand into the magic purse, already shuffling for a bottle of water and, with any luck, a tranquilizer dart.

There were very few instances when Madison ever lost her cool. She always kept the public in mind. She took her role as an ambassador of Hamilton Holdings, Inc., very seriously. She worked hard to project a professional, refined image. But when her nerves *did* snap, when she bared her teeth and assumed what Park and Lex called the "attack position," trouble usually ensued.

"Move back," Park said to Lex with a fluttery wave of her hand.

Madison extended her right arm and clamped her hand over the maid's white T-shirt, lacing her fingers around the fabric at the woman's neck. Then she gently but firmly shoved the little woman against the wall.

"Please!" the woman cried. "Don't hurt me."

"Listen to me and listen well," Madison said through gritted teeth. "In exactly *five* seconds, you're going to take us to Concetta. *Then* you're going to leave us alone with

Concetta. *Then* you're going to come back down here and forget that *any* of this ever happened, and if you don't do as I say, you're going to be sitting on top of a hot dog cart in Central Park, because I'm going to twist you into a pretzel! Got it?"

The woman nodded, her eyes glazing over. "I'm sorry," she said breathlessly. "I didn't mean to get you mad."

Madison growled again, then released her hold on the woman's shirt.

Park stepped in between them. She smiled brightly at the woman. "I apologize for that," she said with a chuckle. "My sister just found out she has the same hairdresser as Mariah Carey, so you can understand why she's so upset. Please don't take it personally."

The woman took a deep breath and smoothed a hand over her white shirt.

Lex yanked Madison to her side. She immediately began dabbing lotion onto Madison's cheeks. "It's Bliss Fatigue Fighter," Lex said, working quickly. "You're all flushed and blotchy and stressed."

"*That's* what happens when people push me too far." Madison threw her head back and fanned herself with her purse. Then she stared at the maid and said, "Take us to Concetta. *Now.*"

"Yes, okay." The maid nodded nervously. "But be advised that Mr. and Mrs. Canoli don't want anyone here because they're afraid the *real* killer might be coming after Concetta. And we have private security here in the house, so if Concetta's upset, you might all be thrown out on your butts."

Park smiled. "We'll take our chances. Thank you."

The maid led them through the living and dining rooms, into the kitchen, and up the back staircase. When they were all standing in a bright hall, the maid pointed to the closed door at the very end. "Concetta's in there. But she's very upset. Please knock first. Please—"

"We'll take it from here," Madison snapped. She grunted a third time. Then she tightened her grip on her purse, stormed down the hall, and threw open the door.

# 12

# A Killer Speaks

Concetta was lying on the king-sized bed, dressed in a gray Moreno wool sweat suit, surrounded by open boxes of chocolate. She popped up with a gasp. "Madison!" she cried. "Park! Lex! Oh—I'm so glad to see you!" She rolled off the bed, her big hips wobbling.

"Don't play nice girl with us, Concetta," Madison said forcefully.

Concetta, jarred by the words, stepped back against the bureau and shook her head. "What—what do you mean? I *am* a nice girl! Why would you say something like that to me? You don't . . ." She cupped a hand over her mouth, smearing a line of chocolate across her chin. "You don't *really* believe I'm guilty, do you?"

Park batted a hand against Madison's shoulder, instructing her to stay quiet.

Madison gave a quick, understanding nod. She stepped back and stood beside Lex and folded her arms over her chest.

They knew that when it came to interrogating suspects, Park was the expert.

"You think I'm some sort of psycho!" Concetta yelled. "A cold-blooded killer! Well, I'm not!" Her voice broke. "I'm . . . not."

Park walked over to her—a steady, fearless stride. She threw her arms around Concetta and held her. "You have to get ahold of yourself, honey," Park whispered. She looked Concetta in the eyes. "It's not that we necessarily think you're psycho; it's just that we have no other *choice* but to think that. We came here to talk to you and to help you. But you have to answer some questions."

Concetta shook her head vehemently. She pushed past Park, stomped around to the opposite side of the bed, and stared out the window. "I'm tired of answering questions," she said. "I've been put through hell and no one cares! Everyone keeps saying the same stupid things! I'm tired of hearing them!"

"The shoes, Concetta," Lex said firmly. "Where the *hell* did you get those awful stilettos? That's the one question you will *absolutely* answer!"

"Those were my good luck shoes," Concetta said quickly. "I know it sounds strange, but I wore them only twice before, and both times I got a little attention from the boys in the room. The first time was at my uncle Vito's wedding in Florence. The second was at my father's fiftieth birthday party in Las Vegas. I know the shoes are kind of . . . loud . . . but I thought they would bring me luck last night. It sounds stupid, but it's true."

"You mean you thought maybe you'd have a little luck with Damien," Park said.

Concetta didn't answer.

Park motioned for Madison and Lex to stay quiet. Silence, Park knew from reading countless books on criminal investigations, was what often forced a suspect to speak.

After a minute of steady quiet, Concetta turned and faced them. "What's true is that I was in love with Damien," she said. "That much I can admit. I tried everything to get him to like me. I really did. But he just . . . didn't. But I know in time I would've accepted that. I didn't kill him. It wasn't a crime of passion like they keep saying on TV." She ran her sleeve over her cheeks, wiping away tears. "I guess I was stupid to even think a duke—someone with royal blood—would be interested in me romantically. I'm just . . . fat. I'm fat and blubbery and ugly!" She buried her face in her hands and started sobbing.

Lex ran to her, throwing her arms out. "Oh, honey. Please don't talk like that. You're not fat. You're just . . ." She scanned the room as if looking for an answer. "You're just . . . *roundly sexy.*"

"Voluptuous," Park offered.

And Madison, feeling genuinely bad for Concetta in these pathetic moments, took a step toward her and said, "Robust and fashionably full-bodied."

"No I'm not!" Concetta screeched. "I'm just a big pig! That's why I'm always on the Worst Dressed List in *Star* magazine!"

Park put her hands on Concetta's shoulders and eased

her into the plush chair at the foot of the bed. Looking down at Concetta, Park said, "You have to tell us everything that happened last night at Cleopatra. We don't *want* to think you're guilty, Concetta. Maybe if you explain yourself to us, we can help."

"The cops didn't believe a word I told them!" she cried. "And neither will you! I haven't slept all night. They had me in a stinky interrogation room and treated me like some sort of serial killer. They even came here and tore my house apart."

"And they found some chemicals in here," Madison said. "Chemicals that are used to make dynamite, Concetta. How did that stuff get here if you didn't bring it in?"

"I don't know!" Concetta wailed. "Someone must've planted it in here to frame me!"

It was the open highway Park needed. She stared down at Concetta and leaned in close to her. "You mean, you think one of the members of the Black Cry Affair framed you?"

Concetta gasped. Her face went from droopy and sad to tight and shocked. "How—how do you know about . . . that?"

"We know about the club," Park said. She stood straight and began pacing the floor. "We know that Emmett McQueen and Jessica Paderman and Julian Simmons are members. And we know Damien was a member too."

"But . . . *how?*" Concetta whispered. "It's a secret. We work so hard to keep it hidden from everyone. How . . . ?"

"It's not important how we found out. What's important is that we know about it." Park crossed her arms over her chest. "You didn't tell the cops anything about the club?"

Concetta shook her head. "No, I didn't. I was going to,

but then I remembered the oath. Every member of the Black Cry Affair takes an oath of silence and honor when they join. I respected that oath. I'll always respect it. I *can't* talk about it."

"Even if it means the difference between living a normal life or spending your entire life behind bars?" Park asked her flatly.

"You *don't* want to go to jail," Lex said, giving Concetta's shoulder a shake. "They'll make you wear unflattering jumpsuits and generic sneakers."

"And they'll make you sleep on a twin-sized mattress." Madison shuddered. "You think about *that.*"

Concetta apparently did think about it. As the words sank into her brain, she gulped nervously.

"Why don't you tell us how it all began?" Park said. "When did the club form? How did you even get the idea to start it?"

"Please, don't do this." Concetta's voice was faint. "I'm so tired. I can't answer any more questions. I feel like crap."

"That's because you don't look your best." Without needing to be prodded, Lex reached into the magic purse and pulled out a hairbrush, compact, and nail file. "Here, let me help you relax. Just sit back." She handed the nail file to Madison, then began running the brush through Concetta's thick, tangled hair.

Madison kneeled down in front of the chair. She cupped Concetta's right hand in hers and began to work the tips of Concetta's nails with the file.

"Maybe . . . maybe I do need a little primping," Concetta said.

Madison nodded. "Of course you do," she replied soothingly. "No matter what happens, you'll be in a lot of pictures and magazines these next few weeks."

"Tell me," Park began again, "how did the Black Cry Affair start?"

"First tell me how you found out about it!" Concetta screamed. "No one knew!"

Park remained silent, her eyes as sharp as daggers.

Concetta licked her lips nervously. "Okay. Fine. Back when Emmett's dad was charged with extortion and all those icky things, Emmett really relied on me to help him get through it. And I did. He spent a lot of time here. We watched movies and listened to music and all that normal stuff, but then we started getting into deep, serious conversations. And one of the topics we always came back to was how cool it would be to just have the power to escape into another world or another body—ya know, to just *be* someone or something else." A pause. "Emmett said he would give anything to just escape from the scandal, from all the stress. He wanted to become another person for a while. I understood that, because I've always wanted to be thin and pretty, or a real bitch who gets all the attention, ya know? So one night, it just all sort of . . . happened. We assumed different roles. We got into it. I mean, *really* into it." She cracked a ghost of a smile. "And it was awesome. I'd never experienced anything like it. For a couple of hours, I really felt like I was Queen Elizabeth. I forgot my life. I forgot everything."

Park nodded. "And then you and Emmett continued to role-play," she said.

"Yeah. It was like an addiction. But a good kind of addiction, because it really helped Emmett get through those stressful weeks." Concetta sniffled. "And it made me feel great too."

"How did Damien and Julian and Jessica get into the club?" Park asked.

"Lex," Madison said quietly, interrupting the flow as gently as possible. "May I please have some nail polish?"

"Not anything too red," Concetta muttered. "I don't like my nails red."

"I have a lovely Picasso-brown Chanel," Lex whispered, passing the bottle to Madison.

"Thank you." Concetta nodded. She stared up at Park. "Anyway . . . well . . . one day Emmett and Damien were hanging out at school, playing chess, I think, and they started talking about stuff. One thing led to another and Emmett told Damien about the club. Damien wanted in. He came and told me himself."

"Did he tell you *why* he wanted in?" Park asked.

"He just said he thought it sounded fun. And it *was*. Damien was a natural. He fell right into our role-playing sessions. He loved being anyone other than who he was." Concetta closed her eyes, gulped, then opened them. "A few weeks after that, I was at a small antiques shop in the Village, buying things we needed for the club. Earrings, necklaces, swords, costumes—stuff I thought would make our sessions more authentic. We don't play Dungeons and Dragons, but costumes are fun. Anyway, Julian Simmons happened to be there at the shop. He saw all the stuff I was buying—a lot of it was pretty strange—and he just started questioning me. I asked him if he'd ever participated in a role-playing game; he told me he hadn't, but that he'd always wanted to. So he joined us too."

"And Jessica Paderman?" Park asked. "How'd she get into the club?"

"I invited Jessica into the club myself," Concetta replied. "She and I have always been friendly. She saw the stamp—our official seal—of the Roman coin on my palm one day and asked me about it. She loves being a member too. We *all* love it. And so did Damien."

"Where do you guys meet? Where's the Chamber?"

"Downstairs," Concetta said quietly. "The basement. But you *still* haven't told me how you know about the club. Why?"

Park stopped pacing. She ignored the question. She clasped her hands behind her back and fixed Concetta with a hard, don't-bullshit-me stare. "And that's *all* that goes on during these sessions? Simple and innocent role-playing?" she asked, an edge of suspicion in her tone. "That's all the Black Cry Affair is about?"

"Role-playing. There's nothing else." Concetta bent her head to one side as Lex pulled her hair up and continued to brush it out. "Lex, I hate having all these messy curls. Is there any way you can tame it down?"

"Of course!" Lex answered brightly. She dug into the magic purse and found several hairpins and a rubber band.

"Thank you." Concetta sniffled again.

"Fast-forward to last night," Park said. "You and Damien are dancing in the cage. What happened?"

"We were dancing and having a good time," Concetta began. "The lights were really bright—those strobes are too strong, by the way—and there were moments when I couldn't even see Damien. But he laughed when we bumped into each other. I took off my shoes so that I'd be able to dance better. Then there was this point when I saw him—his face—and I didn't like it. He looked sick. Pale. He started to stumble. He started to cough. Then he leaned over and grabbed on to the cage's bars to steady himself."

Madison had stopped painting Concetta's nails. "Did Damien say anything?" she asked.

"No." Concetta leaned her head back as Lex tugged at her hair. "He looked like he was having trouble breathing. And even if he *did* say something, how would I have heard it? The music was blaring. I got really scared and panicky. He fell down on the floor of the cage. So I turned around and slipped my foot into my shoe. The lights were spinning and flashing so much, I couldn't see my *other* shoe. Instead of looking for it, I ran out of the cage and down the stairs and into the bathroom. I was gonna get Damien some water, I was gonna get help." She pressed her lips together, clamping down on a sob.

"Go on," Park said firmly. "And then what happened?"

"And then somebody locked me in the bathroom!" Concetta cried, her head straining against the force of Lex's experienced hands. "The door totally wouldn't open! I was the only one in there and I kept banging on it and screaming for help, but no one heard me! I was in there for about three minutes before I heard the Requiem and the commotion. I got so nervous I tore my dress. I started crying. I even tripped because I was wearing only one stiletto. It was *horrible*." She took a deep breath. "Some-one else ran into the cage and hit Damien in the head with my shoe!"

Park shot Madison a questioning glance.

Madison's expression said: *I don't know what to believe.*

Lex, immersed in the nearly impossible task of working curls into a smooth French twist, looked at Park and shrugged slowly.

Park mentally scanned her brain, reviewing everything she'd read about how to question suspects in a homicide investigation. A big part of any successful interrogation was instinct—gut instinct. And Park's gut was telling her that Concetta hadn't spilled all her diamonds.

"Please," Concetta whispered. "You have to believe me."

Park leaned down and rested her hands on the arms of the chair. She brought her face to within an inch of Concetta's and said, "I don't believe you."

*"What?"* Concetta's head bounced up.

Lex let go of her hair.

"How could you not believe me?" Concetta cried. "It's the truth! I've told you everything that happened! I haven't held anything back! You *honestly* think I killed Damien?"

"I don't know whether or not I believe you killed Damien," Park said, backing away from the chair. "But you're expecting us to buy a pretty far-fetched story."

"Damien was physically ill," Concetta pressed. "He had blotches and weird hives all over his face. And even though he was weak, someone with a lot more strength than me had to have killed him!"

"One powerful blow to his temple was all it took to smash his brains in," Park replied sharply.

Concetta shot out of the chair. Seething with rage, she

held out her arms and gave them a shake, the sleeves of her sweatshirt falling past her knuckles. "You see this?" she cried. "I'll tell you why I couldn't have killed Damien! I'll tell you what no one else knows—it's the most humiliating thing in the world!" And then she shoved her hands out from under the sleeves of the oversized shirt and splayed her fingers slowly, showing more than just her newly polished nails. "I have rheumatoid arthritis! I can barely hold a pen some days, let alone pick up a stiletto and smash someone in the head!"

"Oh!" Lex gasped. "You do? Since when?"

"Since two years ago!" Concetta ranted. "Everyone thinks only old people get arthritis, but that's not true. Lots of young people like us get it. It's the most painful thing in the world! I have to get cortisone shots in my joints—which doesn't exactly help how I look, ya know! Sometimes I wake up crying because of the pain, and some days I don't want anyone to see my wrists or knees or anything because they're so swollen. That's why sometimes I can't hold a pen straight or put on my own earrings or clasp a bracelet around my wrist. Half the time, I can't even hold a spoon! And it's the reason I *couldn't* have killed Damien! There's no way I would've been able to hold on to that stiletto and swing it at his head!"

"Concetta, I'm so sorry," Madison whispered. "Did you . . . tell that to the police?"

"Yes," she answered, hiccuping, dropping back down into the chair. "My parents made me. And you know what? The police still don't buy it! They charged me with Damien's murder anyway! They said that according to my medical records, my arthritis isn't *that* advanced and that someone who only gets cortisone shots once every few months could still have done it!"

"But they released you on bail," Madison said. "That counts for a lot. That has to mean something."

"But look at my wrists!" Concetta held them out and up again. "You can see where they're swollen. Do any of *you* think it's possible? Do you still think I'm lying?"

Park stared at her. "I can't really blame the cops," she said. "I mean, you admitted that you and Damien were dancing, which isn't something a person in lots of pain can do. But what I really think is that there's something you're not telling me about the Black Cry Affair." She paused. She slipped her hands into the pockets of her jeans. "Someone in the club had a motive to kill Damien, and you know what that motive is, Concetta."

Madison quickly applied the last coat of polish to Concetta's nails, then capped the bottle and stood up.

Lex twisted the last piece of hair into place. She tightened it with the rubber band and pinned it down, then walked around the chair to join her sisters.

Concetta stared at each of them, her eyes wide and glassy, her breathing shallow. "I took an oath with my friends when I formed the Black Cry Affair," she whispered, as if that would explain everything away.

"Yeah, you all took an oath," Park said. "But I have a feeling Damien wanted to break that oath, that he wanted out of the game. And you, Emmett, Julian, and Jessica didn't want that to happen, did you?"

"Maybe you were all afraid that Damien would blab about some of the things you guys do in the club,"

Madison added. "Things that might embarrass you, or even get you into trouble."

Lex clucked her tongue. "People don't like their secrets being revealed. Some people will do *anything* to keep things private."

Patting her hand nonchalantly over her hair, Concetta looked away from them. She was clearly uncomfortable. She kept shifting in the chair. She blew on her nails and flexed her fingers to study the brown polish.

"We're waiting, Concetta," Park said firmly. "Spill it. If you don't, you'll carry that sacred oath with you right into a trial and probably even a murder conviction."

Concetta rose out of the chair. She turned and stared out the window again. She said quietly, "Damien got bored with the club. He started arguing with us, with everyone. I don't know what his problem was, but . . . but I think he saw something he didn't like. Or he experienced something that bothered him. I don't know. But yes—we were all scared that he might leave the club and talk about it to people."

"Okay. I hear that." Park took a step toward her. "Does anyone in the club use glitter?"

*"Glitter?"* Concetta repeated the word as if it were an obscenity. She looked at Park and crinkled her nose. "What the hell do you mean?"

"Like hair gel or hairspray with glitter in it, or *anything* with glitter in it," Park replied.

Concetta thought about it for a few moments. Then she said, "Julian polishes his gold chains with some sort of oily glitter. Why?"

Park felt Madison and Lex staring at her intently. "By any chance, did Julian and Damien maybe not get along?"

"They had an argument yesterday," Concetta said, her voice low, her tone reluctant. "I heard them in the Chamber. It was after we'd finished up our session. Julian was really pissed off that Damien wanted out of the club. And, ya know, Julian's so *strong*—those big muscles."

"And what did you hear?"

"Emmett and I heard them arguing. It got pretty loud. Julian kept asking Damien why he wanted out, why he wanted to leave the club."

Park, growing more impatient by the second, nearly lost her cool. She sighed, then quickly regained her composure. "And what exactly did Damien say to that?"

"I don't know," Concetta said tersely, clearly irritated. "I . . . I really wasn't listening that much."

"*Think*, Concetta."

She huffed. "Damien kept calling Julian a liar. That's all I remember."

"Has Julian ever said anything about . . . explosives?" Madison asked her, trying to sound offhanded. "Or about any of the chemicals that were found here in your house?"

Concetta shrugged. "He's always saying he wants to blow up the school. But everyone says that when they get annoyed."

Madison gasped.

"And *you* claim you don't know where those chemicals came from," Park said. "So if you're being framed, one of your fellow Black Cry Affair role-players is framing you. Maybe it's Julian."

"I won't believe that," Concetta whispered. "I'll *never* believe that."

"Maybe you should start thinking about it," Park

continued. "If you want anyone to believe your story, then someone else had to have killed Damien, right?"

"Yes, but that could've been anybody at Cleopatra!" Concetta screamed.

"No, it couldn't have." Madison shook her head, thinking about the break-in at St. Cecilia's, the dynamite mixture, and the glitter found in Mother Margaret's office. "Everything ties back to the Black Cry Affair. But the police might not see it that way. As far as the law is concerned, you killed Damien in a fit of passion. And the fact that traces of those chemicals were found in this house just makes you look like more of a psycho."

Concetta was silent, trying to avoid their eyes.

"You can't afford not to listen to us, Concetta," Park said. "In a matter of days, a trial date will be set for you, and with the way it looks right now, you're going straight to jail."

"I told you what happened! I ran out of that cage!" she ranted.

Park sighed. "But who besides us is going to believe that?"

"So then . . ." Concetta gulped. She took a step toward them. "You'll help me?"

Madison and Park glanced at each other.

"When's the club's next meeting?" Lex asked.

"We're supposed to meet tomorrow night," Concetta said. "I can't leave the house because of the court's orders, and my parents have to meet with our attorneys tomorrow night. Emmett called me and said we should still meet. But maybe we won't. I'm not sure yet, with all that's happened. . . ."

"No," Madison told her. "You should *totally* meet tomorrow."

"Why?"

Park smiled. "Because whether or not you like it, Concetta, we'll be there. We're the newest members of the Black Cry Affair."

# 13

# The Deal

"Trail him," Lex said firmly.

She was sitting alone in the back of the limo, staring out the tinted windows at the muscular, well-built figure striding up West Eighty-fourth Street. She slipped on her sunglasses and draped her favorite black silk scarf over her head for added effect. If she needed to set off on foot, she would do so without being recognized.

Julian Simmons had just emerged from his town house. He was dressed in gray jeans, a white tank top, and scuffed Timberlands. In the late-afternoon light, he looked like an ordinary New Yorker headed for a walk. Maybe he was going to Zabar's for salmon and a loaf of fresh French bread. Maybe he was joining a girl for a sunset stroll in Central Park.

*Or maybe,* Lex thought, *he's out to accomplish something far more sinister.*

She'd dropped Madison and Park off at the penthouse and told them she had errands to run. Then she'd given Donnie strict orders to cut across to the West Side and park a few spaces behind the Simmons town house. They'd waited for nearly an hour before Julian finally came outside.

Now Donnie was driving slowly up West Eighty-fourth Street, hot on Julian's tail.

"Don't lose him," Lex said. She was hanging over the partition as she stared out the windshield. She kept moving her head from side to side, trying her best to keep a close eye on Julian even as pedestrians cut through her field of vision. It wasn't easy. A warm Saturday in Manhattan, people revving up for a night on the town. The crowds were thickening.

"Let's hope he starts walking a little faster," Donnie said. "I'm tying up traffic driving ten miles an hour."

Lex frowned. "Just ignore the honking. It's mostly cabs, anyway, and *they* wreak havoc on the streets all the time. Let 'em sweat it out."

"Okay." Donnie settled more comfortably into the seat. He kept the limo moving at a slow pace as Julian continued walking east.

Lex kept her gaze focused on his firm butt. It was a perfectly nice butt, obviously the result of a hundred daily power-squats, but she wasn't about to let her attention slide. Not even a little bit. There was still too much to investigate. And there were still too many unanswered questions swirling around.

An image of Concetta flashed through Lex's mind: the tears on her face, the fear in her eyes, the way she'd held out her hands when telling them about her arthritis. And the desperation in her voice, the conviction she'd used when speaking those four powerful words: *I didn't kill him.*

Even now, Lex couldn't help but feel sorry for Concetta: the poor girl was living through a nightmare, and she wasn't off the hook by any means. She was still the main suspect. She was still the Mozart Murderer and the Canoli Killer. The police were keeping Concetta under house arrest because they didn't believe her story, nor did they view her as a girl with a handicap, incapable of delivering that fatal blow.

This last bit of information intrigued Lex most. Truth was, she didn't blame the cops. No matter how you looked at it, Concetta was still surrounded by elements of guilt. Her disease didn't release her from the place of the damned—it actually heightened the suspicion being cast on her. The cortisone shots. Regular medical visits. Hospitals and doctors and pharmacists. Concetta had direct access to certain drugs, certain chemicals and mixtures. What if sodium carbonate was one of them? What if she *had* been mixing stuff up in a clandestine laboratory like those Park had read about on the ATF Web site? And why?

And then there was the matter of her condition. How advanced was her arthritis? Did she really suffer stiffening pain on a daily basis? If she'd been able to dance and walk around in stilettos, couldn't she have slammed Damien in the head?

Probably.

But the motive for the crime—passion?—just didn't compute.

There was more to Damien's murder, and if Concetta had a *different* reason for wanting him dead, she wasn't spilling it.

But she had pointed the case in a whole new direction.

According to Concetta, Julian used a glittery substance to polish his jewelry. Julian had argued with Damien only hours before the murder. And Julian, whether consciously or unconsciously, had voiced a desire to blow up the school.

When you rolled all that into a pretty little bunch, what you got was suspicion.

At least Lex thought so. It was really more of a hunch on her part, a nagging sensation that wouldn't dissipate. Why had Damien wanted out of the club? Why had the thought of Damien's departure angered Julian?

*The club,* Lex thought. *It's not just a group of role-players. There's more to it than any of us knows. There's danger in the Chamber.*

Now she shivered as the words danced through her mind. Tomorrow, she, Madison, and Park would be invading the Black Cry Affair, walking directly into the eye of the storm. It was a necessary step, but also a frightening one. Lex couldn't help but wonder if Concetta's willingness to let them into the club was a trap. What if something truly evil awaited them in the Chamber? What if Damien was only the *first* victim?

She forced the thought from her mind and kept her eyes locked on Julian. "He's making a left on Central Park West," she said, tapping Donnie's shoulder.

"I got him," Donnie replied, quickly following suit.

The limo trailed Julian for another ten minutes as he

continued walking north. When he reached the corner of 103rd Street, he hailed a cab and climbed inside.

"Now that's strange," Lex said. "Why wouldn't he just get in a cab right near home? Why walk almost twenty blocks to do it?"

"Pretty weird," Donnie murmured.

Lex, still leaning over the partition, gave Donnie's shoulder another tap. "Follow that cab!"

He glanced at her. "Seriously?"

"Of course! How else would we trail him?"

Donnie gave a little shrug, then said, "Okay."

Lex nodded as the limo sped up. Her pulse quickened, adrenaline replacing the chilly stabs of fear. She stared out the windshield, squinting to get a closer look into the back of the cab. The images were bouncy and chaotic, but she thought she saw Julian pull a bandana around his head. Why? To disguise his identity?

They cut across to the East Side.

"They're getting on the FDR Drive," Donnie commented in his usual monotone.

"Follow them." Lex's fingers tightened around the edge of the partition.

Donnie kept the limo at a comfortable distance from the cab, staying several cars behind it. The traffic lightened as they drove uptown. Most people were coming into Manhattan, not leaving it.

The cab stayed left, crossing the bridge and continuing onto Bruckner Boulevard.

Lex sat back for a minute and glanced out the window. To her right, the sky was a canvas of color: purple and pink as the sun began to set in the west, white and bright where the light reflected off buildings and rooftops. Airplanes circled LaGuardia Airport. A helicopter thrummed overhead.

Five minutes later, the limo was exiting the three-lane highway. Lex spotted the cab four cars in front: it made a sharp right off the ramp and then continued through the inner-city neighborhood. They were in the Bronx. Narrow streets, small apartment buildings going gray with neglect. Kids were playing on sidewalks as an open fire hydrant spewed cold water into the air. Where on earth was Julian going?

As she stared out the windows at their surroundings, Lex felt a quick stab of panic. The limo had never looked so out of place. She caught pedestrians turning to stare at it as they drove by. Had the cab driver noticed them on his tail?

The cab came to a sudden stop in front of a small corner bodega.

"Damn," Donnie said. He couldn't pull over without blowing their cover, so he drove past the cab and turned onto a side street and cut the headlights.

Lex peered out the back window just as Julian got out of the cab and ran into the bodega. He was wearing a bandana over his head, and sunglasses shielded his eyes. Why had he gone into the bodega? She hated that she couldn't see him. A full minute ticked by. She was about to climb out of the limo for a closer look when Julian appeared again, darting back into the cab with a water bottle in his right hand.

*That's it?*

Lex bit down on her lip. Poland Spring was crappy, but surely Julian hadn't gone all the way to the Bronx to avoid being seen buying it. There had to be more to his little trip. Her hunch was burning.

The cab shot past them again.

Without needing to be prodded, Donnie hit the lights and started trailing it.

They drove in concentrated silence for several minutes, winding deeper into the unfamiliar streets. The squat apartment buildings and two-story houses disappeared as the landscape changed to flat, concrete parking lots and industrial yards. Lex lowered the window and inhaled the scent of diesel fuel and trash. A briny scent also filled her nostrils. A few seconds later she realized why: straight ahead was the river, its flat surface gleaming as it caught the last rays of sunlight.

The cab turned into a wide lot packed with cars. It was a construction site complete with two hulking cranes, scaffolding, and dozens of men walking around in orange hard hats.

Donnie cut the headlights and pulled over. He turned around. "You don't want me to drive in there, do you? They'd definitely notice a limo."

"I know." Lex weighed her options. The cab was out of sight now, but she knew it couldn't have gone far: the lot was bordered by water and the entrance and exit points were probably one and the same.

Donnie was staring at her intently.

Lex grabbed her purse and tightened the scarf around her head. "Wait for me here," she said quickly. "If I'm not back in five minutes, come look for me."

"Wait." Donnie held up a hand. "You really think it's safe? Let me come with you."

"No." Lex shook her head. "I'll be fine. I can run faster

in heels than any woman in New York." She popped the door handle and climbed onto the tarmac. A mild breeze swept past her, sticky and damp. The sunglasses darkened her view, but they were an absolute necessity.

She threw a fast glance over her shoulder. She ran to the beginning of the lot and hung a right. She crouched down when she spotted the cab.

Julian got out. He said something to the driver, then turned and started walking toward the far end of the parking lot.

Smoke billowed in the air as a jackhammer tore up the pavement. Two construction workers were screaming commands at each other. Lex darted in between two cars and followed the row toward Julian. Her head was already beginning to ache from the noise. She looked over her shoulder again to make sure she hadn't been spotted. That was when she realized how fast her heart was beating. The adrenaline, now laced with fear, was giving her the shakes. She thought about running back to the limo, then scrapped the thought. No. She wouldn't turn into a wimp. She had survived far more dangerous situations than this—Fashion Week, Saks in December, the Latin Grammy Awards afterparty—and she wasn't about to get intimidated.

She took a deep breath and powered along the edge of the lot. Julian was walking faster now. She watched as he made subtle gestures to a tall white guy in a construction hat waiting beside a green SUV—a guy who seemed to recognize Julian at once. Julian raised his right hand in salute and nodded twice. The tall white guy did the same.

Lex reached the end of the lot. There was nowhere else to go except straight ahead—and into Julian's field of vision. Then she spotted the two Porta Potties to her right. The thought of standing anywhere *near* a portable toilet made her stomach lurch, but she had no choice. She wouldn't be able to see Julian and the other guy clearly without standing upright.

*Damn.*

Clutching her purse tightly, she dashed to the first stall and pressed herself up against it. The light was dying, the shadows long and deep. She inched her way to the door, yanked it open, and climbed inside. The space was claustrophobically small—and it smelled unlike anything she had ever experienced before. It was a massive, cloying, impossibly offensive odor. In that moment, Lex decided that every member of the male species should be barred from ingesting prunes.

Her eyes began to tear. She slid the door open a few inches and realized that she'd made the right decision: she had a clear, unobstructed view of Julian and the other guy.

They were walking toward each other in the shadow of the scaffolding.

A chorus of jackhammers started beating the air again, but Lex didn't move to cover her ears. Instead, she reached into the magic purse and pulled out a bottle of custom-mixed perfume. She sprayed some of it into her scarf, quickly pressing it over her nose and mouth. Then she trained her eyes on what was going on outside.

Julian and the guy quickly shook hands. Backlit by the purple sky and the shimmering surface of the water, their movements were entirely visible. Their meeting happened in a matter of seconds.

The guy glanced around and dug a hand into the pocket of his jeans.

Julian did the same, pulled out a thick wad of cash, and handed it over.

The guy accepted the cash with his left hand. He pulled his right hand out of his pocket and dropped something into Julian's palm.

A small, square plastic bag.

Even from her position several feet away, Lex saw the quick flash of white from inside the bag before Julian deposited it in his back pocket.

Then the guy turned around and started back to his SUV.

Julian started walking back across the lot.

Lex quietly closed the door of the Porta Potti. She held her breath, weighing what she had just witnessed. A drug deal, obviously. She wondered if Julian had purchased cocaine or Ecstasy, then found herself gasping for air. Throwing open the door, she stumbled outside into the damp breeze, grateful for the noise of the jackhammers and the caw of seagulls overhead. Had her heels touched that godforsaken toilet? She hoped not. She'd have to chuck the shoes before going back into the penthouse. She clamped a hand over her nose and mouth as the stranger skidded off in his SUV. Full night was only a few minutes away. She caught a fleeting glimpse of Julian as he turned left at the end of the lot and continued back to the waiting cab. All around her, the construction site was quieting down. Men were yelling orders and coming off the rig parked out on the river.

*Time to bounce,* Lex thought. She darted across the lot.

She squeezed in between cars and hopped onto bumpers. The front of the lot was only twenty yards away, but it felt like the longest distance she had ever known. She wanted to get back to the limo and out of here. She wanted to call Madison and Park and report her findings. Maybe they would be able to add this little nugget of information to the whole picture. Julian buying drugs—what did it mean?

The question was floating through her mind so intensely, she didn't notice the short fat guy directly in front of her. Lex slammed into him with a startled "Oh!" and then jumped back, clutching the purse to her chest.

The little guy gave her a once-over and smiled. He was an older man, dressed in a dirty T-shirt and jeans. The orange construction hat gave away his job description. "You should watch where you're going, little lady," he said calmly as he opened the door of his truck.

"I'm sorry." Lex gulped. She knew her voice sounded frightened. She cleared her throat and assumed a confident posture. "I was just hurrying back to my car."

"You looking for somebody here?" the guy asked.

"Um, no." She shook her head. "I was just coming to see if the new condo complex was up yet. That's what you're building here, right?"

A hearty laugh escaped the man's lips. "Condo complex? No, honey. We're here widening a water tunnel. It's a good thing you weren't here earlier—we were blasting away at all that rock those environmental people were fighting to keep."

Lex smiled politely and slipped past him. And then she stopped dead in her tracks and spun around. "Did you say you guys were *blasting* down here today?"

"Yeah." The man nodded vigorously. "Why? You here to protest or something? You one of those tree huggers?"

"No, of course not," Lex replied quickly. "I guess I just got lost—I'm in the wrong place. Um . . . so . . . you guys were using explosives, right?"

"No, we were using chewing gum." The man rolled his eyes, chuckled, and then took off his hard hat and threw it onto the front seat of his truck. "If you're gonna blast something, of course you use explosives. Jeez . . ."

Lex backed away and watched as the man drove off. She was so dazed by the facts swimming in her brain that she actually had to steady herself against the side of a red Honda Civic.

Julian hadn't come here to buy drugs. He had come here to buy explosives. Or the chemicals that would make explosives. That was the transaction she had witnessed.

The little plastic bag. The white powder.

*Oh, my God.*

She wondered in that moment if Damien had witnessed the same thing.

Her heart slamming in her chest, she steadied herself and dashed back to the edge of the lot. She hung a left just as the yellow cab drove away. "Shit," she muttered, realizing that she was too late, that she and Donnie wouldn't be able to trail Julian to wherever else he was going.

She clenched her fists. There were several cars moving in and out of the lot now. Instead of rushing, Lex decided to walk back to the limo at a normal pace. If she looked calm and cool, no one would notice her. She lowered her sunglasses onto the bridge of her nose and scanned the lot, trying to give off the impression that she was searching for her car.

That was when Lex noticed the familiar figure standing at the southern end of the lot—a tall, slim, black-clothed woman leaning against the open door of a pickup truck. She was talking into a cell phone and digging through a light blue tote bag.

Lex blinked once, then gasped.

Sister Brittany had just lit a cigarette.

# 14

# Someone's Big Muscles

The little diner on Second Avenue was exactly what Madison wanted: it was quiet and cozy and tucked in between two apartment buildings, and the old waitresses working the floor looked worn out and uninterested in their customers. After the stress of the day, Madison needed to be in a place where she could just relax. But her nerves were wound too tightly, and she kept rearranging the food on her plate.

"Are you ever gonna eat that?" Theo asked. He was sitting directly across from her, happily chomping down on a thick hamburger piled with tomatoes, onions, mozzarella, and ketchup.

"I *am* eating," Madison shot back. She popped a french fry into her mouth. She pushed her fork around her Caesar salad. It was no good. Her stomach was in knots and she couldn't stop thinking about Concetta, about Damien, and about what awaited her, Park, and Lex tomorrow in the Chamber.

She and Theo were sitting at a corner table beside one of the windows. It was dusk. The sky was shot with streaks of purple, the skyscrapers still burning with lights. A comfortable Saturday evening in June. If her mind weren't so focused on the murder investigation, Madison knew she and Theo would probably be hitting a club or a party, or eating dinner at a trendy restaurant on West Broadway. She felt guilty for making him come here to this greasy, nondescript diner. She just wasn't in the mood for photographers or reporters or curious onlookers. And besides, she and Theo really hadn't had a quiet night alone together in a long time.

She was sitting at their little square table in a boyish green T-shirt and jeans, a Yankees baseball cap pulled over her head. The casual disguise seemed to be working. When she looked up from her plate, she saw Theo staring at her intently. "What is it?" she asked, instinctively running her napkin across her lips.

"Nothing. You just seem so . . . out of it." He frowned.

"Oh. I thought I had ketchup on my face or something."

"You'd still look hot if you did."

"Thanks." She smiled wearily. "I know I'm not being the best girlfriend tonight. I'm sorry for that."

"I know you liked Damien a lot," Theo said quietly. "I

don't blame you for being down in the dumps. I still can't believe what happened. I mean, I wish I'd known him better, but we never really clicked. He was just so crazy."

"He had that kind of personality," Madison replied. "Always trying to make people laugh."

"Or cry."

"Yeah, but never in a vicious way. That's what I liked about him."

Theo finished the rest of his burger, then gulped down his soda. "Now, I knew Concetta a little better," he said. "Nice girl. A little weird, but she always seemed cool. I can't *believe* she actually killed Damien like that."

Madison stayed quiet. She poked at the salad with her fork again. *Maybe. But maybe not.*

"I mean, under all that nice-girl stuff, she was hiding a psychopathic personality," Theo said. "So Damien didn't like her enough to be romantically involved with her. Big deal. That's no reason to kill the poor guy. Like, get over it."

Madison took a deep breath. She pushed the plate to the side of the table.

"And what the hell was with that whole Mozart playing on the speakers?" he continued. "So stupid. Did she really think she'd get away with it?"

Madison glanced away, her eyes scanning the traffic on Second Avenue. Night was falling slowly and she suddenly felt very warm.

"Mads? Hello?"

"What?"

"Why are you acting so strange?" he asked her sharply. "Look at me."

She did. "What do you want me to say? I'm just upset."

"You're hiding something from me."

*Damn.* She clenched her fists at her sides. Sometimes she hated that Theo was so perceptive when it came to figuring her out. He could take one look at her and know she wasn't feeling well or that she'd had an argument with Park or Lex. He could spot an excited gleam in her eyes and guess that she had good news to share with him. She, on the other hand, had never had that ability. She wasn't good at deciphering a person's mood, and she was even worse at hiding her own emotions.

Now she glanced away from him again. She couldn't spill the facts that she, Park, and Lex had uncovered. She couldn't talk about the theft at St. Cecilia's or about the traces of dynamite found in Mother Margaret's office. She hated keeping secrets, but Theo didn't exactly have a steel tongue: he'd end up blabbing the facts to everyone, albeit inadvertently. "I'm not hiding anything," she muttered.

"Yes you are." Theo leaned across the table and planted a kiss on her cheek. "What is it? Are you worried that the media is gonna screw up the chance for Cleopatra to be the most popular nightclub on the planet? It might happen, ya know. It'll be forever known as the site of a gory murder."

"I'm not really worried about that," she said. "And with how crazy people are, Damien's murder will probably bring more clubgoers to Cleopatra. You know how morbid public curiosity is. Everyone will probably want to dance in the cages just to say they did it."

"Yeah, you have a point there. So then, what is it? You worried about all the negative publicity our little school is gonna get? Don't be. St. Cecilia's will survive. And once Concetta's in the slammer and justice is served, everything will work itself out."

"Don't talk like that, okay?" she snapped. And immediately regretted it.

"Whoa. What did I say?"

Madison sighed. She ran her hands over her face. "I just don't want to hear any bad things about Concetta, that's all."

"*What?*" Theo sat back in his chair, a shocked expression on his face. "Are you nuts? You should be happy to hear bad things about Concetta after what she did."

"Well, I'm not."

"Oh, no? You mean you think she's still gonna be your friend from death row?"

"Theo, stop."

"I just don't get it," he ranted. "You knew Damien pretty well, and then he gets killed and everyone knows who killed him and you don't seem angry at Concetta at all. I'd totally want to pop her head off."

An image flashed before Madison's eyes: the splayed, chubby fingers of Concetta's hands, and Concetta's desperate tear-streaked face. *I didn't kill him. I didn't kill him.* Madison couldn't help but imagine Concetta dancing happily in that cage at Cleopatra one minute and then dashing down the staircase in panic the next, limping on one stiletto as the strobe lights spun wildly, her big body wobbling. The whole scenario *was* plausible. But had Julian Simmons—angry with Damien and having dropped a comment about wanting to blow up the school—run up the stairs and committed murder in cold blood instead?

She didn't know. She wouldn't know until after the Black Cry Affair was fully revealed to her.

"I mean, the horror of it all," Theo was saying, "is just unbelievable. My mom called Damien's parents this morning, and she said Damien's mom was beside herself."

Madison looked at Theo. "Did Damien's mom say anything else?"

"Just that they were waiting for his body to be released from the morgue," Theo said. "And that it would be flown to England for proper services. But apparently the body isn't being released anytime soon, and no one knows why. Damien's mom said that agents from New Scotland Yard had been in their town house all night, trying to make sense of things."

"And did they? The agents, I mean. New Scotland Yard."

"I guess so. Damien's mom said she felt guilty because Damien had been acting weird lately."

Madison perked up. "Weird in what way?"

"I don't know. I think she told my mom that Damien had been edgy and nervous. Something like that. But when did Damien ever sit still?"

Madison fell silent as Theo waved the waitress over and paid their bill. Then she followed him outside, into the night, and hand in hand they began walking down Second Avenue.

"So I've been thinking," Theo said. "After you get back from visiting your mom in Italy, maybe we can go on a quick vacation. My father's just completed construction on a new hotel in Antigua—it's *amazing*. We could get the penthouse suite."

"Sure," Madison replied, not really paying him much mind. *Why had Damien been edgy and nervous?* she wondered. *Had he been that upset about something he'd seen in the club?*

They walked past crowded restaurants and bars, crossing to the opposite side of the street.

Madison knew it was unwise to steer a conversation back in the direction of the murder investigation, but she couldn't help herself. "Theo," she said, trying to sound nonchalant, "how do you feel about Julian Simmons?"

"Okay, I guess. He's always been cool to me."

"Anything strange about him?"

"Like in what way?"

She hesitated for a few seconds. "I don't know. Guys talk to each other in weird ways. Like . . . has Julian ever said anything about Damien that you might've overheard?"

"Never." The reply was quick and assured.

Madison nodded slowly. "Okay. How about his personality? You both play on the lacrosse team. Haven't you ever held a real conversation with him?"

"Not more than casually. Julian's always talking about his career, about his music. Why?"

"Just wondering." She cleared her throat and counted off five seconds. "Can you think of any reason why Julian would be upset with the school, or with one of our teachers?" *Or any reason why he might be experimenting with explosives?*

Theo shrugged. "No. I mean, he pretty much got suspended back in February, but that's all over with now."

Madison stopped walking.

Theo stopped too. Then he looked at Madison and bit down on his upper lip. "Shit. I wasn't supposed to say that."

"Why not?"

"Just because it's like . . . a secret. I'm the only other person who knows."

"Who knows *what*?" She tugged at his sleeve. "Why was Julian suspended? And why do you know?"

A long, drawn-out sigh passed through Theo's lips. "My big stupid mouth. I swear, I'm just going to have my lips glued shut one of these days."

"Fine. But tell me about Julian first."

"One day back in February, he and I were both in the locker room getting changed," Theo began. "Our lockers are actually side by side. We were bullshitting and talking, and then Coach Wender came in and told us to hurry up. It was late, and we had just finished a long workout. Anyway, Coach was sweeping up the floor right beside us, and that was when Julian reached into his gym bag to pull out his jeans. And when he pulled out his jeans, a syringe popped out right along with them."

"A syringe?" Madison's voice hit a high note.

"Yeah," Theo said. "Turns out Julian was taking steroids. Coach saw it and *freaked* out. It didn't really surprise me because Julian's arms—his muscles—are so huge. But Coach hauled Julian right up to Mother Margaret's office, and I had to go along too as a witness."

"And?" Madison pressed. "What happened after that?"

"Julian admitted to using steroids. Mother Margaret freaked out, called his parents. She and Coach kept asking Julian where he got the steroids, but he wouldn't spill. Mother Margaret said he'd be suspended. Then she told me not to say anything to anyone, so I didn't."

"But I don't remember Julian ever being suspended," Madison said.

"That's because he wasn't—not literally, at least." Theo chuckled. "You know how things are at St. Cecilia's, Mads. Julian's parents probably made a huge donation to the school and everything was forgotten."

As she stood there, her stiff body being bumped by dozens of passersby, Madison realized she was sweating. Her heart was whacking in her chest. "So, Julian never said anything to you about it after that?"

"Two or three days later he did. He told me everything was cool and that he wasn't in any trouble. And he wanted to make sure I'd stay quiet about it. Which I have."

"You've managed to stay quiet about *that*," Madison snapped. "But everything else I tell you—or anyone tells you—ends up in the papers. How did you manage not to blab that dirt on Julian? You have the biggest mouth!"

Theo shrugged again. "Look, I'm not saying what Julian did was right, but using steroids, unfortunately, isn't really all that uncommon. Jocks shoot up all the time. Julian's not the first, and he won't be the last. Besides . . . me keeping this a secret is different from any of the other things I've blabbed about."

"How so?"

Theo stared at her, and the look in his eyes was both apologetic and relaxed. "It's a guy thing. Guys don't go around squealing on each other."

Madison gasped. "That's *exactly* why men are always in trouble!" She folded her arms across her chest. "Tell me something—that day in Mother Margaret's office, after the steroids had been found, did you see Mother Margaret actually write out a suspension report?"

Theo nodded. "Yeah. She wrote the whole thing out

while she screamed at Julian. She even stood up and waved the paper in his face, trying to get him to spill the beans about where he'd gotten the steroids." He looked at the flashing crosswalk. "Anyway, why the hell are we standing here? And why all the interest in Julian Simmons?"

Madison's mind was racing a mile a minute. She saw several little pieces of the puzzle fall into place. More to herself than to Theo she said, "If it was ever made public that Julian Simmons was on steroids, his career would suffer . . . a *lot*. And even though his parents paid off the school to keep quiet about it, I'll bet anything in the world that Mother Margaret refused to get rid of that suspension report. You know how meticulous and organized she is. She's got stuff on file about all of us—stuff we probably wouldn't even remember."

"That sounds about right," Theo commented. "But it would help if you told me what this is all about. You think Julian is somehow involved in Damien's murder?"

Madison mentally slapped herself. "No, no," she said. "I'm just . . . wondering about stuff, that's all. I'm just saying that Julian knows Mother Margaret's antics as well as we do; he knows that suspension report detailing the steroid use is—or was—probably in her files." *And sometime in March, he broke into her office and stole the documents from the cabinets. And because he was experimenting with explosives, he left a trail of those chemicals everywhere.*

She looked back at Theo. "And you're sure that you and Julian and Coach Wender were the *only* ones in the locker room that night?"

Theo stared across the street, rapt in thought. When

219

he finally glanced back at her, the expression on his face was tense. "Kind of," he said.

"What does that mean?"

Theo sighed. "I know where you're going with this, and it's so *wrong*. But—okay—that night in the locker room? Damien Kittle was also there, but he was, like, fifteen lockers away from us, and Coach Wender didn't even see him."

"But *you* saw Damien standing at his own locker when the syringe came out of Julian's bag, right? And while Julian was getting yelled at by Coach Wender?"

Theo nodded. "Yeah. I saw Damien out of the corner of my eye. But he walked into the bathroom really quietly while Coach Wender was yelling."

Madison gasped. "So then Julian saw Damien too, right? And Damien overheard the whole thing?"

"Again . . . yes. Can we stop talking about this?"

Madison felt a rush of pure adrenaline course through her blood. Was that it? Had she solved the crime? She pictured herself busting into Julian's house, tackling him to the ground, and slipping handcuffs over his wrists. She so totally wished she had a badge.

Exasperated, Theo threw his arms around her waist and clamped his lips over hers.

Madison was taken aback by the kiss, but she melted into it without hesitation.

"There," Theo whispered, drawing his face away from hers. "Maybe *that* will get your mind focused on me now."

Madison blushed. She loved these hot, tender little moments. And she loved Theo's tendency to be spontaneous when it came to affection. "It worked," she answered quietly. As she stared up into his eyes, she forgot about the loud traffic and the pushy pedestrians. She almost forgot about Julian Simmons too.

"You won't tell me why you're asking all these strange questions, so I had to improvise." Theo winked. "Unless you want to tell me what's going on in that mind of yours?"

"Nothing's going on. Like I said, I'm just thinking about things."

Theo glanced at his watch. "Are we going downtown to hang out with Park and Jeremy or what? You promised me we'd get to see the set of his new movie."

"Yeah. Come on, let's go." Madison walked to the edge of the curb and shot an arm into the air. A cab skidded to a stop and she and Theo climbed inside. Madison took off the baseball cap, shook her hair out, and then fixed her makeup.

Ten minutes later, they were pushing through the crowds on West Houston Street, trying to make it to one of the blue barricades sealing off the set. Huge bright lights illuminated the hundreds of fans eager to catch a glimpse of the moviemaking magic. Several onlookers called Madison's name as she walked past. She gave them a warm wave. Cameras flashed in the corners of her eyes. Then she spotted Park standing beside one of the long trailers.

"Excuse me," Madison said, tapping a production assistant on the shoulder.

The young guy recognized her instantly and waved her forward, moving one of the barricades as he did so.

"Thanks." Holding fast to Theo's hand, Madison raced across the street, cutting a direct line through the set. The blinding overhead lights made it feel like early morning instead of early evening.

"Hey," Park said, spotting them and waving. "I didn't think you were coming."

"We almost didn't." Theo pointed at Madison. "Your sister got into one of her police interrogation moods."

"I did not," Madison said. She looked at Park, locking eyes with her. "I was just gathering information."

Park nodded, a smile tugging at her lips. "Gotcha."

As Theo stared around the set, Madison mouthed the words *I have something to tell you* at Park.

"Hey," Theo asked. "Where's Jeremy?"

Park shook her head and pointed straight up at the sky.

Theo and Madison both gasped when they spotted Jeremy standing on the ledge of a tall building.

"It's another one of those jumping scenes," Park said, more than a little annoyed. "I just don't get it."

"Action!" a voice suddenly boomed over the street.

The cameras began rolling. The crowds of onlookers silently stared at the star above them. Jeremy moved along the ledge; he feigned a stumble and a few seconds later was plummeting toward the ground at breakneck speed.

"Jesus!" Theo shouted.

"And there goes the inflatable device," Park said a moment before the huge cushiony thing broke Jeremy's fall.

Madison rubbed a hand over her stomach. "That's twisted."

"Tell me about it. There's no way I'd ever be able to do that." Park sighed. "I'd totally need a stunt double."

Jeremy came strolling toward them, pulling away from the makeup artist who was dabbing more blood onto his face. He pushed past a little knot of production assistants and sound technicians. "Dude!" he said, offering his hand to Theo. "Thanks for coming!" He bent down and kissed Madison's cheek. "So did you guys like my fall?"

"Freaking awesome," Theo raved.

Madison crinkled her nose. "It was a little much for me."

Jeremy laughed. If he felt odd standing there with a torn and bloodied shirt and a fake purple gash etched onto the side of his face, it didn't show. "Hey, where's Lex?"

"She's home, designing," Madison answered.

"Too bad," Jeremy said. "I wish she could've seen that stunt. It was actually my last skydive for a couple of weeks."

"Thank God," Park mumbled.

Jeremy threw an arm around her shoulder. "So did you guys hear? Park got her first official acting lesson this afternoon."

"Oh!" Madison's jaw dropped. She slugged Park in the arm. "You didn't tell me that!"

"It's not true," Park said with a dismissive wave of her hand. "All I did was read parts of the script aloud. And I haven't signed on any dotted line."

"So not true." Jeremy shook his head. "I saw you reading that script. You were *totally* into it."

"Oh, man, I would give anything to star in a movie," Theo said.

"Dude! You should try it!" Jeremy reached into the pocket of his jeans and lit a cigarette.

"*Ugh*," Park said, pinching her nostrils as a plume of smoke drifted past her face. "Do I *have* to get used to kissing an ashtray?"

Theo and Jeremy launched into their own conversation, and Madison pulled Park off to one side. "You're not going to believe this," she whispered.

"Tell me."

Madison excitedly told Park about Julian Simmons, the steroids, his suspension, and the apparent cover-up. "So Julian probably wanted to get rid of any documents that detailed his steroid use," she said firmly.

Park nodded. "And when you put it together with what Lex saw today, the glitter that was found in Mother Margaret's office you just might get a killer!"

"What did Lex find?" Madison asked quickly.

"Lex called me a while ago," Park said. And then she rehashed Lex's trip to the Bronx, where she trailed Julian to the construction site that had explosives on hand.

"Oh my God!" Madison shouted. Then she cupped her hand over her mouth and took a long, deep breath.

"It makes sense," Park said calmly. "But the thing is, I've been thinking a lot about what Concetta told us today. *Her* version of what happened. And something's bothering me."

"What is it?"

Park threw a quick glance over her shoulder to make sure Jeremy and Theo weren't listening. She said, "If Damien collapsed in that cage like Concetta told us he did, then someone clocked him in the head *after* he fell down."

Madison winced. "You mean he was killed *twice*? Why would somebody do that?"

"For only one reason," Park replied. "To throw off the police. To throw off an investigation. And to hide Damien's *real* cause of death."

# *15*

# Double Dead

"**A** postmortem wound," Lex said.

She was standing in her bedroom, a ruler in one hand and a pencil in the other. A pair of black rectangular reading glasses sat on top of her head. She had been sitting at her desk for the past two hours, sketching new designs for the Triple Threat label, enjoying the solitude of her own company, when Madison and Park burst into the apartment like two tourists at a sample sale. Now Lex knew she would never get her work done.

Walking slowly back to her desk, she sat down and let the weight of her own words settle into her brain. *A postmortem wound.* Was it possible, or had Madison and Park flown off the deep end?

"You have to think about it in a broad context," Park said, sitting on the edge of Lex's bed. "It's not so far-fetched."

"No, it isn't," Madison agreed. "And if we've decided that we're going to believe Concetta's story, then we *have* to believe that the wound was inflicted after Damien fell to the floor of the cage."

"Wait." Lex held up a hand. "We have to piece this together chronologically. Otherwise it won't make sense."

"Fine." Madison plopped onto the bed, sliding a pillow under her chin. "Where do we start?"

"I know *exactly* where to start," Park said. She nodded. "Last night, when we first got to Cleopatra, we ran up to the fourth level to get rid of those ugly floral arrangements, remember? That was when we saw Damien—he came right up to us and started acting like his old self, right? But he didn't *look* well. Remember? I asked him if he was feeling okay?"

"Yes, I do," Lex replied. She dropped the pencil and ruler and flipped her sketchpad closed. "He was pale and sweating a lot—"

"And he had hives," Madison cut in.

"Right." Park snapped her fingers. "So we know Damien wasn't feeling well. Then Concetta and Emmett showed up, and Emmett did his catwalk modeling thing to show off the Triple Threat suit he was wearing. And Julian came by too."

"And Concetta started flirting with Damien immediately," Lex said. "Damien wanted to dance, and the two of them ran off together."

"Obviously to the cages," Madison added.

"Yes. And then we went down to the main level to make our appearance on the stage." Park closed her eyes, trying to remember every last detail. "And I remember looking out on the crowd—I didn't see Damien and Concetta."

"Me neither." Madison scowled. "I started speaking and then Lex nearly knocked me down to get her own airtime."

"I *apologized* for that," Lex said. "And right after my scream, the music started up. Madison, you joined Theo on the dance floor, and Park and I hung out for like a minute on the stage."

"Okay, stop." Park stood up. She started pacing the floor. "This is where it'll get tricky. We were all on that dance floor on the main level for at least an hour and a half, right?"

Lex nodded. "Definitely."

"And in that span of time, which of our classmates did we see dancing beside us, or at least on the main floor?" Park asked.

"Better yet, which ones *didn't* we see?" Madison rolled into a sitting position on the very edge of the mattress. "Did any of us see Julian?"

Lex shook her head.

So did Park.

"I saw Emmett dancing beside us at some point," Madison said. "That much I know."

"And Jessica?" Park asked.

"Negative on that one." Lex sat back in her swivel chair.

Madison and Park both agreed.

"Okay," Park said. "So in keeping with the hypothetical thing, none of us saw Julian or Jessica on the main floor. That doesn't mean they weren't there, but let's stay with that for a minute. Let's say either one of them was up on the fourth level, which is where you gain entrance to the cages from the catwalk. Either one of them could've been watching Damien and Concetta dance."

"And witnessed what Concetta said happened—Damien collapsing, her running out of the cage and down the staircase," Madison offered.

"Which would've given either one of them a chance to dash up the stairs and into the cage," Lex said. "Let's say it was Julian. He jumps into the cage, sees the stiletto, and bashes Damien in the head. Then he runs back down the stairs. Bam, and it's done."

"Shit," Park whispered through gritted teeth. "I just wish I'd been glancing at my watch more last night. I hate that we can't piece this together into a real time frame."

"Oh!" The little shout of joy was Madison's. She popped up, her mouth wide open. "We *can*! The music was all timed. It was all played in sets, one song after another. Dad didn't want the DJs to have free reign with the music. Weeks ago, he made them put together a list of songs."

"Madison," Park said slowly, trying to contain her excitement. "You're the most professionally organized person I know—except for that floral fiasco. *Please* tell me you have that list."

"Of *course* I do." Madison looked genuinely offended. "I keep my files immaculate." She dashed out of the bedroom.

"I really hope this works," Lex said. "At least with that list we'd be able to know what was going on *when*."

"Exactly." Park nervously ran her hands through her hair.

Two minutes later, Madison returned holding several manila files. She laid them out on the bed neatly, scanning each one. "Here's the first guest list," she said, turning over a page. "Here's the second one. Here's the *final* one." Her fingers worked swiftly. "Here's the bill for the catering staff, the florals . . . I'll have to call *them* on Monday. . . ."

"Hurry," Park said impatiently.

"I'm trying . . . Aha!" Madison held up two sheets of paper that were stapled together. "*Here* it is! A complete rundown of every song that was played, along with its approximate time."

"Thank *God* for modern technology." Lex ran out of the chair and stood beside Park.

"Excellent," Park said, scanning the pages. "Madison, how long was your speech supposed to be?"

"About two minutes."

"Okay, so the end of your speech was the DJs' cue to begin playing the music." Park pointed at Lex. "Then *you* jump-started the party. So let's just assume that each of these play times is about two minutes off. Okay. Here. The music officially started at ten-thirty-five p.m. According to the list, it began with a thirty-minute set of electronica."

"So let's say we got onto the dance floor at ten-forty," Lex said. "At five after eleven the set would've changed to what?"

"Thirty minutes of pop." Park turned the sheet over.

"Here—oh, I remember this. It started with Beyoncé and the Killers, then look—they played Beck and the Postal Service and the Guns. Then it ended with Justin—"

"That's it!" Madison cried. "I remember seeing Emmett when Justin was playing. I looked across the floor and saw Emmett dancing and mouthing the words to the song. I remember."

Lex ran back to her desk and grabbed a pen and her sketchpad. "So let's see, that would've put a sighting of Emmett at about eleven-thirty-five p.m." She jotted it down on a clean sheet.

"Yes," Park said. "Because then a round of trance started at about eleven-thirty-eight, and that lasted for twenty minutes. Then at midnight the music went back to pop."

"And the last song that was playing before the cage came down with Damien's body in it was Gwen," Madison said. "I remember it now."

"So do I!" Lex cried.

"Okay then—that would've been . . ." Park scanned the page. "Here. Gwen Stefani, and they played it at twelve-twenty-six a.m. Concetta said she heard the commotion and the Requiem playing from the bathroom after about three minutes of being locked in. So take off two minutes because Madison didn't make her speech and that leaves us at twelve-twenty-four."

"So let's say the cage came down at about twelve-twenty-five." Lex nodded. "Concetta would have already been in the bathroom for like three minutes."

"So she got into the bathroom at about twelve-twenty-two," Madison said.

"It would've taken her about a minute to limp down the stairs," Park said. "So let's say twelve-twenty-one.

And let's say Damien collapses at around twelve-twenty. Concetta leaves the cage right then, which basically gives the killer almost five minutes to whack Damien with the shoe and disappear back into the crowd. Because the cage descended at around twelve-twenty-five."

"And that's when the Requiem started playing." Lex shuddered. "And just a few seconds before that, the killer popped into the DJ booth and knocked them out."

Park started pacing again. She shook her head. "No, wait. It's all too random. It's starting to not make sense."

"That's because we haven't discussed *why* the killer would have wanted to hit Damien in the head *after* he collapsed," Madison said.

"I thought you guys said the killer did that to throw off the police." Lex sounded confused. "Right?"

"Yeah, but the killer couldn't have known Concetta was going to lose her shoe in that cage," Park explained. "The fact that she ran out of there limping was just something that *happened.*"

"So the killer was watching Concetta and Damien," Lex said, "already *knowing* that Damien was going to collapse. And when he—or she—sees Concetta running out of the cage limping, the killer grabs the opportunity to cover up the *real* cause of death by whacking Damien in the head." She smiled brightly. Then the smiled faded. "Does that make any sense?"

"Actually, it does. Sort of." Park resumed her pacing. "But that still leaves us without a cause of death. Did someone shoot Damien from the rafters, for God's sake? Was that a bullet wound? What is it? I just don't get it."

"But . . ." Madison clamped her mouth shut and looked away.

"But what?" Park asked.

Madison sighed. "I mean, the autopsy would've been completed by now, right?"

"Right."

"So an official cause of death has been issued—we just don't know it. And if the cause of death *is* blunt impact trauma from the shoe, then Damien's body would be released to the family, right?"

Park nodded. "I assume so. Why?"

"Theo told me that his mom spoke to Damien's mom this afternoon," Madison said. "And Mrs. Kittle told Theo's mom that Damien's body isn't being released. The medical examiner is, like, holding it."

"That doesn't sound right." Lex scratched her head. "Especially because Damien is English royalty. They would want that body flown back to England as soon as possible."

"If that's the case—that Damien's body isn't being released—then I'd bet anything it's because we're on the right track," Park said. "The autopsy probably revealed that the stiletto couldn't have killed him—or something else."

"Like what?" Lex sat back down again.

"Like another cause of death," Park explained. She walked to the windows at the far end of the room and stared outside. "And here's the *really* big question. With what we know so far, Julian Simmons is a total suspect— but did he kill Damien because Damien knew about the steroids? Is that really enough of a reason? Is that Julian's motive?"

"Look, we know Damien wanted out of the club," Madison said. "That's probably reason enough for someone to kill him."

"Yeah, but *why* did Damien want out of the club?" Park asked, frustrated. "And what the hell does this club do behind closed doors that's worth killing for?"

"We'll know soon enough," Madison whispered.

"Maybe not," Lex said. "I mean, if I witnessed Julian buying *explosives* today, should we really be going to the Chamber tomorrow?"

"Of course!" Park nodded. "How else will we know what's really going on?"

"But what if he tries to blow us all up?" Madison asked. "What if that's his plan?"

"It's not," Park said calmly, firmly. "We have to find out what this is really all about, and that means taking risks. We've come this far, and we're *not* turning back."

Lex flipped open her cell phone and punched in a number. "Hello, Donnie? I know you're supposed to be off duty in about ten minutes, but I might have to ask you to do a little overtime. Can you come upstairs? Thanks."

"What's going on?" Madison asked.

Lex got up and slipped into a comfortable pair of shoes. She went to the mirror and checked her makeup, adding more blush to her cheeks. "There's only one way to settle this," she said.

"And what's that?" Park cut her a suspicious stare.

Three minutes later, they all heard Lupe open the front door. There was a bit of mumbled conversation, and then Donnie appeared at Lex's bedroom door.

He stood on the threshold with his head bent and his eyes cast downward. "Uh, hello?" he said in his typically shy voice.

"Come on in, Donnie," Lex replied cheerfully.

He stepped into the bedroom, smiling vaguely at Madison and Park. But he wouldn't move five feet beyond the door. He stood there looking like a guilty schoolboy.

"Lex, are you going to tell us what this is all about?" Park demanded.

Lex walked over to Donnie and threw her arms around him. "You've been *so* good to us!" she said. "And I want you to know how much we all appreciate your hard work. You're always there when we need you." She stood on her tiptoes and planted a kiss on his cheek.

Donnie turned redder than a tomato. He gulped and cracked a grin. "Thanks."

"But now I need to ask you for a *really* big favor," Lex said. She reached for the magic purse and flung it over her shoulder. "You're probably the best former medical student in the whole city, and I know you still have some nice connections."

Donnie smirked. "A few."

"Good." Lex motioned her head at Park, then stared up at Donnie. "I need you to break us into the morgue."

"*What?*" Madison screeched. "*Eeeewwww.*"

"Lex . . ." Park said.

"Uh . . . I don't know if I can do that." It was one of the longest sentences Donnie had ever spoken. He said the words quietly, apologetically . . . but not altogether firmly.

"Of course you can't!" Madison shrieked. "It's too disgusting!"

Lex rolled her eyes. "Stop being such a baby, Madison. How else are we going to find out what we need to find out?"

"How about waiting for the media to release Damien's

cause of death?" Madison shot back. "It'll be in the papers eventually."

"*Eventually* might be too late." Park suddenly sounded intrigued. She stared at Donnie, her eyes asking the obvious question: *Can you do it? Can you break us into the morgue?*

He cleared his throat nervously. "I mean . . . it's not gonna be easy," he said. "And if we get caught, your . . . um . . . your dad would have to pay a really big fine, 'cause I sure as hell won't be able to pay it."

"I'll give you a blank check drawn on my own bank account," Park said seriously. "That way, if we do get caught, you won't have to worry about paying for a thing."

"But how the hell are you going to do this, Donnie?" Madison's voice cracked. Her cheeks flushed in the heat of her fear. "You're talking about the office of the chief medical examiner. Isn't there, like, security everywhere?"

"Yeah," Donnie replied. "But I got a friend who works there. All I'm saying is that we could try, if you really want to."

"We want to!" Lex reached into the magic purse, pulled out five crisp one-hundred-dollar bills, and slipped them into Donnie's shirt pocket.

"You're all crazy!" Madison shrieked. "I'm not going to any morgue! Forget it!"

"You don't have to," Park said calmly, patting Madison's shoulder. "But if Lex and I aren't back in two hours, call our attorneys, 'cause it probably means we got arrested."

# 16

# The Body

In the back of the limo, Park and Lex changed into fresh blue surgical scrubs Donnie had pulled from his backpack; cheap, flimsy, and just a wee bit stinky, the scrubs were a necessary disguise—you couldn't break into a morgue dressed in Triple Threat daywear. Thankfully, Donnie still had a small stash of them from his medical school days.

Park finished first. Sitting on the edge of her seat, she cinched the drawstring into a bow and tied it as tightly as possible. Then she pulled the plastic mask over her head and let it hang around her neck. The little surgical cap didn't quite fit over the bun she had fashioned with hairpins, but it hid most of her dark locks. "There," she said, "that's not so bad."

"Not so bad?" Lex shrieked. "Are you kidding me?" She was struggling to roll up the oversized scrub pants so that they wouldn't drag when she walked. The shirt hung on her lean frame like a poncho; she couldn't imagine stepping outside like that, so she tied it in a knot just above her waist. "These things are hideous!"

"Well, what did you expect? Designer scrubs?" Park chuckled.

"It'd be a start! I mean, how do people walk around in these things—they're so ugly, and so poorly made." Lex pointed to the bunchy pants. "Look—there's not even a seam!"

"Doctors and nurses need to be able to move around," Park explained. "These do the job, I guess. But they really are kind of itchy."

"They're more than just itchy," Lex snapped. "They happen to smell."

"Sorry about that," Donnie called from the driver's seat. "That smell is what you call cheap detergent. The no-frills kind."

Lex shook her head to keep from fainting. "How low have we stooped?" she whispered to Park. "If I'm ever photographed wearing these, it's all over."

"It could be a fashion statement, ya know." Park pointed to her own scrubs. "Someone might think it's cool."

"As if." When the limo slowed to a crawl, nearing the corner of First Avenue and Thirty-first Street, Lex reached into the magic purse and pulled out several items. She opened her compact and checked her reflection; she winced, horrified by the pale blue color of the scrubs. She swept her long hair up in a leopard-print clip, then tied the surgical cap over it. She didn't care how plain the uniform was supposed to look—it needed accessories. She fastened a smallish Cartier diamond brooch to the left side of the shirt and knotted a black silk scarf around her waist to hold up her pants better. She yanked two thick strands of hair out from under the cap and let them dangle along the sides of her face.

Now, at least, she had some semblance of style.

Donnie parked the limo on First Avenue. He pulled on his white lab coat, stepped outside, and opened the back door for Park and Lex. Seeing Lex—the accessories and, most of all, the big purse hanging from her right shoulder—he said, "Um, you might want to leave that in here."

"My purse?" Lex raised her eyebrows. Had he really uttered those blasphemous words?

"Yeah," Donnie said. "It just doesn't look right."

"I agree," Park mumbled.

"Well, I hate to disappoint both of you, but I'm not going *anywhere* without my purse." Lex held on to the strap. "For God's sake, we could need something in here!"

"Like what?" Donnie asked quietly.

"Like more things than you can possibly imagine," Park answered, patting his shoulder. "Let's just try and do this before I lose my courage, okay?"

With Donnie in the lead, they crossed the street. Park and Lex fixed the surgical masks over their faces as they went up the front steps and into the muggy main lobby of the office of the chief medical examiner.

Lex felt her heart slamming in her chest. In that

moment—seeing the tall security guards and the two uniformed police officers at the desk—she almost stopped short and turned around. It was unlike her to lose her cool. It was unlike her to think that the task at hand couldn't be accomplished. But this was way different from scaling the fire escape and breaking into St. Cecilia's Prep. The OCME was as serious as things got; a restricted, internationally renowned forensic facility, it was home to scientists, FBI agents, and countless death-challenged corpses. Getting caught tonight would mean riding yet another wave of scandal.

She glanced at Park and felt a twinge of reassurance.

Her head held high, her eyes gleaming above the mask, Park looked completely in her element as she followed Donnie up to the front desk and waited at his side.

Donnie and one of the security guards exchanged words, and then a buzzer sounded and two big double doors swung open.

Lex tried to keep her knees locked as she followed them to the elevator banks. She was impressed by Donnie's reserve, his professional air. The shy, introverted twenty-seven-year-old definitely looked more like a serious doctor than a chauffeur.

The elevator doors yawned open. Lex and Park followed Donnie inside. They both winced when he hit the down button and they descended into the morgue.

The first blast of foul air hit Lex like a huge fist: it was the smell of formaldehyde and rotting flesh. The cold nearly made her teeth chatter. She shook her head as they walked out of the elevator and into a gleaming white-tiled hallway.

Park, standing rail-straight, coughed and clamped a hand over her mask to further blot out the odor.

Donnie was moving more quickly now. He seemed to know his way around. He ducked into an office, yanked a white lab coat from a wall, and held it out to Park. "Here," he whispered. "Put this on."

She slipped into it, relieved that it fit her slim frame perfectly.

They continued down the corridor until they reached another set of double doors. The words AUTOPSY BAY were printed in big block letters on the wall.

Lex felt her stomach flip into her throat. She accepted the packet of latex gloves Donnie handed to her, tearing it open and fitting her fingers into the rubbery texture.

As they neared another door, Donnie paused and scanned the long corkboard mounted to one wall. It was filled with clipboards and sheets of paper, everything classified by a specific code. On the left were the cases marked *H* for homicide. Donnie grabbed one of the clipboards and scanned it. He found what he was looking for, pointing to the name *Damien Kittle*.

"What does that mean?" Park asked, her voice a whisper.

"It means Damien was autopsied this morning," Donnie explained. "And according to these notes, his body is in drawer four-D."

*"Drawer?"* Lex put a hand on her stomach.

"Yeah," Donnie said. "It's like a freezer."

"Does it say the cause of death on that clipboard?" Park asked.

Donnie shook his head. "See here?" He pointed again,

this time at an empty box beside Damien's name. "This means Damien's death was ruled a homicide by the medical examiner, but in order to see the actual cause of death we need to go inside there." He motioned his head at the closed door.

Park nodded. She and Lex followed Donnie into a large square room lined with steel autopsy tables, stainless steel sinks, and bright overhead lamps. The smell was unreal—an entity all its own. Lex nearly gagged and Park had to reposition the mask over her nose and mouth.

Worst of all, though, were the bodies lying on the tables: stiff human shapes beneath white sheets, bare feet sticking out, every big toe tagged and numbered.

"This is *so* gross," Lex whispered.

Donnie pointed to the wall at the very end of the autopsy bay, where the drawers were located.

Park followed him. Her arms were straight at her sides, her body movements cautious and rigid. She didn't want to rub up against anything that would make her barf later on. Or right now. She scanned the rows of closed body drawers slowly.

Lex moved to the far end of the wall. She saw a letter *D* stamped on one of the drawers and instantly wrapped her fingers around the handle. She turned it; the drawer yawned open with a blast of cold, foul air. A stab of fear made her pause. She didn't want to see Damien dead. She didn't want to see his familiar face all blue and frozen and stiff. *But I have to,* she thought. *I can't be afraid.*

Gulping, she looked down.

The dead face staring back at her was that of an elderly black man.

She gasped and jumped to the side, the Cartier pendant shaking where it was pinned to her shirt.

"Lex!"

Park's low, sharp voice echoed from the other end of the wall. She waved Lex over to where she and Donnie were standing.

Lex realized she had acted too quickly—opening up the first drawer she saw. She stared regretfully at the man. "Sorry about that," she muttered, and shoved the drawer shut with her hip.

"We found Damien," Park said quietly.

Lex nodded.

And Donnie yanked the drawer open.

Damien's face stared back at them, his eyes taped closed, his blue lips parted slightly. The wound on the side of his head was crusted with dried blood. And a single speck of glitter was still shining on a strand of dark hair.

Park pointed down at it. "See? The medical examiner must've taken the rest of the glitter we saw as a sample."

"There was definitely a lot more last night," Lex said.

Park saw the clipboard hanging off to one side of the drawer. She reached for it, flipped it open. Her eyes scanned the small print. "Listen," she said quietly, reading from the official autopsy facesheet. " 'The wound on the right side of the victim's head measures two inches wide and five inches deep, and is consistent with the measurements of the aforementioned weapon, a size-twelve shoe with a stiletto heel, classified as Exhibit A.' "

"Damn, that was a hard hit to his head," Lex said impatiently, loosening the silk scarf from around her waist and dropping it over her shoulders.

Park continued scanning the document. " 'Victim measured five feet nine inches tall and was . . .' " She flipped to the second page. "Here. Okay. 'Further forensic evaluation of Exhibit A is *inconsistent* with blunt impact trauma, due to Exhibit's size and point of impact.' " She gasped. "You see—we're right. It says right here the stiletto couldn't have killed him!"

"But what *did* kill him?" Lex asked.

Park read more of the report. " 'Internal examination of the victim revealed pulmonary edema and hemorrhaging, as well as severe dehydration and lesions on both the brain and lungs.' " She paused and looked up.

"Oh my God," Lex whispered. "That's horrible."

"I know." Park repositioned the mask, giving herself more room to breathe. Then she again lowered her eyes to the sheet. " 'Pending further toxicological analysis, the victim appears to have died as a result of . . . *poisoning*.' "

"Jesus Christ!" Lex lowered the mask from around her ears. "I can't believe it! So Concetta *is* telling the truth!"

"It appears that way," Park replied, her voice flat and unemotional. "And right down here, it says Damien looks like he died from . . . *ingestion of abrin*. That must be the poison."

"Abrin? Where's it come from? What is it?" Lex scanned the report, looking for a clue.

"It doesn't say anything else about the poison. But look—it says right here that this autopsy was completed at eleven-forty-five this morning. And look—a carbon copy of this report has already been sent to the NYPD, the FBI, the ATF, and New Scotland Yard."

"So this is news. They found all this out after they interrogated Concetta." Lex yanked the mask back over her ears. "So the cops must know by now that she didn't kill him."

"Not necessarily," Park replied. "The cops know the blow to his head didn't kill Damien. But they might still believe that Concetta's the one who swung the stiletto, and they might believe that she's the one who poisoned him."

Lex stared at her. "Do you think she poisoned him?"

Park thought about it, then shook her head slowly. "No, I don't. It doesn't make sense that she would poison him and then clock him in the head with her own shoe. The whole point of the stiletto was to throw off the investigation. From the perspective of criminal psychology, a powerful blow to the head with a blunt object might pretty well fall in line with a crime of passion, but that's not what this is. Whoever poisoned Damien did it for other reasons."

"What's that?" Lex pointed to the bottom of the page, where the words *Trace Evidence* were highlighted in bold print.

Park read through the few lines. And her heart nearly stopped. "Holy shit!" she yelped.

"Park—be quiet," Donnie warned.

Lex tried to read the intricate wording in the report. "What is it?"

Park cupped a hand to her mouth. "Okay—this part refers to trace evidence, which is evidence that's not often seen with the naked eye because it's usually totally microscopic. It says here that the only piece of trace evidence found at the scene of the crime—meaning in the cage—were two strands of *bright red hair.*"

Lex's eyes widened. It took her a few seconds to draw the link. Then her eyes lit up and she said, "Jessica Paderman."

"Bingo."

"So—wait—this means that Jessica was in the cage?" Lex asked.

"Only a DNA test could prove that it's actually *her* hair," Park explained. "But come on—who else's hair could it be? It's too much of a coincidence."

"But Concetta said she and Damien were the only ones dancing in the cage. She would've told us if Jessica had joined them."

"I think so too. Which means that Jessica would have to have entered the cage *after* Concetta left it."

"Just like the killer," Lex whispered. "Now, if Jessica used any kind of glitter product and had a reason to break into Mother Margaret's office and steal confidential school documents, she'd be as much a suspect as Julian."

Park frowned. "The fact that Jessica's hair was found at the scene of the crime makes her even *more* of a suspect. No one has to guess as to her whereabouts. Even if she says she was dancing on the main level of Cleopatra, this trace evidence places her otherwise."

"Goddamn," Lex murmured, and shook her head.

Suddenly, the door to the autopsy bay swung open.

Donnie went rigid.

Park slipped the clipboard back into place and pushed the drawer shut. Then she and Lex turned around.

The young man staring back at them was dressed in

the same ugly blue scrubs. He was short and thin, his red hair buzz-cut. For a moment he simply stared at them. Then his face relaxed and he set his eyes on Park. "Oh, Doctor Sanjay," he said. "I'm glad I found you. I thought you had left. Anyway, I wanted you to take a look at this victim."

Park blinked. She felt Lex and Donnie fidgeting nervously behind her. She glanced down at her white coat and saw the name badge on her lapel: *Sunjita Sanjay, MD.* Her mind went blank.

"Doctor Sanjay?" the young man said again.

Park lifted her head up high and walked toward him. *Acting,* she thought. *If you're going to be in a movie, you might as well start now.* She cleared her throat and assumed her best Indian accent. "Yiis," she replied. "I vvwould be glad to *hilp* you."

The young man nodded. He shot a curious glance at Lex, and another at Donnie.

When Park reached the body in question, she curled her fingers around the edge of the steel autopsy table and stared across it at the young man's name badge.

*William Billard, Forensic Technician.*

"Deese are my colleagues," Park said, gesturing her head at Donnie and Lex. "Dis is Ducta Halstrom, and dis is Nurse . . . Lexana."

William Billard nodded at them.

"Hey," Donnie said.

"Vvwhat seems to be da problem?" Park asked.

"Well, I just needed your take on this case." William Billard pointed at the body underneath the white sheet. "The police think the bite marks on this victim were made by a pit bull, but when I was hosing the body down, I caught a look at them, and I don't think these are pit bull bite marks. They look a lot . . . worse."

Park nodded.

William Billard pulled back the white sheet. The body was that of a middle-aged white man, and he appeared normal . . . except for a chunk of mottled muscle just above his left knee.

Park's eyes met the gory reddish purple injury. She gasped and swayed, tightening her grip on the edge of the table. The immediate image that leaped into her mind was of chopped meat.

Beside her, Donnie said, "Wow."

Lex was breathing heavily, her eyes focused on the ceiling.

"Yiis," Park said. "Dat looks like berry bat bite."

"A bat bite?" William Billard asked.

"Oh, you tink it's bat bite?" Park stared at him.

"No. Yes. No, I meant . . ." William cleared his throat nervously. "Did you say *bat* bite?"

"No. *You* said bat bite."

"No, I didn't. I thought that's what *you* said."

The phonetic equation finally clicked into place. "Oh," Park said. "No. I said *bad* bite. Berry berry bad."

"And do you think this looks like a pit bull bite?"

"Uh . . . *yiis.* Could be. Maybe. Berry ugly."

William Billard was clearly growing agitated. He sighed. "Could you just give me your professional opinion, Doctor?"

Park nodded as she felt Lex tug at the sleeve of the white coat. "Uh . . . My professional opinion is . . ." She looked up. She gulped. She looked back down at the table and pointed. She said, "My opinion is dat dis patient . . . he vill not vwalk anytime soon."

"What?" William Billard snapped.

Lex and Donnie had already begun walking toward the door.

"I'm sorry." Park shrugged. "I'm late for meeting. Have to *skee-dattle.*" And with that, she dashed out of the bay and into the corridor. She broke into a run, Lex and Donnie at her heels. She yanked off the white coat and chucked it onto the first chair she saw.

An elevator was waiting for them, its doors open.

They jumped inside.

Lex jammed her fingers on the lobby button.

"Shit," Park said, resuming her own voice. "That was close."

"It was *too* close." Lex stared up at the numbers as the elevator began to move.

"Wow, Park, I'm impressed." Donnie Halstrom smiled. "That was mighty good acting."

"Thanks." She smiled from behind the mask. "I think so too."

When the elevator doors opened, they poked their heads out to check that the coast was clear.

"Okay," Donnie whispered. "Now just walk out without looking at anyone. If the guards ask you to stop, tell them you're running to an emergency."

Park and Lex nodded. They squared their shoulders and walked through the double doors and out into the lobby.

And stopped dead in their tracks.

Standing off to the left, a few feet from the main exit, was a circle of bodyguards: they were all dressed in suits, earpieces strapped to the sides of their heads. Several of them were talking. Outside on the street, cameras were flashing.

And in the middle of the security circle was David Gordon, prime minister of England. He was a handsome man, but as he stood with his arms at his sides and his eyes fixed on the floor, he looked grim.

Lex moaned. She leaned in close to Park and said wearily, "I think we're busted again."

"No way," Park whispered back. "He can't recognize us. We're wearing masks and caps on our heads."

Donnie was standing behind them. He gave their shoulders a nudge.

Lex was solid as stone. She couldn't believe her eyes. She didn't move a muscle until she felt Park's hand snap around her wrist and lead her outside—past the news vans and reporters, past the photographers, and into the safety of the limousine. She didn't speak for the first several minutes of the ride back home. Then, as she peeled the mask off her face and yanked the cap from her head, she looked at Park and said, "I'm never breaking into a morgue again!"

Park shook out her hair. "It was your idea. A close call, but I'm glad we came," she said simply, calmly. "And I don't think they've figured it out yet. The school, the police, the prime minister—they don't know there's a biochemical killer on the loose."

"A biochemical killer?" Lex asked.

"Yep." Park applied a fresh coat of gloss to her lips,

then snapped open her compact. "Someone who knows about poisons and chemistry and how to make dynamite. Someone who has a secret little laboratory hidden somewhere. And tomorrow, you, Madison, and I are going to flush the creep out."

# 17

# In the Club

At precisely eight o'clock on Sunday night, Madison, Park, and Lex walked up the steps of the Canoli town house on East Sixty-fifth Street.

Dressed casually in jeans and tank tops, they stood shoulder to shoulder in the heavy air, anxious and fidgety and not quite knowing what to say. They were certain that down in the Chamber, a killer was waiting for them. They also knew that if they didn't solve Damien's murder soon, St. Cecilia's Prep probably wouldn't have much of a commencement ceremony on Monday afternoon. St. Cecilia's might not even survive the forthcoming media backlash—a dead student, an accused student, and an unknown chemical criminal on the loose. A crappier graduation day you just wouldn't find.

It was Park who had the most relaxed look on her face. As she rang the bell, she said, "Remember, just play it cool and go along with the game."

"Wait," Madison burst out nervously. "What if this is all a plot to silence us? What if we go in there and they just chop our heads off?"

"Look on the bright side—at least we're all wearing nice earrings." Lex rolled her eyes. "Calm down, will you? Nothing bad is going to happen. And besides, Donnie is waiting in the limo at the corner. He knows we're here. And this *was* our idea, remember?"

The front door opened. Concetta appeared on the threshold. She was dressed in jeans and a pink blouse. She met their eyes and smiled.

"Hi," Park said brightly. "You seem a lot better today, Concetta."

"I'm feeling a little better." She stepped back and waved them inside, then closed the door. "We have to hurry—I don't want the maids knowing that I'm receiving guests. My parents think only Emmett is here."

Lex took off her sunglasses. She stared at Concetta. "So is everything . . . *okay*?"

"I think so," Concetta answered, shrugging. "Today's a big day. We haven't initiated any new members of the club since Jessica. And now we have three all at once."

Park stepped closer to her. "Does this mean you kept our conversation private?" she asked. "You didn't tell any of the other members what we discussed yesterday?"

"Of course not," Concetta said. "Do you think any of

them would've agreed to show up here and have one of our regular Sunday-night sessions if I told them you thought one of us was guilty?"

"So what *did* you tell them?" Lex asked.

Concetta ran a hand through her hair and cleared her throat nervously. "Just that I've been wanting the three of you to be in the club for a while now, and that it was finally time to do it. I told them I approached you last week and talked to you about it."

"And they bought it?"

"I think so. They're all just relieved that I didn't blab to the cops. Apparently they all thought I would've buckled under the pressure. But, ya know, I didn't. And no one's going to argue with me, because *I'm* the one who created this club. Besides, it's not like you'll tell me how you found out about the club anyway. But I have an idea."

"What's your idea?" Park asked cautiously.

Concetta stared at Madison a bit coldly. "I think Damien told you. I know how much he liked you, Madison. How much he loved making you laugh. Maybe he broke our sacred oath."

Madison felt a chill snake along her spine. She didn't say anything.

"Well," Park said, "I guess we should get started."

Concetta led Madison, Park, and Lex to the bathroom in the nearest corridor. "Your costumes are hanging up behind the door, with your names on them. Put them on, then come back out here."

Madison, Park, and Lex did as they were instructed. They stepped into the bathroom together and closed the door behind them.

"This is creepy!" Madison whispered. "I don't know if I can go through with it!"

"Of course you can." Park found the costume with her name on it, then handed Lex and Madison their own.

They changed quickly, not stopping to look at one another.

A minute later, the door opened and Concetta barged in. She was dressed in a brown monk's robe and holding three identical robes in the crook of her right arm. "Put these on over your costumes," she told them.

Lex held her robe in her hands. "Excuse me—is this polyester?"

"I think so," Concetta replied. "Just put it on and let's go. We're wasting time."

When they had each slipped on a robe, Madison, Park, and Lex walked back out into the corridor.

"Now we're ready," Concetta said dramatically, already falling into whatever role she was to play. "Come along now—let us enter the Chamber."

Lex shot an uncertain look at Madison, and Madison's eyes held the same fearful glint. Park fell in step behind Concetta as they hurried down the corridor, into the kitchen, and through the basement door.

The staircase was pitch-black. Concetta lit a candle and led the way down into the Chamber.

Park couldn't see much of it—the soft firelight illuminated only the immediate space they were standing in: a hardwood floor, a beamed ceiling, a chandelier. She could feel drafts of air moving right and left, so she knew the basement had to be very large—at least as large as the first floor of the town house.

Madison and Lex stood beside Park, looking spooked

in their brown monks' robes. They kept exchanging glances—looking around, trying to dissect the darkness. But it was impossible to see beyond the candle. Madison squeezed Lex's hand in a silent gesture of fear. "We're alone down here," she whispered anxiously.

Lex simply blinked, unable to move.

Concetta began the Black Cry Affair initiation ritual by circling Madison, Park, and Lex twice. Her gaze was hard and unsettling, and Park found herself wondering if Concetta was merely in character or expressing her unconscious rage at everything that had happened since Friday night.

"You have entered the Chamber," Concetta said dramatically, loudly. "You have chosen of your own free will to be members of the Black Cry Affair. In doing so, you have told me, mistress of the court, that you wish to relinquish all inhibitions and fears and prejudices. Is this so?"

The question took them all by surprise. They glanced at one another, and then Madison said, "Yes, that is so."

"Good." Concetta stopped circling them. She held the candle up and out and tossed her head back. "I now call upon the court to enter the Chamber!" Her words echoed through the open, unseen space.

One by one, three doors opened on both sides of the basement, the darkness immediately retreating as three figures emerged from the shadows, each holding a candle. They were dressed in the same long monkish robes.

Park recognized Julian Simmons beneath the droopy hood of his robe. She then stared in the other direction and saw Jessica Paderman and Emmett McQueen walking toward the circle.

Madison nudged Park's shoulder—another clear gesture of fear.

Lex, standing stock-still, had no emotion on her face, though she had moved her arms and was now clasping her hands together over her middle.

Concetta, Emmett, Julian, and Jessica each held out their candles. Then Emmett lifted his left arm and held his hand up: in it was a small video camera. He brought the lens to his eye and began recording.

Concetta said, "You stand before your fellow brothers and sisters in the universe of the Black Cry Affair. There is no turning back."

Madison gulped so loudly, the sound actually reverberated through the basement.

The hooded figures began walking around Madison, Park, and Lex, making a continuous circle.

Concetta held out her left hand.

From his side, Julian raised a long sword and held it up and out, its gleaming tip stopping only inches from Lex's face.

The weapon caught Lex by surprise. She jerked her head back, then quickly regained her composure and fixed Julian with a don't-mess-with-me stare.

He moved the sword to the edge of Park's face, then moved it to Madison's.

"You will now take the sacred oath of secrecy," Concetta said. She held out her right hand and pointed a finger at Madison, Park, and Lex. "In this, the Chamber of the Black Cry Affair, there are no limits or inhibitions. There are no fears. Do you solemnly swear and promise to abide by our rules and to keep the practices of the Black Cry Affair secret—*under penalty of death?*"

"Yes," Park answered quickly. "We do."

"The oath of loyalty," Concetta whispered.

It was apparently Jessica's cue to speak up. She held the candle firmly in her hands as she locked eyes with Lex. "Do you promise and swear to honor your fellow brothers and sisters outside of the Black Cry Affair, just as you would inside the Chamber—under penalty of death?"

"We do."

"The oath of transformation," Concetta said quietly.

Emmett's candle shook slightly as he balanced the small camera against his left eye. "Do y'all promise to share with your brothers and sisters in the Black Cry Affair your deepest and most personal experiences of self-transformation and change? Self-transformation is inevitable, and your oath requires you to speak of it while in the Chamber. Under penalty of death."

Park nodded. "We do."

Concetta said, "The oath of inhibition."

Julian moved the sword back and forth, its pointed tip almost grazing Madison's chin, Lex's cheek, and Park's nose. His eyes seemed to hold an almost predatory look. "Do you promise to let go of your fears and insecurities, your shame, your prejudices and judgments, while in the Chamber? Inhibition has no place in role-playing. Do you swear to this oath, under penalty of death?"

Again, Park nodded. "We do." This time, when she spoke the words, her voice held a confidence that hadn't been there a moment or two ago.

Concetta stopped walking.

Emmett lowered the camera from his eye and clicked it off.

And Julian finally dropped the sword.

"Welcome," Jessica whispered. She walked forward and pointed to their hands.

Madison, Park, and Lex held out their palms.

Using a small stamp, Jessica branded them with the Roman coin symbol. Then she stepped back and blew out her candle.

Every candle was blown out after that.

The room plunged into complete darkness.

Park gave Madison's hand a reassuring squeeze and nudged Lex's shoulder with her own.

Lex responded, nudging Park's shoulder twice.

Then an earsplitting scream tore through the air. Someone clapped twice and the Chamber was flooded with instant light.

Madison was the first one to gasp. She couldn't believe her eyes.

The Chamber was literally another world: colored crystals hung from the beamed ceiling, catching the light of the chandelier and creating a radiant prism that stretched across the floor. One of the walls had been painted to look like a medieval gauntlet. Another held several ancient weapons—swords, a crossbow, a Viking dagger, a spiked flail, and a Damascus blade. There was also an entire suit of armor along with a gleaming knight's shield. Across the room, the scenery changed entirely; here, it was more modern, with a grand piano, a long marble table, and an artist's easel. Farther back, almost out of sight, stood a plasma TV and a disco ball.

"Concetta," Madison said. "This is amazing! How did you do this?"

Concetta's face contorted. "I'm not Concetta!" she

yelled sharply. "I am mistress of the court! And now the games shall begin!" She unzipped the long brown robe and dropped it to the floor, revealing a skin-tight red velvet gown that trailed over her feet; bright yellow feathers stuck out at the shoulders. Around her neck were several gold chains, denoting a woman of noble rank.

Jessica let her robe drop as well. Her mane of long, flaming red hair tumbled down to the middle of her back. The sultry, determined expression on her face matched her costume: a black corset that hugged her waist and lifted her breasts, black fishnet stockings, and black heels. She struck a seductive pose. Closing her eyes, she slipped into character and sighed.

Lex nodded to herself. The usually reserved and nerdy Jessica Paderman certainly didn't have any inhibitions here in the Chamber. In fact, Jessica looked like a total tramp—a role Lex would never have imagined her playing.

The shock intensified when Emmett dropped his robe. Gone were the accessories and accoutrements of a flamboyant, self-avowed social queen. His long, lean body was wrapped in the steel armor of a knight, a sword at his side and the trademark helmet cradled in the crook of his right arm. He exuded power and masculinity. There wasn't a trace of the real Emmett anywhere in the room.

"Wow," Madison said under her breath. "Who knew there was a real guy attached to the man-purse?" Then she felt Park elbow her in the ribs and clamped her mouth shut.

Julian let go of his robe. The droopy hood came off first, revealing a blond wig of curly hair. His face was painted exquisitely—bright strokes of blush across his cheeks, long fake eyelashes, red lipstick. The dress wrapping his body was a long and elegant pink-sequined frock. He looked totally female.

Park had to stop herself from reacting. Never in a million years would she have imagined that the macho, lady-loving hip-hop star also moonlighted as a cross-dresser. She was struck by the irony of it and shocked by the reality of it. Julian made a beautiful woman. Once you looked past the thick muscles bulging out of the delicate fabric of the dress, of course.

Madison and Lex were staring at him, eyes wide and lips slightly parted in surprise. The looks on their faces said it all: *Where have our classmates gone? Who the hell are these people?*

Concetta brought them back to the moment. She pointed at them and said, "Remove your robes and enter the game."

Madison was grateful for the order. She had begun to sweat beneath the heavy robe. She thrust it off her shoulders to reveal the costume Concetta had chosen for her, not caring about how ridiculous she looked in the trampy leather dress and garter belt and boots. Her right hand held a whip. She still couldn't figure out if she was supposed to be a prostitute of the long-ago Roman era or a circus lion-tamer. And now, trying not to appear self-conscious, she wondered if she'd be able to role-play either one.

With an irritated sigh, Lex let go of her robe. She rolled her eyes and kept them locked on the ceiling as her short, white, and very cheap-looking toga came into view.

There was nothing to it—just an ugly and flimsy piece of fabric thrown over her head. No sash or belt. Not even a brooch. Even now, away from her magic purse, she fought the urge to accessorize. She looked like she was wearing bedding.

Park was the last of the group to do away with the robe. And she did this slowly, dramatically, slipping out one shoulder at a time and keeping her head held high. She looked stoic as her gladiator costume was unveiled—the maroon tunic and pants, the body armor with its resin casting, the two fur armbands and shin guards. Like a soldier getting ready for battle, she took one step forward and planted her fists on her hips. She was clearly in character.

*Let the game begin.*

Concetta circled the court. Stepping around her fellow role-players, she focused her gaze on Emmett, pointing at him. "*You*, Knight of Enoch!" she shouted angrily. "You come here and demand that I release your slaves after I rescued them from your failed army? Is that what you wish?" She grabbed Madison and Lex by their arms and roughly shoved them to where Jessica was standing.

Madison stumbled.

Lex, nearly crashing face-first into the floor, turned around and shot Concetta a cold stare. "Watch it!" she snapped.

Concetta's mouth fell open. She slapped Lex with the drooping ends of her sleeves. "How *dare* you speak to your master that way? Don't repeat the mistake!" She slapped her a second time with the big sleeves, clear across the face.

Lex flinched at the whack. She looked at Madison, her eyes wide with shock. "That bitch is totally asking for it," she muttered, gesturing her head at Concetta.

"And, excuse me—she just called us *slaves.*" Madison shook her head.

Emmett stepped forward, his body armor rustling. "I *do* demand that you return them!" he screamed. His voice was guttural and raw, all traces of the southern twang gone. "By the order of my king I come to collect them! They are *my* slaves. Not yours!"

"Ha!" Concetta tossed her head back. "These slaves have found service in my court, and I shall keep them!"

"And *I* shall *fight* to keep them!" Park's voice boomed through the Chamber. She took a step toward Emmett and cast him a dirty look. "You swine! Coming into our court and making demands! Did you think you would do it without a battle?" She jerked her head at him.

"You've got to be kidding me," Lex whispered.

Emmett smiled. "Well, well." He lifted his sword with his right hand and let the blade rest in his left. "It looks as though I've met a fellow warrior."

"Indeed," Park replied coldly. "You have."

Suddenly, Jessica ran to Park and fell to her knees. She yanked at the ends of Park's tunic. "Please, don't let the Knight of Enoch take us!" she cried. "He shall enslave us again in the worst way possible!"

"Fear not, my child," Park whispered, patting Jessica's head. "I shall rescue you from the evil of Enoch's kingdom."

Madison nudged Lex. "Where the hell is Park getting this stuff?"

"I don't know," Lex whispered back. "But I don't like it. If she doesn't get out of character soon, I'm going to call the paramedics."

With a feminine flick of his hand, Julian pranced across the floor—a slow, measured sashay. He stood beside Emmett. "These little beggars think they can outrank us, do they?" He chuckled. "They don't know the power we wield! As queen of my kingdom, I alone can squash you!"

Concetta seemed to be weighing Queen Julian's words. She nodded and began circling the court again. This time, she stopped beside Madison and Lex. "And what say the slaves?" she asked, flicking their shoulders.

Lex glanced nervously at Madison, then Park. But Park, falling deeper into the role of a warrior, kept her expression stony. Lex licked her lips and said, "I . . . I say no fighting! It's . . . it's totally violent!"

"Agreed." Madison waved her hand in a poor display of acting. "Let's all play nice."

"Nice?" Concetta shook her head at them. "Perhaps the two of you aren't even worthy of my warrior's courage!"

Madison and Lex winced at the severity of her voice.

"No, wait." With long, even strides, Park walked over to them. She stared at Concetta. "May I speak to the slaves, master?"

Concetta frowned. "I suppose you may."

"Thank you." Focusing her gaze on Lex, Park said, "If you go back to the kingdom of Enoch, you shall be denied everything. No more shelter or food. No more protection. *And no more shopping excursions in the town square.*"

The last comment struck Lex like a bolt of lightning.

Those horrendous words made her forget the game altogether. Denying anyone the freedom to shop was by far the cruelest punishment in any kingdom. "What!" she shrieked. "Don't you dare!" She fell into an instant panic, running her hands through her hair and fidgeting with the ends of the toga. "Okay! Please, *please* rescue us from that awful place! Don't make us go back!" She tugged at Park's arm.

"It's only a game, you idiot," Madison whispered, slapping Lex in the back of the head.

Lex stared at her, whimpering. "No more shopping," she cried. "I can't deal with that—not even in a game."

Park set her gaze on Madison. "And *you*," she said. "If you return to the kingdom of Enoch, you shall be denied everything too! No more makeup for your little excursions. No more perfumed pillows and bed sheets. *And no more champagne.*"

Madison gritted her teeth. "You really are good at this," she muttered, casting Park a cold glance. "*No one* denies me champagne." She took several deep breaths, as if battling with reality and the fantasy. Finally, the threat of not guzzling Dom Perignon on Friday nights or having any to mix with a tall glass of milk won out. She bowed her head and touched the armor shielding Park's chest. "I implore you to fight for us," she said.

Park smiled. She turned around and walked back to her place in the center of the court.

Julian stared her down. "Come!" he screamed in a high-pitched voice. He pointed at the floor. "Kneel before me, as I am queen!"

"I shall *not* kneel before a *bogus* queen!" Park shot back.

Julian gasped.

Concetta laughed out loud.

And Emmett raised his sword. "The battle commences!" he bellowed in the thunderous, manly voice. "No one speaks to my queen that way!"

Park looked at Jessica and motioned at the wall that held the weapons.

Jessica ran to it and lifted a heavy, bejeweled sword from its holder.

Extending both her arms, Park accepted the sword, circling her fingers around the thick cold handle. She drove the point of it against the ground and traced a straight line to Concetta. "My master," Park whispered, her tone grave, "I shall go into battle for you now."

Concetta sniffled, feigning tears. She pulled a white handkerchief out from between her boobs and blew her nose. "Oh, my dear warrior princess," she replied quietly. "I thank you for fighting in my name and honor."

Park bowed her head. Then she turned and faced Emmett. She lifted the sword with one arm and held up her shield with the other.

Emmett assumed the position of battle. With a roar, he charged forward and swung the sword at Park.

Park ducked to avoid the blow and instantly brought her own sword up in defense.

"Oh my God!" Madison said. "Those are, like, real swords. I think he just tried to kill her!"

"I know." Lex nodded, growing pale. "But do you see how heavy they look? I just hope Park doesn't break a nail."

As the battle ensued, the rest of the players began circling Park and Emmett.

Park lifted her sword. She lowered it and swung it and turned it sideways, fighting off Emmett's attempts to win the battle. When his weapon came charging at her from an unexpected angle, she thrust her shield forward, nearly toppling over from the force of his blow.

"Fight, my princess!" Concetta screamed again.

Madison shook her head. Watching the battle unfold, she couldn't help feeling as though she were trapped in a time warp. Park and Emmett really looked like medieval warriors. Concetta looked like a baroque noblewoman. Jessica looked like a turn-of-the-century New Orleans tramp. Lex looked like a typical Roman slave and Julian looked like a high-society socialite with an odd penchant for weight lifting. And *she* looked like a dominatrix from one of those icky adult movie channels. Her mind was being pulled back and forth through the centuries. She didn't like it.

And neither, apparently, did Lex: she kept bouncing up and down, rolling and unrolling the ends of her toga nervously. "Oh!" she screamed as Emmett's sword narrowly missed Park's left shoulder.

The battle raged on for several more minutes. Park was drenched in sweat and Emmett was breathing heavily. They never took their eyes off each other, circling the floor like wolves from rival packs, grunting and sighing.

Then Emmett made a cruel move. Dashing quickly to one side of the room, he grabbed Madison and pulled her to him.

"Here!" Emmett cried. He held the sword up to Madison's throat. "Do you still wish to fight, O warrior princess?"

Park lowered her sword. Her chest rose and fell. Her face registered hatred and shock and a smidgen of fear. "You play by cowardly rules," she said. "Let the slave go."

Emmett inched the sword closer to Madison's neck.

"Hey!" Madison screamed. "Go easy! If you scar my neck I'll have to wear chokers for the rest of my life!"

"Oh!" Concetta sighed, cupping a hand to her mouth. "Don't spill the child's blood!"

"I will," Emmett whispered. "And then my queen and I shall overtake your entire court."

"I don't think so." As the words left Park's lips, she made a lighting-quick move and grabbed Julian by the arm. She yanked him forward with all her might, tripping him with the edge of her boot.

He stumbled to his knees. The wig slipped off his bald head and onto his face. He righted it, then stared up at Park.

Suddenly, Jessica ran across the room and grabbed Lex from behind, holding her in a bear hug. Jessica pulled a dagger from the middle of her corset and pressed it to Lex's neck.

"Ow!" Lex said.

"Let the queen go!" Jessica screamed. "Or I swear I'll rip her throat open!"

Concetta gasped. "A betrayal!" she screeched. She took two steps toward Jessica and cast her a scornful look. "How dare a slave betray her master!"

"Hey there!" Lex waved her arms out. "You're really hurting me. Can you please let go?"

"Let us both go!" Madison yelled, squirming against Emmett.

Julian, trying to shake the wig into place on his head, said, "Kill the warrior princess! She has no right!"

"Let the queen go!" Jessica shouted again. She tightened her hold around Lex's neck and shoulders.

"Bitch, you are *so* going to pay for this," Lex said.

It all came down to Park. Still breathing heavily, she glanced around the court, at Concetta's wide eyes and Madison's pleading face. Her sword was in perfect position against Julian's neck. She could have ended the game by pretending to kill the queen right then and there, but her instincts steered her away from instant bloodshed. She thrust Julian forward, toward Emmett, and then went down on her knees.

"Ha!" Emmett cried triumphantly. "The warrior princess loses!" He let go of Madison, paying her no mind as she flogged him with her whip and scurried away. He lowered his sword to his side and smiled.

Julian pranced around him, pulling rose petals out of a pocket of the dress and sprinkling them into the air.

With a cry of victory, Jessica let go of Lex, spinning her around and shoving her as she did so.

Lex, off balance, twirled and slammed into Concetta.

"I do surrender," Park said solemnly. "My life is now in your hands, O great Knight of Enoch. I pray you spare me more humiliation."

Emmett stood up a little straighter as he stared down at Park. When he opened his mouth to speak, a floating rose petal landed on his tongue and he gagged, trying to spit it out.

"Oh, my great Knight," Jessica cooed, wrapping her arms around Emmett. She rubbed up against him, playing her trampy role for all it was worth.

Emmett kissed her passionately, his lips moving from her mouth to her neck. "I've been waiting to do that for a long time," he said.

Park lifted her sword, letting it rest flat in both her palms. In her mind's eye she pictured a camera rolling, a director watching her from his chair, and her own face on a big screen. She liked the image a lot. She liked it so much, in fact, that she didn't want the game to end. But she knew it had to. And so in final tribute to her first official role, she let out a warrior's cry and knocked Emmett off his feet. She wasn't about to accept defeat so easily. She sprang up as a chorus of startled cries rocked the Chamber.

Emmett stared at her from the floor, a stunned look on his face. He was lying flat on his back.

"Good-bye, O great Knight." Park swung the sword over her head. Looking directly at Julian and Jessica, she said, "No crime ever goes unpunished." Then she brought the sword down and slammed it into the floor an inch from Emmett's neck.

Emmett gurgled and groaned and flopped like a fish out of water for nearly a minute. He forgot to take into account the fact that he had just been beheaded.

Concetta raised her arms up. "The Chamber closes," she said, clapping her hands.

In the instant before the lights went out, Park caught the look on Julian's face—it was the narrow-eyed look of rage and suspicion. Her last, purposeful comment had not been a part of the game, and he had understood that.

Darkness fell. Then came the sounds: costumes brushing against each other and metal clanging, a stampede of footsteps scurrying up the stairs. When complete silence returned, Park clapped her hands.

The lights went on again.

"Oh, thank God!" Madison cried. She and Lex were huddling in a corner, hunched down on their knees.

They were alone in the chamber.

"Where is everyone?" Lex asked.

"Didn't you hear the sounds? They all ran up the stairs." Madison chucked her whip to the floor and ran a hand over her face.

"The Knight is dead, and I have done my duty," Park said stoically. She raised her sword into the air, staring into space.

"What?" Lex blinked and stared. "What the hell did you just say?"

Park lifted her shield from the floor. "The warrior princess reigns over the kingdom."

"Oh. My. *God.*" Lex strangled the ends of her toga as she glanced worriedly at Madison. "Are you seeing this? She's lost her mind. Oh—be careful. She might chop you with the sword!"

In no mood to continue on with the game, Madison charged across the floor, clamped her hands on Park's shoulders, and gave her a hard shake. "Wake up!" she yelled. "You. Are. Not. A. Warrior. Princess!"

Park's head bobbed back and forth, her hair whipping her face. "Oh," she said. "Oh my God. I'm sorry." She stepped back and took a deep breath. "I don't know what just happened. I just . . . couldn't stop acting."

"Well, save it for the movie set, okay? I want to get out of here." Madison was already unbuttoning her costume.

The basement door swung open. "Hey, girls?"

Concetta's voice echoed down the long staircase. "Don't you want to come up and change?"

"Yes," Madison said. "We're coming right now." She charged toward the staircase, Park and Lex following her.

◇   ◇   ◇

Five minutes later, dressed in their own clothes, they met Concetta at the front door.

Still in costume, she stood with her arms at her sides, a pensive look on her face. "I hope you had fun," she said quietly.

"We totally did." Park smiled.

"Did everyone already leave?" Madison asked.

Concetta nodded. "Yes. That's one of our rules. When the game ends, it *ends*. We don't hang around and talk about it." She stared at them intently. "So now do you believe me? Don't you see that we're an innocent club?"

Madison didn't reply. She clutched her purse and stormed out of the town house.

"I'll see you soon," Lex muttered, following Madison.

Noting the confusion on Concetta's face, Park said, "I think they're both just a little out of it. We really did have fun. We'll see you guys soon." And with that, Park walked through the foyer and into the humid evening.

"If either of you thinks I'm ever doing that again, you're nuts," Madison said as they headed for the limo. "That was freaky."

"Lighten up, will you?" Park answered. "It wasn't that bad."

"That's because you got to act." Lex knocked on the

driver's side of the limo and waved at Donnie. "For me and Madison, it was total torture."

"I mean, *really*," Madison said. "I'll need another massage just to loosen the muscles in my neck. The level of dark in that room was almost poisonous."

"So *that's* the big secret?" Lex shrugged. "The Black Cry Affair really is a role-playing club and not a terrorist ring?"

Park folded her arms over her chest. "Did either one of you see the look on Julian's face when I said that no crime goes unpunished? He's freaking out because he knows we know something."

"And I think we know enough," Lex said. "It's time to tell Mother Margaret what's going on. And it's time to find out what the hell Sister Brittany is up to. The last thing we need is Julian trying to poison us."

The locks to the back door popped up, and Park and Lex climbed into the limo.

But Madison didn't move. She was staring across the street, where Jessica Paderman was waiting for the cross-walk signal to change.

"Hey, you coming in?" Park called out.

Madison studied Jessica's proper plain jeans and white dress shirt. But it was her tote bag that made Madison's heart skip a beat.

"Madison? What's wrong?"

Forgetting the limo, Madison walked calmly across the street. Her eyes locked on the tote bag, and on the name printed in block letters across the front: PADERMAN PHARMACEUTICALS WORLDWIDE.

And in that moment, everything clicked into place.

"Hey, Jessica?"

Jessica Paderman spun around. "Oh, hi," she said, a little too pensively.

There was no time for polite introductions, so Madison dropped the bomb without pretense. "Did Damien Kittle know you were supplying Julian Simmons with steroids?" she asked, her rage boiling over. "Did he know that you have direct access to nitroglycerin and a whole lot of other dangerous shit?"

# 18

# Little Black Book

Jessica Paderman was trembling. Sitting in the back of the limo, clutching the tote bag to her chest, she stared at Madison, Park, and Lex and kept shaking her head. "You've got it all wrong," she said. "I didn't kill Damien." Tears poured over her face. A little line of spittle streamed down the side of her chin. "You have to believe me."

"No, we don't." Madison's voice was sharp. She pointed to the tote bag. "I can't believe it took me—us—this long to make the connection. But now it all makes sense. You were Julian's dealer. That's where he got the steroids. That's why he was suspended."

"No one's supposed to know about that!" Jessica yelled.

"Well, *we* know about it, and so will the police soon enough." Lex shook her head. "So Damien found out about it and threatened to expose you, and you killed him. Case closed."

"No!" Jessica wailed. "That's not it! Stop accusing me! I don't do bad things! I'm not that kind of girl!"

Madison sniffed.

Park, jumping into her interrogation mode, leaned forward and put a hand on Jessica's arm. "Let's start at the beginning, honey," she said. "Why did you traffic steroids for Julian?"

"Oh, God. You make it sound so *illegal.* Like I'm some drug lord." Jessica reached into the tote bag and pulled out a tissue. She held it to her nose. "Julian and I have always been friends. A lot of people don't know this, but his father and my father went to college together, so Julian and I have kind of known each other since we were little kids. But anyway . . . it was no big deal. Back in January, Julian was getting ready to shoot a new video for his upcoming album, and he was upset by the way he looked. He said he wasn't pumped up enough. He wanted to look better— fitter, I guess. One day he asked me if I'd be able to get my hands on some steroids and I told him the truth—that I could. That it would be easy for me."

"How is it easy for you?" Park asked.

"Paderman Pharmaceuticals has a laboratory in New Jersey," Jessica replied, sniffling. "I've been working there part-time on the weekends and during the summer for almost two years now. It's great for college applications, and I want to be a doctor anyway. I know where all the drugs are."

"So you smuggled steroids out for Julian and gave

them to him." Park shrugged, trying to make it sound casual. "But you did it more than once, right?"

A pause. Then Jessica looked down. "Yes."

"Why?"

"Because Julian kept telling me he needed them. We fought about it once, and he sort of threatened me. He told me that if I didn't get him some more, he'd tell my dad about it." She looked up. "I didn't want that to happen. Do you know how crazy things have been for me lately? With my parents getting divorced and all?"

Park nodded. "I know. You must've freaked out when Julian told you he got caught."

"I did. But then it all went away—his parents made a nice donation to St. Cecilia's and Julian didn't actually get suspended."

"Are steroids the only drugs Julian takes?" Lex demanded.

Jessica bit down on her lip. "I don't think so. I think he smokes pot and does Ecstasy now and then."

"So he has another dealer for those drugs?" Lex asked.

Jessica nodded. "But I don't know anything about that. I swear. I've tried to tell Julian to stop, but he won't listen."

"So when was the last time you got him steroids?" Lex asked.

"A few weeks ago," Jessica said. "I know it was stupid, but like I said—it was no big deal."

"Did Damien know about this?" Madison asked gently.

Jessica looked out the window, her eyes glassing up again. "He knew. He found out. But I swear—he wasn't angry about it. This has nothing to do with his murder. I didn't kill him."

"Did you ever smuggle out anything else for Julian?"

"What do you mean? Like what?"

"Like nitroglycerin and sodium carbonate and diatomaceous earth," Park said.

Jessica's eyes flew wide open. "Are you crazy?" she shouted. "That's for making dynamite! I don't know how it ended up in Concetta's house—unless she's plotting to blow us all up. That's all I kept thinking about today—that we were in the Chamber with a murderer who likes explosives. I was a wreck."

"We know it's used for making dynamite," Lex whispered. "And we think maybe Damien knew too. Did you supply Julian with those chemicals?"

"Never! Of course not! Why would I carry around nitroglycerin? Why would *anyone*? You'd kill yourself."

*Spoken like an excellent chemistry student,* Park thought. She said, "But Damien wanted out of the club, right?"

"Yes."

"Why?"

"I don't know! He didn't tell me. He just started to get all weird in the last few weeks." Jessica huffed and closed her eyes. There was a steady stream of silence. Then she looked at Madison, Park, and Lex and fixed them with an angry stare. "And *anyway,* why the hell are you accusing *me* of killing Damien? Concetta's the one who did it! Everyone knows that!"

"Not really." Park kept her voice even and calm. "Jessica, two strands of long red hair were found in the cage where Damien was killed. Any idea how they got there?"

Jessica didn't answer. She looked away.

"Now, DNA tests will prove whether or not those hairs are yours," Madison said. "But we're going to have to call the police and tell them not to go crazy looking for the redhead. You were probably the only redhead at Cleopatra who knew Damien."

Jessica took a long, loud breath. Trying to move quickly, she threw her left arm against the door and reached for the handle.

Lex lurched forward and pulled the door back. "Donnie!" she called out.

"I gotcha," Donnie answered from the front seat.

The automatic locks slammed into place.

"You can't hold me hostage in here!" Jessica screeched. "I'm not a prisoner! Let me out!"

"Puh-lease." Madison held up a hand. "We're probably doing you a favor by holding you in here. The cops will be knocking on your door any minute."

"That's not true," Jessica shot back. "Concetta didn't tell them anything about the club. Oh, I *knew* letting you guys in was a bad idea!"

"Sorry to have disappointed you," Park said. "But you still haven't answered my question. How did your hair get into the cage?"

"It's called *trace evidence.*" Lex smiled smugly. Her tone held a hint of superiority.

Jessica didn't seem to care about that. The anger left her face and she stared out the window again, not bothering to wipe away the tears that dripped down to her chin. "I loved Damien," she said quietly. "And I think maybe he was starting to love me too."

Park felt Madison and Lex staring at her. "So, you and Damien were dating?"

"I don't know if you'd call it that," Jessica replied. "We kissed a few times. We went out for coffee and lunch, but that was it." She shifted in the seat. "The funny thing was that I never knew Damien had such a serious side to his personality. That was what he never showed people. But he showed it to me. We talked a lot. We went to the Museum of Natural History once. That was where we first kissed. But that was it."

"No kidding." Lex sounded amazed. "You and Damien?"

"He was only a *quarter* gay!" Jessica shot back defensively. "And when you do the math—"

"—it only comes out to about three times a year," Madison said, nodding her head in agreement. "No big deal."

"Never mind that. What happened? Why didn't your relationship . . . progress?" Park asked.

Jessica shook her head. "I don't know. It just . . . didn't. Damien started to act all weird. He said I was too involved with the club because I didn't want Concetta or Emmett or Julian to know about us. I didn't want anyone to know. I mean, me with a clownish guy like Damien? And I didn't want to risk losing my place in the club. Damien was a different story. I mean, he liked being a member and all, but he didn't take it as seriously as the rest of us. If Damien wanted to act a certain way or wear certain clothing or do something crazy, he just *did* it. Emmett and Julian and Concetta and I . . . I guess we're just not as free and open with ourselves. That's why we're so protective about the club. It's our own little world."

"But Damien *did* find out that you were supplying Julian with steroids," Madison stated flatly.

"Yes. Once, Damien saw them in Julian's gym bag when we were in the Chamber," Jessica explained. "When Damien told me about it, I confessed. He was upset with me and all, but I really don't think he gave it much thought after that. He didn't care all that much."

"What about Sister Brittany?" Lex asked quickly. "Does she know anything about Julian's problems? Do you talk to her at all?"

"Sister Brittany?" Jessica made a sour face. "*Please.* I can't stand that woman. She's always trying to talk to me, trying to find things out. Julian doesn't like her either. Why would anyone?"

"Friday night, Jessica," Park said. "Cleopatra. The cage."

Jessica took another deep breath. "Okay. Yes—those were my hairs. But I didn't kill Damien. I was dancing on the third level, going a little crazy, and I don't know what made me look up. But I did—it was just a glance, and in between the flashes from the strobes, I saw Damien lying in the cage. Or—I mean, I saw his hand on the floor. So I ran up the steps and into the cage and then . . ." She shook her head, trying to blot out the image filling her mind. "I saw him lying there, and all the blood, the shoe . . ."

"So why didn't you scream for help? Why didn't you *say* something?" Madison asked, her tone incredulous.

"Because when I realized that Damien was dead, I panicked. I saw everything flash in front of me—the club, the two of us together, the steroids—and I didn't know what to do." She sobbed and blew her nose. "And . . . I was standing over him and the lights were spinning and the music was so loud and then I . . . saw his little black book."

Madison, Park, and Lex leaned forward in unison. "What little black book?" Lex asked.

"Damien always had it on him," Jessica explained. "He kept phone numbers and appointments and everything in it. When he fell, it must've fallen out of his jacket, because it was lying just beside his arm. And in that moment—it was so crazy—I didn't want anyone seeing the little black book . . . and my name in it . . . and the few dates he and I went on. I thought it would make me a suspect or get me into trouble and I pictured myself having to tell the cops about the club, and being so embarrassed . . . and I . . . I bent down and picked it up. And I got blood on my fingers and under my nails!"

"The little black book?" Park's voice was hopeful. "You picked it up?"

Jessica nodded, her bottom lip trembling. "And as I was standing up, the cage started to move—it started to, like, shake because I think it was starting to descend and I—I jumped out of it, and a few strands of my hair got snagged on one of the bars—but I just kept moving. Down the catwalk and down the stairs. Two seconds later, the Requiem started playing and the cage was being lowered."

"Okay. Wait." Madison held up both her hands. "So you never saw Concetta run out of the cage?"

"No."

"And you didn't see anyone coming down the stairs as you were running up the stairs?"

"No."

"Were you dancing with Julian?" Park asked.

"No. I was dancing alone. I *wanted* to dance alone. I never felt confident enough to do anything like that, but ever since the club . . . I've been feeling better about myself. Freer. I was dancing and listening to the music and I didn't care about anything. Until I looked up and saw Damien."

Lex stretched her arm up over her head and directed one of the air-conditioning vents at Jessica. "So, um . . . where's Damien's little black book?"

Jessica reached back into the tote bag, shuffled stuff around, and then pulled out the item in question.

It was, in fact, a little black leather-bound book.

"I was going to throw it away, but I just couldn't," Jessica sobbed. She opened the book and flipped to one of the pages. She held it out to them. "Look. It broke my heart when I saw this."

Park clasped the book in her right hand. The page Jessica had pointed to was dated May 29, and there, in the six o'clock time slot, was Jessica's name, followed by a series of small hearts Damien had doodled beside it.

"Oh, how *sweet,*" Lex whispered.

"Very sweet." Madison reached for the box of tissues on top of the bar. She fluffed one out and dabbed it under her eyes.

"He drew hearts everywhere he wrote my name," Jessica said. "So I know he was starting to like me. And he—he was the only boy who's ever liked me." She glanced down. "I didn't kill him. I had no motive. And even if Damien *had* left the club and started talking about how crazy I am, I wouldn't have resorted to murder. I'm not that stupid and heartless. I would've just sucked up the criticism and dealt with it."

It was another open highway, and Park jumped right

into it. "How about Julian?" she asked. "Do you think Julian would've just . . . sucked it up and dealt with it?"

"Are you kidding?" Jessica's voice rose as she wrapped her finger inside a tissue and shoved it up her nose. "That's Julian's worst fear—being exposed. A macho hip-hop star who likes to cross-dress? Who has a submissive side? Julian would've . . ." Jessica let her words hang in the air.

"Julian would've what?" Lex asked.

"Well . . ." Jessica sniffled. "I was going to say that Julian would've killed someone before letting that bit of news leak out. But, you know, I don't really *mean* that."

"You told us before that Damien had been acting weird," Madison said. "In the past few weeks, had he mentioned anything about Julian?"

"Just that Julian has a tendency to be a bully," Jessica replied. "Damien made it known that he was thinking of dropping out of the club, and it was Julian who got the most scared by that."

"Maybe even scared enough to kill him," Park said.

Jessica simply stared at her. "I don't understand what you're talking about. Even if I believed Julian was capable of killing someone in order to keep his little private side private, it wouldn't change the fact that Concetta was in that cage with Damien. That her shoe is the murder weapon. Hello?"

"You're a really good chemistry student, Jessica," Madison said. "Can you answer me one question? What do you know about *abrin*?"

"Abrin!" Jessica blinked, stunned by the question. "Abrin is highly toxic. It's a poison. If you ingest or even inhale enough of it, you die."

"What else?"

Jessica shrugged. "It's derived from a plant called jequirity. Sometimes it's called crab's eye, or rosary pea, or Indian licorice. The plant is pretty ugly. It looks kind of like a fern, but inside the leaves are small seeds—red seeds that have a black spot in the middle."

"And the plant is poisonous?" Lex asked.

Jessica shook her head. "Not the plant. The seeds. You have to grind the seeds down to a powder. But the shells are hard. The plant is indigenous to tropical areas. Sometimes the seeds are used to make jewelry—like necklaces and bracelets. It's not harmful unless the seed is ground down to a powder."

"So someone would have to sprinkle some of that powder into a drink or food in order to kill someone." Park scratched her head. "Or a victim would have to inhale the powder."

"Right."

"And what happens once a person ingests it?"

"Oh, a whole lot happens." Jessica blew her nose again. "There's no antidote for abrin poisoning. A person who ingests it would break out in a rash, have difficulty breathing, all sorts of things. But mainly, they'd just die. Abrin gets all caught up in the cells, and prevents them from absorbing protein."

"So death would be pretty immediate," Lex said.

"No, it wouldn't," Jessica answered. "It usually takes at least eight hours for a person who's ingested abrin to feel its effects."

"No way!" Madison blurted out. "Are you serious?"

"Yes. If a person's ingested or inhaled a large amount,

eight hours will probably do the job. But—why all these questions? Do you . . . does this have anything to do with Damien's death?"

Lex looked at Park. Park looked at Madison.

Madison looked at Jessica. "Let's just say that maybe it does. Is abrin hard to come by?"

Jessica shrugged. "Yes and no. If you're vacationing on a tropical island and you buy one of those pretty necklaces or bracelets made from the jequirity plant, you could easily wear it under your clothes and pass through customs. And once you have a single seed, you can always grow more."

Park held up Damien Kittle's little black book. "Can I keep this, just for tonight? I promise I won't lose it."

"No!" Jessica cried. "You can't! If someone sees it—"

"No one's going to see it except us," Lex cut in. "We promise."

Jessica clutched the tote bag. "Does this mean you believe me? You know I didn't kill Damien?"

"Sure," Park said, sounding a little too offhanded.

"But you think Julian killed Damien, and not Concetta."

Madison said, "It's not important what we think right now. What's important is that we find answers to the questions we have. Don't forget, Jessica—Cleopatra belongs to us. We do have a right to know exactly what went on in that club."

"Yeah," Jessica answered, sniffling again. "I hear that."

"Good." Park smiled and held up the little black book. "So I can keep it for tonight?"

"On one condition," Jessica said. "That you guys be

with me when I explain my side of the story to the cops. Deal?"

"Deal." Park nodded. "We'll see you at graduation tomorrow, right?"

"Yeah." Jessica started moving out of the seat, her hand on the door handle.

"I'm sorry if I sounded a little rough before," Madison said. "I was just upset."

Jessica looked down and nodded.

"Donnie?" Lex called out.

"I hear ya," he called back.

The locks sprang up.

Jessica shoved the door open and climbed out onto the sidewalk without saying good-bye.

Pulling the door closed, Madison dropped the bright, apologetic look from her face. "So is Jessica going to run and call Julian now?"

"Wouldn't surprise me if she does," Park said, flipping through the little black book. "But unless the cops find Julian's clandestine laboratory where he's growing a jequirity plant and engineering dynamite, they'll have a hard time charging him with anything."

"Maybe he has the laboratory in his house," Lex suggested as the limo started moving. "I mean, would we have ever known what goes on in Concetta's house if we hadn't seen it ourselves today?"

"I don't buy it." Park scanned a page of the black book. "Julian might be totally nuts, but I don't think he'd risk blowing up his house and potentially killing his own family in the process. If he has a clandestine lab, it has to be somewhere else, somewhere out of the way."

"What really gets me is the dynamite," Lex said. "I mean, we know why the poison was used. But the dynamite?"

"Well, *duh.*" Madison rolled her eyes. "Because he wants to blow something up."

"But what would he gain from blowing up the school?" Lex screamed. "I just don't get it! And what I saw yesterday—did Julian buy drugs or chemicals at that construction site?" She banged the palm of her hand against her forehead.

"Look at this," Park said, holding the little black book open. "The last entry in this book was made on Friday. Damien wrote down an address—one-nineteen East Ninety-first Street. I wonder what that means."

"It's probably one of his parents' apartments," Lex told her. "They have three here in the city."

"Do they?"

Lex nodded. "One is right by the United Nations, some diplomat thing. The other two are here on the Upper East Side."

Madison cleared her throat. "Did you all hear what Jessica said about the poison? Eight or nine hours for it to take effect. We deduced last night that Damien died shortly after midnight, which means he would have had to ingest the poison at around three o'clock Friday afternoon."

Park and Lex looked up.

"Shit," Park said. "I hadn't even thought of that."

"Three o'clock was around the time I saw Damien in the student lounge," Madison continued. "Right before Lex and I met up to see Mother Margaret."

"Where was Damien right before he came to the student lounge?" Park asked.

"The principal's office." Madison grabbed another tissue from the bar. "Remember? Mother Margaret said he'd gone in to make an appointment to speak with her. That's how he overheard her telling Mary Grace that Lex and I were expected."

"Funny thing," Park said. "Friday afternoon, I ran into Julian as I was leaving the set of Jeremy's movie."

"In the West Village?"

Park nodded. "It was around four. He told me he'd taken the day off to go shopping."

"Not the whole day," Lex said. "I saw him at around one-thirty, having lunch in the student bistro."

"So he lied," Madison snapped. "Great. He lied *and* he killed Damien. A lovely afternoon we're having."

Lex shivered. "I totally need some moisturizer." She dipped into the magic purse, fishing for her heavy-duty Bliss hand cream. A minute later she gasped. "Oh. My. *God.*"

"What is it?" Park looked at her.

Slowly, her lips parting in a grimace, Lex lifted her hand out of the purse. Clutched in her fingers was a wilted stem with a green, fernlike leaf. "Friday night," she whispered. "The ugly flowers that weren't supposed to be on the tables upstairs? Remember, you made me put them in my purse?"

With a flash of recognition, Madison took the stem from Lex's hand. "Could it be?"

Park reached out and tore open one of the leaves. Three small seeds tumbled into her palm.

Red round seeds. Each with a little black spot in the middle.

It was the final piece of the puzzle. And it made Park break out in a sweat.

"Oh my God," she whispered. "That's *it*. How could I have been so stupid?

"What is it?" Madison asked.

Park closed her eyes, then opened them and shook her head. "On Friday afternoon, when I saw Julian on West Houston Street, he was carrying a bag—I saw the hem of the dress he wore today in the club, but I *also* saw leaves. I thought it was just a bouquet of some sort. But it wasn't. It was *these*." She held out her hand. "He had a jequirity plant in his bag. *He had the poison*."

*19*

# Graduating to Terror

They hatched a plan.

It wasn't a big plan, or even a very detailed one. But through the long hours of the night, Madison, Park, and Lex put together a concise chronology of the crime. They worked diligently, quietly, professionally, as if they were drafting a business proposal or a large-scale term paper. Sleep, as Park pointed out, was useless. A generous amount of concealer would hide the dark circles rimming their eyes. So it was after dawn on Monday morning when they finally showered and changed into their best Triple Threat daywear pieces and readied themselves for the task at hand.

And the task was both simple and complex: to catch a killer without ruining the St. Cecilia's Prep commencement ceremony.

At precisely 8:00 a.m., Madison, Park, and Lex walked out of their building and into their waiting limousine. There were no stray reporters milling around, and the weather was mild and sunny. Donnie had the air conditioner turned up high. Three cups of hot espresso were waiting for them on the bar.

As she stirred sugar into hers, Madison reached into her purse and pulled out her notes. "Okay," she said, "let's do a quick review before we take him down."

Park sipped her espresso and then set it back down on the bar.

Lex downed hers in a single gulp. "Go."

"On the afternoon of March twelfth, Julian Simmons is brought up to the principal's office because steroids are found in his gym bag," Madison began. "He refuses to name his dealer. Damien probably overheard that little fiasco in the locker room when it happened. Mother Margaret suspends Julian and writes out a report of that suspension."

"And files it in her cabinets," Park said.

"Right." Madison checked off that point on her notepad. "A day or two later, Julian's parents make a donation to the school and Julian's suspension is lifted—"

"Total hush money," Lex cut in.

"Total," Madison replied. "Fast-forward to the next weekend, the weekend of March eighteenth. Julian breaks into the school and steals private documents from the cabinets in the office—obviously the suspension report

Mother Margaret had filed, and some other important stuff that makes it look like he wasn't only interested in the report detailing his steroid use. He leaves traces of dangerous chemicals on the floor, along with glitter on the file cabinet."

"But we still don't know exactly why he's experimenting with dynamite," Lex said brightly. "Although blowing up the school is a definite possibility."

Park nodded. "Fast-forward to sometime in the last two weeks. Damien Kittle begins threatening to leave the Black Cry Affair. This causes total distress among the other members, who don't want their secret role-playing lives exposed. Especially Julian, because a hip-hop star who moonlights as a cross-dresser is absolutely *not* making it to the Grammys."

"Or even the MTV Music Awards," Lex threw in.

"You don't think MTV would love a cross-dressing hip-hop star?" Madison asked thoughtfully.

Lex thought about it for a moment. Then she shrugged. "Yeah, you're right. He would've made it to the MTV Awards."

"I agree," Park said, then snapped back to business. "Okay—there is a span of tense days in the Black Cry Affair. Everyone's worried that Damien's going to push the button and talk about things. Tension, tension. And Julian begins thinking about how he can silence Damien."

"Julian can't just kill him in cold blood." Lex picked up the conversation. "So he weighs his options and decides that poisoning Damien is the best way possible. And he has the means to do it—he's an excellent chemistry student, and he's probably been experimenting with the idea of abrin for a long time. He has a plant or two of jequirity in his clandestine lab that he probably brought back from one of his holidays in the Caribbean."

"He figures the best place to have Damien die would be at the opening of Cleopatra," Madison said. "Spinning lights, tons of people—and Julian's there, so he has a lot of alibis."

"Fast-forward to sometime on Thursday night," Lex said. "Julian grinds the jequirity seeds into a powder. He knows that in order for Damien to die sometime Friday night, he has to feed Damien the poison on Friday afternoon."

"Fast-forward to Friday afternoon." Park reached for her cup of espresso again. "At around two o'clock, probably in the student bistro or maybe somewhere else in the school, Julian dumps the mixture into whatever Damien's drinking. Then Julian cuts out of school and heads to the Village for some shopping. I run into him by chance—and I spot a dress *and* another jequirity plant in his bag."

"A fatal error," Lex whispered. "But looking at it from the point of view of criminal psychology, carrying that plant even though he's just used the poison to commit murder gives him a sense of power and completion. It's his way of silently telling the world that he's hatched what he thinks is the perfect crime."

"And countless killers in history have done the same thing." Park downed the last drops of espresso. "It's a classic form of narcissism. A way to stroke your own ego. And now that he's actually done it, he's probably going to make some more of the poison to kill off a few other people in the near future."

Madison checked off several more points on her notepad. "At around three o'clock, I see Damien in the student lounge. He walks me upstairs, where I meet Lex and Coco."

"Fast-forward to Friday night," Park said. "Julian gets to Cleopatra early and quickly gets rid of the flowers Madison ordered, and drops a few jequirity stems into vases on the tables. He figures that when the cops come and do a sweep of the place, they'll find the plants and eventually connect them to the autopsy's findings—death by poisoning. But as far as the police are concerned, *anyone* could be a suspect, any one of hundreds of guests. It would be almost impossible for them to track Julian to the plants. Except, of course, for the fact that I've spotted him with one."

"Fast-forward a little more," Madison said. "To around twelve-fifteen Friday night."

"Julian's dancing somewhere on the fourth level of Cleopatra," Park said. "He knows Damien and Concetta are in the cage together, and he wants to keep an eye on Damien. He wants to see him collapse. And he *does* see Damien collapse, and Concetta run down the stairs, limping, one of her feet bare."

"And then Julian climbs the stairs, steps into the cage, and sees the stiletto," Lex said gravely. "And it comes to him in a flash—a brilliant little surge of criminal inspiration. He figures that if he hits Damien in the head, the crime will look simple. An open-and-shut case. Blunt impact trauma. He won't even have to worry about the poison being exposed. Damien's already dead on the floor of the cage, and it only takes Julian a few seconds to pick up the stiletto and deliver a steroid-powered blow. *Wham.* And blood starts pooling everywhere."

Madison nodded, staring down at her notes. "And then Julian runs back down the stairs in the nick of time. Maybe ten seconds later, Jessica happens to look up. She sees Damien lying on the floor of the cage and runs in, and strands of her hair, unfortunately, are left at the crime scene."

"It was a really smart move on Julian's part," Park said. "I mean, when you think about it. Delivering that blow to Damien's head with Concetta's stiletto turned his whole crime into something else. He probably figured the cause of death would be obvious, and it was—initially. Everyone points a finger at Concetta."

"But then at some point in the middle of all this, Julian would have had to jump into the DJ booth and knock the two DJs out and pop in the Requiem, which he'd planned on doing anyway," Madison reminded them. "It certainly wasn't on the original play list. Anyway, I guess he'll tell us once we confront him. They always do."

"Which, by the way, we're going to do very casually." Park pointed at Madison and Lex. "Commencement is going on, the prime minister is at the school, and the school doesn't need any more bad publicity. So we're just going to find Julian, take him out into the hall, try to get him to surrender peacefully. There'll be cops everywhere, so we really don't have to worry."

Lex shot a glance at Madison. "What if he doesn't surrender peacefully? I mean, what if he goes ballistic and starts to attack us? How do we keep our cool? How do we not create any more scenes?"

"If he starts attacking us," Park said simply, "we just start screaming. Screw the damn plan." She sighed and stared out the window. She blinked several times. "Donnie? Am I seeing things, or are you going the wrong way?"

"Major detour," he called back from the front seat. "A bunch of streets are closed. I had to go to First and drive all the way back up. Now we'll start heading south again. Sorry."

"It's not your fault." Park leaned back in the seat, but she didn't close her eyes. She was exhausted and on edge. She kept her gaze trained on the street, on the rows of buildings and restaurants and stores.

Horns blared everywhere as the traffic came to a halt.

"Oh, man," Lex said, irritated. "It's freakin' gridlock! We're going to be so late."

Madison sighed. "It'll move soon."

Park continued scanning the street. She wasn't thinking about anything in particular when her eyes stopped on one of the building addresses.

*119 East Ninety-first Street.*

She sat up. Why did the address ring a bell? She stared at the building, half hoping the limo would move. But it didn't. The cacophony of traffic continued.

And then it hit her.

*Damien's little black book.*

Her lips parting, she plunged an arm into her purse and pulled out the little black book. That was it. She had seen the address—119 East Ninety-first Street—last night while flipping through the book. In fact, the address had been Damien's last entry. She flipped to the page and found it.

296

There. Right there.

"Donnie, pull over," Park said.

"Why?" Madison asked.

Park held up the little black book. She pointed to the squat, ugly building directly beyond the windows of the limo. "That's the address Damien wrote down. The one Lex thought was one of his parents' apartments."

"*That* ugly thing?" Lex leaned over and stared out the window. "That's impossible. English royalty wouldn't live in a dump like that."

"It *is* unattractive," Madison said. "But that's probably because it's a rent-controlled building."

Four stories high, the front steps and siding all riddled with cracks, the apartment building looked as though it hadn't undergone maintenance in a hundred years.

Donnie pulled the limo into a wide spot directly in front of a fire hydrant.

Park popped open the door.

"Wait." Madison grabbed her arm. "Where are you going?"

"I've got a hunch," Park said. "This may explain everything. Both of you, come on."

Lex sighed, annoyed. "Donnie, if we're not back in ten minutes, please come and get us."

"Okay."

They dashed up the front steps of the building. The entrance was locked. Park looked at the apartment listings; there were five in all, and only one of the slots, apartment 2B, was missing a surname. She jammed her fingers against all the bells.

"What are you *doing*?" Madison asked.

Park turned to face her. "Let's just hope someone's expecting company so that we can get inside. I have a feeling—"

The door buzzed.

"Oh!" Park threw herself against it and stepped into the dingy hallway.

"Ewww, it stinks in here," Lex said.

"And practically none of the lights work." Madison was looking at the mold-infested ceiling. "I guess it shouldn't surprise me that there isn't a doorman."

The hallway led directly to a staircase on the left; on the right was an apartment door with a welcome mat in front. Remembering the empty name slot, Park raced up the stairs to the second floor. Apartment 2B was just off the landing. She paused when she got to the door.

"Oh God," Lex said nervously. "I think I figured it out too."

"Well, it would be nice if someone explained it to me." Madison slammed her purse against the staircase railing.

Park held her breath and banged on the door. She put her finger to her lips, instructing Madison and Lex to stay quiet.

A minute passed in silence.

Park laced her fingers around the knob; it didn't budge. She gestured her head at Lex. "Open the magic purse. I need a screwdriver. And something heavy."

"I don't know if I have that," Lex said. She started shuffling through the purse, handing Madison her makeup bag, her sunglasses case, her two emergency silk scarves, and a handful of pens. "Okay. Here's something heavy."

Park smiled as Lex handed her a big steel paperweight

with the Hamilton Holdings, Inc., insignia emblazoned on the front. The damn thing had to weigh four pounds, and it was solid.

"My *God*," Madison gasped. "You have more shit in that purse than a sewer! First thing tonight, you're going to clean it out. You're going to totally mess up your back."

Lex was still straining to sift her way down to the bottom of the purse. When she did, she yanked out her hand and revealed a small pair of pliers.

Park stepped back and leveled the paperweight in her right hand. Then she slammed it against the little circular space directly above the knob.

The door shook.

She repeated the process several more times until a chunk of the old wood came splintering off.

"Breaking and entering twice in one weekend is *not* smart," Madison snapped. "We're going to get busted."

Park ignored those words. A sheen of sweat had developed along her neck and she was almost out of breath. She jammed the paperweight against the space of the doorknob one last time, then jumped back when it gave way.

She stood with her arms outstretched in a defensive position. But in this case, she was defending Madison and Lex from a potential blast. None came. Everything was silent around them.

Handing the paperweight back to Lex, she nudged the door open with her toe.

A narrow foyer came into view.

Park inched her way inside, moving with her back to the wall. "Julian?" she called out, knowing she wouldn't get a reply.

Madison and Lex tiptoed inside the apartment.

Just beyond the foyer was a big square room, a studio with three small windows and dingy patches of light. There was a tattered couch, two chairs, and a long large desk against the far wall. The air smelled sulfurous and musty.

Park froze when she spotted the dozens of test tubes and chemical tray holders, the books on explosives, the portable burners, and two jequirity plants. There was a spatter of something powdery on the floor. She said, "Nobody move."

Lex froze beside her.

Madison, still staring around the apartment, was shaking her head. "So this is it," she whispered. "This is the clandestine lab where Julian operates."

"And there . . ." Park gulped and pointed. "Right there on the table is what looks like a completed stick of dynamite."

"*What?*" Madison cupped a hand to her mouth. The fear in her eyes was palpable.

"Uh, Park?" Lex spoke quietly. "Didn't you say that nitroglycerin is shock sensitive?"

"Yes, you have to be very careful when transporting it."

"Or what?" Madison asked.

"Or it'll just blow up. The slightest movement could set it off."

"Well, for God's sake, what are we supposed to do? Just stand here until the police arrive?" Madison snapped. She had backed herself up against the wall closest to the sealed window; leaning into it, she turned sideways, cowering, lifting her arms up over her head.

Park nodded. She took a deep breath, then took a step

toward the desk. She felt like she was standing in the laboratory where Frankenstein's monster had been fused together, or in one of the classrooms at Hogwarts. But this was no fantasy. She stared down at the small open cardboard boxes and the pieces of paper strewn across the floor, trying to imagine the extent of danger that this small, nondescript studio apartment posed.

"Look at the corner of the desk," Lex said. "It's pieces of tinfoil wrapped around a fuse."

Park tried to control the trembling in her arms and legs. "Don't go near that," she warned. She patted the drops of sweat from her forehead. She was afraid to move, afraid to even breathe.

"Park?" Lex whispered.

"I'm okay." Park looked at Madison, still backed against the wall, and blinked. And blinked again. And again. As if trying to make sense of what she was seeing. For a moment, the fearful expression on her face disappeared and was replaced by one of astonishment. "Madison," she said quietly, "you're . . . glittering."

"What?" Madison pressed herself deeper against the wall. Then she looked down at her clothes and gasped. The bottom of her shirt was glittering. The tips of her shoes were glittering. And there, in the ends of her hair, was a sparkle that caught the slats of light burning in through the shaded window.

Flecks of glitter, as bright as diamonds. Twinkling like stars on a moonless night.

"Holy shit," Lex said.

Gasping a second time, Madison stepped away from the wall and ran her hands down the side of her shirt. "It's all over me," she said. "Even on my shoulders. What the hell is it? I didn't touch anything."

Moving slowly and carefully, Park went to Madison's side and inspected the back of her blouse. A rainbow of glitter arced over the delicate fabric. Park turned and stared at the bare wall: it was a yellowish shade, the paint peeling and crumbling, tiny chips falling to the floor. She touched her hand to cold plaster, then inspected her palm.

It was glittering.

"It's the paint," she said. "These walls have glitter paint on them. Look." She held up her hand. "It's probably all over the place because the walls are so old. You so much as brush up against them and the glitter falls out with the paint chips."

A long line of light suddenly cut through the shadowy space. Lex had pulled down on one of the shades, and now she was inching it up over the window slowly, not wanting to disturb the air in the room. The light spread across the walls. The air churned with dust motes and tiny, shiny specks. The glitter was etched into the walls, an ingredient of the paint that had probably been white once upon a time, back when this apartment served as an actual living space and not a musty clandestine laboratory.

"You're right," Lex said, her eyes widening. "It's everywhere." She glanced at her own palms and nodded when she saw the glittery specks on her fingertips. "I pulled up the shade, and now I'm glittering too."

"And I guess if you spend a lot of time here, you kind of become immune to it," Madison suggested. "I mean, the paint on these walls is saturated with glitter, but if

Park hadn't mentioned it, I probably wouldn't have noticed it myself."

"And Julian obviously didn't notice it either." Park backed away from the window. "It's in the air. We're, like, breathing it in."

"We're also wasting time," Lex snapped. "Come on—we either look around or we split. Personally, I feel like splitting. This place is creepy."

"I'm going to look through that pile of papers," Madison said, making the decision for them as she pointed to the messy stack beside the couch. "Lex, see what you can find."

Park took several more steps toward the table. As it came fully into view, she saw the other test tubes and bottles of chemicals, the crystallized hairpins that had been used to measure a particular mixture's detonation capacity. She was both transfixed and horrified. She would have reached out and grabbed for one of the books, but Lex's voice broke through the silence.

"We were wrong."

Park spun around quickly. "What?"

Lex was standing beside one of the chairs. Her expression was stony, and her eyes were locked on the familiar Prada man-purse pressed into a corner of the room. She went to it and picked it up. Then she held it out like Exhibit A in a courtroom. "This isn't Julian's."

Park shook her head. "No," she whispered. "That—that has to be a mistake. It—it can't be."

"It's Emmett McQueen's purse." Lex unzipped it and angrily dumped its contents onto the floor: a hairbrush, a bottle of hair spray, several pens, and the clearest proof of all—Emmett's St. Cecilia's Prep ID.

"I d-don't understand," Park stammered. "Why is that here? Is Emmett part of this? Is it . . . *two* criminals we're supposed to catch?"

Madison stood up from where she'd been squatting. "No, it's just one." Her lips had gone ashen. "It's Emmett, for God's sake. It's not Julian. And here's the proof." She waved several sheets of paper in the air. "These are the documents that were stolen from Mother Margaret's office. Look. It's all a bunch of financial info about the school. Receipts, credit slips, endowment reports—"

"So what?" Park snapped. "How does that prove it's Emmett who's behind all this?"

"This sheet explains it all." Madison held out a single piece of paper and pointed to it. Her voice low and trembling, she said, "This is a receipt for a two-million-dollar check written by Emmett's father, Warren McQueen, last October. And look—it bounced. The sheet has a note scrawled at the bottom, and it's signed by Mother Margaret."

Lex shook her head. "And?"

"And don't you see what it says?" Madison said impatiently. "Look! It says right here that Mother Margaret reported the matter to the Internal Revenue Service for review. And look here—three more of his checks bounced in the two weeks before that. Warren McQueen was writing checks on a phony account because he already knew he was in financial trouble."

"And it was Mother Margaret who reported him to the IRS," Park said. "And Mother Margaret who sparked the investigation that led to Warren McQueen's disastrous downfall."

Madison shook the papers at them. "Exactly. Emmett

must've suspected it, so he broke into the office and stole these documents to confirm his suspicions. Remember what he used to say back when his dad was on trial? He used to go around telling everyone that *someone* would pay for it one day."

"But why was that someone Damien?" Park asked.

"Damien was an obstacle," Madison said. "He probably figured out to some extent what Emmett was up to."

"About the dynamite?" Lex crinkled her nose.

"I guess so! Look around you!" Madison flicked the pieces of paper to the floor. "Damien must've caught on. *That's* why Damien was killed—because he knew Emmett was up to something totally sick! This address was in his little date book! And he knew that, more than anything, Emmett wanted revenge for what was done to his father, his family."

"Oh my God," Lex whispered. "*Emmett?* How could it be? Why would he be doing this?"

"Damien wrote this address down in his little black book because he must've suspected Emmett was up to something, and Damien probably followed him here one day."

"But there's no way Damien knew what was in here," Lex said. "He would never have kept this a secret."

"I don't think so either." Madison let out a long, disappointed breath. "But everything we suspected Julian did? Erase his name from the equation and replace it with Emmett's freakin' name! Dammit." She unzipped her purse. "I guess we should just call the police."

"There's no time for that," Park said. She was backing away from the table slowly, a big sheet of paper in her hands. There was an urgency in her voice that neither Madison nor Lex had ever heard before.

The sheet of paper was a diagram of the St. Cecilia's Prep auditorium exactly as it would look today, at commencement. There were little doodles of chairs and tables, balloons strung along the ceiling. It was, at first glance, a celebratory image. But the words scrawled in Emmett's hand along the side of the sheet told an entirely different story: *impact, detonation, current from the live wire hits the switch.* In the left corner of the diagram was a sketch of the podium; an arrow pointed to the adjustable microphone, and a second arrow, a few inches away, pointed to a wire running along the edge of the floor.

"Holy shit," Madison whispered. "Is that . . . ?"

"It's why Emmett's been experimenting with all these explosive things," Park said, her voice rising. "This diagram spells it all out. It proves what he's planning to do!" The words caught in her throat as she shook the paper in her hands.

Madison raked her hands through her hair. "You don't mean—"

"Yes!" Park shrieked. "He's planning to detonate a bomb at commencement. That's his revenge—*that's* what this is all about! Look—when someone moves the microphone on the podium, the movement will create a current that will detonate an explosive."

"Come on!" Lex turned around and bolted for the door. Her feet barely touched the stairs as she flew down to the first floor. "Hurry! Move! The ceremony starts in *less than ten minutes!*"

# 20

# The Queen's Revenge

The front of St. Cecilia's Prep looked like a fortress: crowds of reporters packed one side of the street and a line of uniformed police officers formed a blue wall across the sidewalk. The school had totally beefed up security in preparation for the prime minister's arrival.

"There's probably a damn sniper on the roof!" Madison said, jumping out of the limo.

"Good! We need all the help we can get!" Park grabbed Lex's hand and together they raced to the edge of the sidewalk.

Madison shoved her way past a cluster of reporters, using her elbows to knock their microphones and cameras out of the way. She kicked at a tripod. She ignored the petite woman calling out her name and shouting a question.

Park and Lex tried to follow suit, but they made it only halfway through the crowd before a sea of bodies washed over them. "Move!" Park screamed. "Please get out of our way!"

"Emergency!" Lex cried.

But the cluster wouldn't break. Park felt one of the reporters reach out and grab her shoulder, and she nearly lost her purse.

"Park!" someone shouted. "Where's your friend Concetta Canoli today?"

"Lex! How do you respond to rumors . . ."

With a burst of energy, Lex slammed herself against Park and simultaneously shoved two reporters out of her way. Microphones jutted out from every angle.

"This is insane!" Park said.

*You have less than two minutes to stop a bomb from exploding,* a voice screamed in Lex's head. *Hurry!*

The old body-pushing approach wasn't working. As the panic swelled inside her, Lex did the only thing she could. She circled her fingers around the strap of the heavy magic purse, lifted it over her head, and swung it propeller-style.

"Get down!" someone yelled.

"Oh my God! Watch it!"

The purse knocked every microphone out of the air in one fell swoop. The reporters bent down to scoop them up, and for a few precious seconds, a path cleared.

Park and Lex raced past several police officers and met Madison at the top of the stairs.

"Excuse me," a male voice said from behind them. "I'll need to search your bags. We have a security checkpoint and—"

"Come with us!" Madison screamed at the security guard. "There's no time to waste!"

"Hey!" the man shouted, chasing the girls down. "Get back here!"

They dashed through the entrance and down the main hallway. Music flooded the air.

"Oh no!" Lex shrieked. "The ceremony's started!"

"Twenty seconds!" Park snapped.

Madison was at the head of the line. She kicked up her speed, her eyes trained on the closed double doors straight ahead.

*A bomb. The school. The prime minister. All the students and guests.*

*Hurry.*

Breathless, Madison slammed against a security guard manning the hall and ignored his shouts of protest.

"Oh!" Park said, biting down on her lip. "Sorry, sir! We'll explain in a minute!"

"Faster!" Lex cried.

Madison reached the double doors to the auditorium first. She shoved them open with a grunt. The music came to an abrupt stop and all eyes turned in her direction—a sea of shocked, startled faces.

Park and Lex jumped on either side of her.

As Madison turned her gaze to the stage, she saw David Gordon, the prime minister, staring at her awkwardly.

He didn't stop walking toward the podium. His right hand went out, mere inches from the microphone.

"Prime Minister Gordon!" Madison shrieked, her voice booming across the auditorium. *"Don't touch the microphone! There's a bomb rigged to it!"*

The prime minister jumped back.

Secret Service agents jumped up like rockets, shoving Madison, Park, and Lex aside.

And every guest started screaming in the mad dash to exit the building.

Madison nearly fainted from fright. Every ounce of energy drained from her body. She felt Park and Lex holding her up as they searched for a way out of the converging mass of bodies.

Someone grabbed Park's arm. She glanced up and saw Sister Brittany looking down at her.

"Are you sure?" Sister Brittany asked nervously.

"Yes!" Park said, lifting her voice above the commotion. "Where's Emmett McQueen?"

"Emmett?" Sister Brittany shook her head. "He left here about two minutes ago. I saw him heading for the side exit."

"He killed Damien—and he rigged the podium with a bomb!" Lex screamed. "We have to find him!"

Sister Brittany's face contorted with rage. *"What?"*

Madison experienced an odd resurgence of energy. Adrenaline hit her nerves like a double espresso, and she grabbed Park and Lex and bolted out of the auditorium. Instead of heading for the main entrance of the school, however, she hung a sharp left, bypassing the music room.

Ahead of them was the little-known side exit.

The door was already open.

They rushed through it and ran out onto the avenue, thankful that the overflowing crowds had engulfed most of the reporters. As they ran across the pavement, thunder cracked overhead, and a sudden downpour drenched the streets.

Lex pointed and said, "Look!"

Madison and Park followed her finger. They both caught a glimpse of Emmett McQueen running into Central Park.

"Get him!" Park screeched.

Lex led the zigzag run through the gridlocked traffic. She stepped on the bumpers of several cars in her mad race to catch up with Emmett, holding tight to the magic purse. The rain beat down hard on them as windshield wipers flicked on and pedestrians hurried into cabs or buildings.

"Be careful!" Madison said, her hair matted to her forehead. "Those heels are gonna break!"

Park was totally drenched. "Come *on!*"

They made it across to the west side of the avenue, and Lex was the first one to dart into the park, stepping into a huge puddle that splattered her with more water.

"Emmett!"

He was a good distance away, but Lex saw him freeze and spin around.

"Don't move!" Park screamed, picking up her pace.

All around them, the park emptied as the few lone joggers and dog-walkers ran for cover from the downpour.

Emmett realized what was happening. He turned and broke into a run, but he stumbled and went down on the ground.

"He's gonna try to make it across the park!" Madison said.

"He won't!" Park shot back.

"Ouch!" Madison stumbled and stopped, her hands flying to her right leg. "Charley horse!"

The path in front of them forked, and they all knew from experience that it converged again just past the meadow. Lex ran right. Madison and Park went left, Madison breaking into a weak limp-trot.

"Stop running, Emmett!" Lex shouted, her own feet pumping the ground. "Everyone knows! You can't get away!"

He powered along the path ahead of her.

Lex was surprised by her own physical stamina. She gulped in huge breaths of air and picked up her pace until she was finally within an arm's length of Emmett's backside. But instead of reaching out and trying to grasp his shirt, she pounced and took to the air—slamming against him with a hard grunt.

They stumbled to the ground in a splash of mud.

"Shit!" Lex screamed, thinking of her clothes and the magic purse.

"Let go of my arm, bitch!" Emmett screamed.

When Lex finally caught her breath, she realized she was under him, his weight pressing down on her and his elbows resting on her shoulders. She tried to squirm and fight, but his body was too long and—surprisingly—too strong. "Just give up!" she said. "Why . . . the hell . . . are you . . . fighting me?"

Emmett managed to yank his arm from her grasp long enough to reach into his back pocket.

A moment later, Lex saw the dagger in his hand; the blade caught a glint of light as the sharp point came down at her.

She flung her body to the left, gasping as the blade dug

into the dirt beside her right shoulder. Rain poured down the side of her dirt-streaked face. An image of a healing mud mask flashed before her eyes, and she stopped worrying about any potential damage to her skin. "You little creep!" she seethed. "Did you actually think you'd get away with it?"

"Revenge," Emmett grunted, "for what that nun did to my family!"

Lex tried to nab him with an uppercut, but missed.

Emmett lifted the blade again.

And in the flash of an instant, everything shifted.

There was a loud *whoosh*, and Lex saw Emmett literally skid off her with a yelp.

Park had used her own body as a battering ram, knocking him onto his back.

"My head!" Emmett screeched, placing a muddy hand on his scalp.

"How could you do it?" Park yelled. "How could you try to blow us all up?" She was kneeling on his chest, angrily batting him with her fists. "That's for Damien!" she screamed, striking Emmett in the jaw. "That's for trying to blow up the school. And *that's* for ruining our clothes!"

Emmett's face registered pain. "It would've worked!" he panted. "If you little *bitches* hadn't butted in! I knew I should have killed you in the Chamber with my sword when I had the chance!"

Park grabbed him by his muddy shirt collar. "And you even betrayed your best friend!" she shrieked. "Concetta would've fried for killing Damien! You pathetic little wimp!" She let go of him and slammed both her fists down on his chest again.

With a loud grunt, Emmett bucked his entire body.

The movement threw Park to the ground. He shot to his feet and held the blade out.

Park jumped up too. She didn't take her eyes off him as she hunched her back and held out her arms like a wrestler who had just entered a ring.

Lex did the same. She took Emmett's left side, blocking his path of escape.

They circled him slowly.

"So," he said between breaths, "which one of y'all wants to get cut first?" He slashed the dagger to his right.

Park jumped back, narrowly avoiding the blade. "Ha!" she said. "Not quick enough, McQueen!" She ran a muddy hand through her muddy hair. "Not smart enough and not quick enough!"

"Like hell I'm not!" In a lightning-quick move, he lashed out at her again, this time grabbing hold of her wrist and nearly pulling her against his chest.

But before he could complete the capture, Park elbowed him in the ribs and broke free. She ducked when she saw the dagger swooping toward her.

"Damn!" Emmett steadied himself on the wet ground. He was out of breath, rain dripping into his eyes and down his face. He stared at Lex—and the stare held a gleam of determined evil.

Before she could even scream, Emmett's left hand grabbed her shoulder. She felt herself being spun around. Then she felt fingers close around her jaw and the sharp tip of the blade against her throat. "Park!" she screamed, helpless.

"Don't struggle!" Park answered back.

Emmett laughed. "Now who's not fast enough, huh?"

He pressed the dagger deeper into the flesh at Lex's throat.

Park froze. For a still, silent moment, she actually felt a spark of panic in her chest. She didn't know what to do. She stared at Lex's tear-streaked face. She stared into Emmett's cold, gleaming eyes. She—

"We got him!" Madison yelled, appearing out of nowhere. She stopped limp-running as she reached the scene, but her shoes slid out from under her and she skidded forward, slamming directly into Emmett, knocking the blade from his hand.

He slammed into Lex.

Lex slammed into Park.

They tumbled to the ground in a knot of arms and legs. Thankfully, Lex landed flat on the magic purse.

"Ouch!" Park screamed. "Get *off* me!"

The instant Madison rolled onto her stomach, something caught her eye. She wiped the mud from her face and stared across the gray, rainy light of midday. As if in slow motion, she saw the figure powering down the path, coming toward them with all the speed of a rocket.

Sister Brittany ran like an athlete in her Roger Vivier platforms. The long ends of her black habit swished and swirled and the Dolce & Gabbana rosary beads bounced against her hip.

Madison was so startled by the surreal image that she didn't see Emmett fish the dagger from the little puddle of brown water.

In one final attempt to salvage what was left of his vengeful plot, Emmett arched over Park. He clasped the dagger between his palms, pulled it up and took aim.

"Don't!" Madison screeched. She lunged forward onto Park, purposely placing her own body in the path of the oncoming blade.

Lex thrust her muddy magic purse up and out, and it caught the blade's impact completely.

Emmett gritted his teeth.

*"Freeze!"* a voice behind them screamed.

Breathless, exhausted, the rain pooling over their muddy faces, they all turned and stared up at Sister Brittany.

The fingers of her right hand held a gun, and it was pointed directly at Emmett. In her left hand was a gold badge. She was FBI.

# 21

# A Star Is Born . . . Again

On Friday afternoon, Park reported to the set of *Short Fuse* for her first official day of filming. It was sunny and hot and busy, a typical June morning in Manhattan. As she stepped through the doors of her own personal trailer, she felt relief wash over her in the form of air-conditioning and several bouquets of red roses. The card in all of them was the same: *Love, Jeremy.*

On the small counter beside the window, Park found a gift basket filled with beauty products, courtesy of Madison and Lex; they hadn't overlooked a single item. Park laughed out loud when she saw the huge tube labeled *Facial Mud Mask.* It was a joke and a reminder of all they had been through.

Park had spent the last three days reading over the script for *Short Fuse* and recovering from her violent and unexpected duel with Emmett McQueen. Madison and Lex were recovering too, but they were looking forward to vacation and the beginning of a very restful summer. Park, on the other hand, would be working for the next six weeks: first here in Manhattan, then out in Los Angeles, where the last quarter of the film was being shot. It was an entirely nerve-wracking experience—memorizing lines, learning how to get into character, fearing that her performance on-screen wouldn't live up to all the media hype—but Park wasn't sweating it. And when the jitters *did* seize her, she thought back to Sunday evening and her performance in the Chamber. How exhilarated she'd felt playing that role, how she'd been able to capture all the little nuances of a character. She hadn't merely been playing a game; she'd been acting out a scene, feeding off everyone else's words and movements and emotions. She'd lost herself in the thrill of it.

So maybe Jeremy was right. Maybe acting really was in her blood.

A knock sounded on the trailer door.

"Come in," Park said.

A woman wearing a headset poked her head in. "We'll be ready for you in five minutes, Park. Hair and makeup in trailer four."

"Thank you." She took a deep breath and reached for the script in her purse. She flipped through it, smirking at the irony of it all. The explosions and mayhem and danger that were all central to the movie. The stunts. Hell, she'd lived this script in the past week. Maybe life really did imitate art.

She went and stood before the full-length mirror at the front of the trailer. She was pleased with her reflection: it radiated strength and confidence and a slight edginess. There was no sense in worrying about her feature film debut. Jeremy had been right all along. A lot of her life *was* about acting. But there was a huge difference between art in front of the camera and life behind it. She was ready to do both.

She opened the door of her trailer and stepped outside. Three photographers were waiting just behind the blue barricade. Park didn't bother to shield her face as the flashes erupted. There was no point in hiding on a movie set. Several onlookers waved and called her name excitedly, and she smiled and waved back.

Jeremy was waiting for her outside the makeup trailer. "Hey, babe," he said, grinning from ear to ear.

"Hey." She slipped into his embrace and held her face up for his kiss.

"So," he said. "You ready?"

"As ready as I'll ever be."

"Long day ahead of us. Press conference after we finish shooting."

She nodded. "Sounds typical. I think I can handle it."

Jeremy stared into her eyes, then arced a finger across her cheek. "We're *officially* a power couple now. If you really don't want to do the press conference, we don't have to. They wait for us, and not the other way around."

She laughed. "It might take me a while to get used to the Hollywood stuff, but I will eventually." She glanced over his shoulder and saw Madison, Lex, and Coco McKaid walking toward her.

"I brought you some extra moisturizer," Lex said. She

had a little trouble digging into her new magic purse—it was bigger than the last one, which had been damaged by the mud and Emmett's dagger—but she was handling the change well. She held out the tube of moisturizer. "All these lights, and being outside in this weather—it'll be hell on your skin."

Park took the tube. "I know. I can already feel the dryness beginning around my eyes."

Madison held up a file folder. "Well, it's all here. The police and the FBI and the ATF finished their investigation."

"Oh!" Park's eyes widened. "So what happened?"

"Everything happened while I was away!" Coco wailed, disappointed. "I swear, I'm never going to a Zen monastery again. They even confiscated my iPod."

"Emmett broke into Mother Margaret's office back in March," Madison explained. "He stole the documents and they confirmed his suspicions—it was Mother Margaret who sparked the investigation into his father's bad business dealings. In fact, Mother Margaret had been cooperating silently with the IRS throughout the whole scandal, but she never thought Emmett would resort to this. It apparently never occurred to her that he would want to take revenge on her or St. Cecilia's Prep."

Lex nodded sadly. "The apartment on Ninety-first Street—the clandestine chemical lab—is actually owned by Emmett's mom. But it's under her maiden name, so it kind of went unnoticed. Emmett had gotten used to staying there alone during the trial. He liked being there as opposed to with his parents, and his mom didn't mind that. But she didn't know what he was up to. He started experimenting with all the explosives back in February, when he began to suspect that St. Cecilia's might've been behind the investigation. That's why traces of it were found in Mother Margaret's office. When he broke in, he'd had some of it on his shoes, maybe on his gloves. Clandestine laboratories, by the way, are fairly common. Criminals have them in their bathrooms and basements and bedrooms. It's a big problem. I guess it was thoughtful of Emmett to at least spare his mother from danger."

"But where was he getting the nitroglycerin?" Park asked.

"He was engineering it *himself*," Madison said. "Literally. I mean, that's how smart he is when it comes to chemistry. He did it by nitrating glycerol, and nitric and sulfuric acids."

Park nodded. "I'm impressed, Madison. Sounds like you understand chemistry a lot more since reading that report, huh?"

Madison beamed. "I'm *so* taking physics or advanced chem next year. But getting back to what I was saying about Emmett and the clandestine laboratory . . . *that's* why the FBI was brought in. In this case, they planted an undercover agent to try to find out what was going on. And that agent was Sister Brittany. Whose real name, by the way, is Special Agent Christine Resnick."

Park sighed. "I *always* thought she was a little bit of a wack-job. She let students get away with too much. I guess she wouldn't make a very good nun. What about everything else?"

"The night Cleopatra opened, Emmett pretty much did exactly what we thought *Julian* did," Madison said.

"He saw Concetta run out of the cage, and his chance to jumble up his own crime, and he used her stiletto to wound Damien after Damien had probably already died from the poison. And it turns out he knocked the DJs out with chloroform, which, for the record, he also made himself." She smiled. "And remember Friday afternoon, when I saw Damien in the student lounge? Well, he had just come from Mother Margaret's office, but he hadn't been alone. Turns out Mary Grace Burns saw Emmett waiting for him in the hall, holding a soda can. That was when Emmett poisoned him."

"Jesus," Jeremy said. "That's so cold."

Lex took the file from Madison and flipped through the legal documents. "On Thursday night, Damien spotted Emmett coming out of the apartment building on East Ninety-first Street. Damien questioned him about it—and he also saw a book on explosives in Emmett's backpack. Damien never really made the connection, but he was probably going to mention it to Mother Margaret. And everyone else."

"Which would've exposed Emmett's plan to seek revenge," Madison said. "So Emmett knew he had to get rid of Damien. Damien was a threat; he was already suspicious of Emmett and things would've only gotten worse. Emmett confessed all of this to the police—he signed a sworn statement and pleaded guilty to avoid a maximum sentence."

"And Julian?" Park asked.

Lex shrugged. "He's okay, but he's spending the summer in rehab. The day I followed him to the Bronx and saw him pay for that little plastic bag down by the construction

322

site? Turns out it was cocaine. And remember the plant you saw in his bag when you met up with him on West Houston Street? It wasn't jequirity. It was actually cannabis."

Park shook her head. "Figures. And I guess Jessica is out in the Hamptons with her family, right?"

"Yes," Madison said. "She wasn't too nice to us when we tried to talk to her the other day. But apparently she's giving up on her plans to study medicine. She wants to take up writing instead, so in the fall she's going to Bennington, not Brown."

A small commotion suddenly erupted behind them. One of the production assistants was trying to keep someone away from the trailer, but that someone shoved her way past the blue barricade with a loud grunt. Concetta Canoli wasn't about to be restrained. She was dressed in a pink sarong and a men's white button-down shirt. She met Park's eyes and smiled pensively. Then she looked at Madison and Lex and waved.

"Concetta!" Park said. "We're so glad to see you!"

She nodded and rushed forward, her head held high, her voluptuous body swaying in typical Concetta fashion. She hugged Park. She air-kissed Madison and Lex. "I know I'm not supposed to be on the set bothering you," she said, clearing her throat nervously, "but I never really got the chance to thank you for saving me. For saving everyone."

"You're not bothering us," Park assured her. "And I'm glad you came. You're looking fabulous."

"I think you look *great* in pink," Lex told her.

"Truly beautiful," Madison said.

"Thank you." Concetta smiled again. Then she turned

around and stared up at Jeremy. Her cheeks flushed. She started twirling a strand of her hair. "Hi," she said breathlessly. "I'm such a big fan of yours."

Jeremy smiled politely. Then he glanced down at Concetta's feet. No stilettos. Relief flooded him.

"Well, I guess that leaves only me to talk about."

They all spun around.

Special Agent Christine Resnick—a.k.a. Sister Brittany—pushed past the security guards as she flashed them her badge. She was dressed in jeans and a black blazer, and her short hair was spiky and actually quite flattering.

"Oh my God!" Lex said. "Sister Brittany!"

Special Agent Resnick laughed. "Not anymore. I'm done with wearing veils."

"Thank you for saving us, by the way," Madison said. "*We* never got a chance to say that to *you*."

"Hey, I never got a chance to thank *you* girls for doing such a great job on this case," Special Agent Resnick replied. "If you hadn't found the jequirity plants or created that time line or invaded Emmett McQueen's secret lab . . . well, we might not all be here today."

The reality of the situation prompted a moment of stunned silence. Madison, Park, and Lex stared down at the ground. So did Coco. Concetta made the sign of the cross without ever taking her eyes off Jeremy.

Special Agent Resnick said, "But the good news is that it all worked out. I hear that because of you girls, the prime minister's wife has begun wearing Triple Threat everywhere in London."

Lex gave a thumbs-up. "It's the only way to dress. And

because of that roll in the mud in Central Park, I've decided to start a new line of cosmetics. My skin's been amazing after that."

"Mine too." Madison nodded. "And the other amazing news is that Cleopatra is reopening next week!"

Special Agent Resnick pulled a miniature bottle of champagne out of her purse and handed it to Park. "I just wanted to say break a leg. I think you're going to be great in this movie."

"*Totally* great," Lex echoed.

Jeremy slipped his arm around Park. "Babe, we've got to get ready. Shooting starts in ten minutes."

"Oh, wait," Special Agent Resnick said. She took a small envelope out of her side pocket and handed it to Madison. "This is actually for you, Park, and Lex. It's some information on a new internship program the FBI is developing for teenagers who are interested in forensics and crime-fighting. The Bureau thinks you girls would be a perfect fit."

Lex gasped. "Give me that envelope!"

"We'll think about it," Madison said with a smile.

"You should." Special Agent Resnick nodded. "Because fashion and forensics *can* go hand in hand."

Madison held out her hand. "We'll be in touch, Agent Resnick." She couldn't help but smile as she watched the ex-nun cross through the barricade and disappear into the thickening crowds.

"You think we'll ever see her again?" Lex asked hopefully.

Madison smirked. "Ya know, for some strange reason, I totally think we will." She turned around suddenly, catching a glimpse of Theo out of the corner of her eye.

He strode toward her carrying a bouquet of red roses, a bottle of champagne, and a quart of milk. He didn't bother to muffle his laughter as he handed the gifts over to her.

"Very funny," Madison snapped.

"Well, I figured you'd need something to keep you calm." He plucked a puffy strand of baby's breath from the bouquet and slipped it into her hair. "Now, *that* looks a lot better than the jequirity plant you had on your head last Friday night."

Madison sighed, then smiled. "*What* am I going to do with you, Theo West?"

Lex didn't say anything as she watched Theo and Madison poke each other and laugh. They really did look happy. She suddenly felt guilty for being so lame about him. When Theo turned to look at her, she frowned and gave his shoulder a slug.

He got the hint. "Thanks," he said quietly.

A minute later, Park came out of the makeup trailer, dressed and primped for filming. She was wearing torn jeans and a bloodstained T-shirt. Dirt matted her face and a fake cut ran across her forehead in an ugly red line.

"Places!" The director's voice boomed across the set.

"Well," Park said, staring at Madison and Lex. "I guess this is it. I guess you guys have to leave to catch your flight to Italy, right? It's going to be a long six weeks without you." She cleared her throat, fighting back tears.

Madison and Lex exchanged a furtive glance.

"Actually, we're not," Madison said. "That's a little surprise. We're not going."

"What?" Park nearly screamed.

"Mom is on her way here," Lex explained. "She said she couldn't imagine not being here to see you make your first movie."

"Oh!" For the first time in a long time, Park lost control of her emotions. Her face lit up happily. "I can't believe it! This makes me feel *so* much better!" She launched into her sisters' arms and held the embrace.

It really did feel good to *finally* have a quiet moment together, to know that everything was okay.

After a long, deep breath, Park turned and ran across the set, taking her place in front of the camera.

"Hey." Theo waved his hand to get their attention. "Anybody want an espresso?"

"Two, please," Madison replied.

Theo nodded and jogged over to one of the production assistants.

"I think it's going to be a good summer," Madison said confidently.

"Yeah, me too." Lex looked at Madison. "But I thought you were going to tell Park the *other* big news. Why didn't you say anything?"

Madison shrugged as the cameras started rolling. "We'll tell her about it later. She's too busy right now. Besides, there's only so much news a girl can take."

"I guess you're right." Lex slipped on her sunglasses. Then she bent her head to one side and listened as a police siren blared in the distance. "Sounds like they're playing our song a few streets over," she said with a chuckle.

Madison winked at her sister. "Proof that New York is our town."

# ACKNOWLEDGMENTS

Talk about being lucky: I get to write about cool characters, hot clubs, and all the adventures that fall in between. But I don't do it alone, and that's what really makes me lucky.

My editor, Krista Marino, is smarter, classier, and cooler than any character I could have imagined. She is a gift and a guiding light. Two words sum her up: *the best*.

Michael Bourret has the difficult job of putting up with me, and he does this with enthusiasm, professionalism, and warmth. I am ever grateful for his support . . . and for his uncanny ability to respond to e-mails within seconds.

Beverly Horowitz and the excellent team at Delacorte Press make it all possible, and I am both honored and humbled to be a part of such a wonderful and vibrant literary community.

Angela Carlino has amazing creative vision and instinct, and so much good cheer. It is always a joy to work with her.

Noreen Marchisi does a masterful job of rousing the crowds and getting the word out. She is every celebutante's dream publicist. (And mine too!)

I am fortunate to have such an extraordinary family and circle of friends. Bless you, one and all.

**Antonio Pagliarulo** was born and raised in New York City. After the publication of *The Celebutantes: On the Avenue*, he acquired his first Dolce & Gabbana suit (along with several Zegna shirts), and gave up window-shopping. When not writing, he's usually lunching in midtown Manhattan. You'll never spot him without a book.

Don't miss Madison, Park, and
Lexington Hamilton in . . .

# TO THE PENTHOUSE
## *the Celebutantes*

*coming in fall 2008*